The Knight's Tale

The Knight's Tale

Book 10 in the Struggle for a Crown Series

By

Griff Hosker

The Knight's Tale

Published by Sword Books Ltd 2024

Copyright ©Griff Hosker First Edition 2024

The author has asserted their moral right under the Copyright, Designs and Patents Act, 1988, to be identified as the author of this work.
All Rights Reserved. No part of this publication may be reproduced, copied, stored in a retrieval system, or transmitted, in any form or by any means, without the prior written consent of the copyright holder, nor be otherwise circulated in any form of binding or cover other than that in which it is published and without a similar condition being imposed on the subsequent purchaser.
A CIP catalogue record for this title is available from the British Library.

Cover by Design for Writers

The Knight's Tale

Dedication

To Michael, my grandson and computer assistant. He has all the potential to be a writer!

Contents

The Knight's Tale i
List of important characters in the novel 3
Prologue 5
Chapter 1 7
Chapter 2 20
Chapter 3 31
Chapter 4 39
Chapter 5 56
Chapter 6 64
Chapter 7 71
Chapter 8 79
Chapter 9 87
Chapter 10 97
Chapter 11 104
Chapter 12 111
Chapter 13 118
Chapter 14 129
Chapter 15 142
Chapter 16 151
Chapter 17 160
Chapter 18 171
Chapter 19 180
Chapter 20 190
Epilogue 200
Glossary 201
Historical Notes 204
Other books by Griff Hosker 206

The Knight's Tale

There was a knight, a most distinguished man,
Who from the day on which he first began
To ride abroad had followed chivalry
Truth, honour, generousness and courtesy.
He had done nobly in his sovereign's war
And ridden into battle, no man more,
As well in Christian and in heathen places
And ever honoured for his noble graces.

The Prologue, Canterbury Tales, Geoffrey Chaucer

List of important characters in the novel

Dowager Queen Catherine - widow of King Henry Vth
Henry VIth King of England
Duke of Bedford - brother of King Henry Vth
Humphrey, Duke of Gloucester - brother of King Henry Vth
Eleanor Cobham - the second wife of the Duke of Gloucester
King Charles of France - brother of Queen Catherine
Edmund Beaufort - Count of Mortain 2nd Duke of Somerset
Jean Poton de Xaintrailles - Seneschal of Limousin
Étienne de Vignolles- La Hire - French commander
Sir John de Cressy
Owen Tudor - grandfather of King Henry VIIth
Edmund, Jasper and Owen - the children of Owen Tudor and Queen Catherine
William Ayscough - Bishop of Salisbury
Sir Thomas Rempston - Captain of Calais
John Sutton - Baron Dudley, Lieutenant of Calais
Richard Neville - Earl of Salisbury
William de la Pole - Earl of Suffolk
Robert Neville - Bishop of Durham
Ralph Neville - 2nd Earl of Westmoreland
Richard Neville - 5th Earl of Salisbury and Warden of the West Marches
Henry Percy - 3rd Earl of Northumberland and Warden of the East Marches
John Beaufort - The 1st Duke of Somerset
Richard, Duke of York
Sir John Talbot - the Lieutenant of France and the leader of the English Armies
Sir Gruffudd Vychan - a Welsh knight and tournament champion

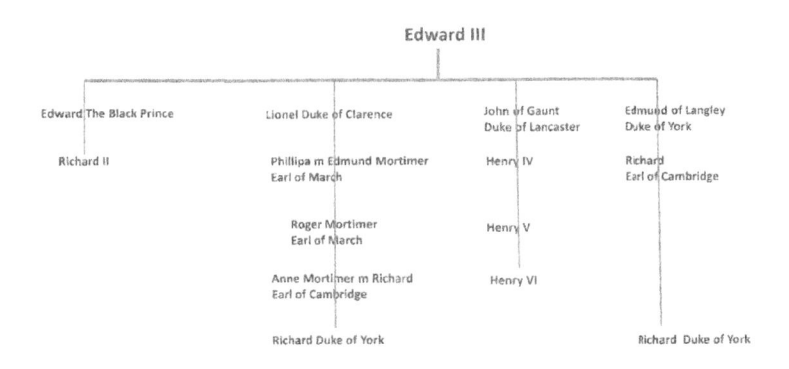

The Knight's Tale

```
                              Edward III
    ┌─────────────────┬─────────────────┬─────────────────┐
Edward The Black Prince  Lionel Duke of Clarence   John of Gaunt        Edmund of Langley
                                                  Duke of Lancaster      Duke of York
    │                         │                       │                       │
 Richard II              Phillipa m Edmund Mortimer   Henry IV              Richard
                         Earl of March                                      Earl of Cambridge
                              │                       │
                         Roger Mortimer               Henry V
                         Earl of March
                              │                       │
                         Anne Mortimer m Richard      Henry VI
                         Earl of Cambridge
                              │
                         Richard Duke of York                         Richard Duke of York
```

Weedon

Houghton Regis

Windsor

Southampton   *London*   *Iden*

Calais

Rouen   *Les Pérets*

12 Miles

Prologue

1437 Houghton Regis

I am Sir Michael of Weedon and I am the knight who was made by Sir William Strongstaff, for me, the greatest knight this land of England has ever seen. His training paid off when Houghton Regis was attacked. After the attack on my home by the Swabians sent by the king's uncle, the Duke of Gloucester, I withdrew from all contact with the court. Queen Catherine had died and I was no longer the Queen's Knight. The Duke of Gloucester had dismissed me as the protector of the king and so I had no responsibilities save those as the lord of four manors. Les Pérets lay in Normandy and was run for me by my wife's uncle, Charles. Iden was close to Rye and Edgar White Streak was my steward. Before Queen Catherine had given me the grand manor of Houghton Regis, I had lived in William Strongstaff's favourite home, Weedon. My former squire John and his wife, my sister-in-law Eleanor, lived there. I had a comfortable life and my three English manors were farmed by former archers and men at arms. They had served both me and Sir William.

In former battles we had won when we were led by the king's father, Henry V[th], but following his death and the rise of the Maid, we had endured defeat after defeat. Although Sir John Talbot, an able commander, still fought the French, it was a losing battle. France was no longer part of the Angevin empire and when we finally lost Normandy, then that empire would be ended.

I was still a soldier but my days of going to war were ended. I ensured that the lands I controlled were at peace and I paid my taxes. I had a son who had been christened Jean but, since we had come to live in England, he was now anglicised as John. He had a younger sister, a baby, Maud. There was another child in our home but she was our secret. Margaret was the daughter of Queen Catherine and Owen Tudor. While the three sons of that liaison were cared for in religious establishments and Owen Tudor languished in Newgate prison, I was obeying the last order from Queen Catherine and raising her daughter as my foster child. Owen Tudor and Father Bertrand had managed to escape from the prison once but they had been hunted, caught and returned there by Humphrey, Duke of Gloucester. I promised to care for Margaret as my own. We had fabricated a story that she was the child of Sarah and that we had adopted her. As Sarah had been her wet nurse and the queen had been ill during the baby's infanthood, Margaret also thought that Sarah was her natural mother. John called her sister. The child did not know her royal antecedents and, as her identity was only known to a handful of people, it would be my decision to either tell her or keep her blissfully in the dark. When I swore an oath I did so for life. Sir William Strongstaff, Rafe and Edgar White Streak had all trained me well.

As we remembered rather than celebrated the death of the queen, I wondered if I would just become a fat old knight who would no longer draw his sword in anger. Would I live in a land blessed by peace with memories of glory in the past? In many ways, I hoped so.

Chapter 1

The summons to ride to Windsor from King Henry VIth came as a shock. I had thought that I was forgotten. I had only been the king's guardian for a short time and the Duke of Gloucester had quickly severed those ties. I had been closer to the king's mother than the king. I had also been closer to the king's father. To me, he was the greatest king that England ever had and when disease took him, it seemed to me that God was punishing England for something, I knew not what.

I no longer had a squire and when the pursuivant had left and I had read the missive which commanded my presence, I used my rock, my wife Isabelle, for council. She read the letter and her face mirrored my dismay. A command from the king never boded well for my family. "We have done naught that is ill, my husband, but I do not like this. Why should he send for you?" Just then there was a squeal from the children as they played in the next room. Houghton Regis was almost palatial compared to Weedon. "It cannot be about Margaret, can it?"

I shook my head, "We have kept the secret well. Apart from Sarah, you and I, the only other who is privy to that knowledge is Father Bertrand and he languishes in prison."

"Her father will know."

She was right. Owen Tudor was also one who might know the existence of the child, but as he had been forbidden by the Duke of Gloucester from visiting the queen in her latter days, it was not a certainty.

"Speculation will not avail me anything. I shall leave on the morrow at dawn. I thought to take Robbie Red Fletch."

She nodded, "He is getting on in years, my husband, but he is a good soldier. You will need another, you know. Someone to attend you as a servant."

I wracked my brains and then it came to me, "Jack."

My wife beamed, "Of course, Jack." Jack was the son of Elizabeth. They had come to us when I had destroyed a nest of bandits. The two had become part of my household and Elizabeth cooked for us while Jack acted as a house servant. He had grown since he had come to us and my wife had ensured that he learned manners and how to be a gentleman. She had even taught him some French. He sparred with me when I needed the exercise and was developing good skills with a blade. He was too old to be trained as an archer but he could be a man at arms.

I called, for he was next door with the children, "Jack!"

He appeared in a flash, "Yes, my lord?"

"We need to ride to Windsor tomorrow. Find Robbie Red Fletch and tell him we are going to visit the king. You will need riding clothes as well as clothes that are suitable for court. See Peter the horse master. I shall take Shadow."

His face lit up, "Yes, my lord."

I sighed as I went to my chamber where my wife was already choosing the clothes that I would need. I was a warrior and not a courtier but I knew that I would have to dress well and be prepared to wait for an inordinately long period of time. Court worked at a different pace from the rest of the world. I would have to endure it for the king was young and I did not know him well. He could take the slightest oversight as a major misdemeanour. England had suffered some kings who were unpredictable and less than fair. The King Henry I had followed to Agincourt was clearly an exception.

"You will need your best hose and doublet. I fear that the journey will crease them. I will pack your new soft boots, too. Do not think to ride whilst wearing them for that would ruin them."

"My love, it will be a brief meeting. I may not even have to stay overnight."

She stopped folding the clothes and stood, "You cannot get there and back in one day. Surely the king will find a bed for you."

I shrugged, "He is young and unpredictable. I have not seen him since, well, a long time ago. Gloucester dispensed with my services before the boy was formed."

She stroked a lock of hair into place, "You have been used, my love. I thought when the queen died, that your service to the crown was done."

"As did I, but the English crown has many claimants. Young King Henry does not sit securely on the throne. When we lose France, and lose it we will, then there will be many who will blame the king for its loss and forget that it was his father who won it. The two sides of the family, those of Lancaster and those of York, do not get on. They vie with each other for position, status and power. Had they not done so, we might have won the war in France." I kissed her on the forehead, "Hopefully, this will be a trivial matter and I shall return here with the news that I am no longer to be used."

I knew the words that I spoke were unrealistic but I wanted my wife to feel less worried. For my part, I imagined all sorts of dire consequences to the meeting.

We were well-wrapped as we left the next morning. It was more than thirty miles to Windsor and we left before dawn. It was cold and the air felt damp. This was England and rain was a constant threat. We each rode wearing an oiled cloak. The bags with our clothes were on our saddles and we each carried a sword. Mine was the weapon of a knight while Robbie and Jack had simple short swords. Robbie had the added burden of his gardyvyan and the longbow in its case. He was an archer and he would no more leave the tools of his trade behind than he would his cloak. I knew that beneath the soft hat he wore would be the spare bow strings. They would be kept dry in case they were needed. I did not think he would need them but, as his arrows had saved my life before now, I did not make a fuss. As the sun rose to reveal a grey day, I spoke to Jack. I had surprised my men at arms with my choice of a boy and while Jack himself was delighted, he too wondered at his inclusion.

"Jack, I chose you because you are clever and you have shown me you can keep your wits about you."

"Thank you, my lord. I will try not to let you down. My mother said that this was an honour and I should be on my best behaviour."

"You will be expected to serve me at the table. You will stand behind me and when the other squires and pages go to the kitchen to fetch the food, you shall follow them and do as they do. You serve me but if any lord asks for something on your platter, you serve them too." He nodded. "While you do this, I would have you remain silent and listen. You will hear things that you think are unimportant. I will decide what is important and what is not."

"Am I your squire then, my lord?"

I shook my head as Robbie laughed, "No Jack, nor my page. Since I gave your namesake the manor of Weedon I have not needed a squire. I may not need one again, for I hope that my days of going to war are gone." I glanced at him and saw the disappointment on his face. "Would you like to be a squire?"

He stared ahead as though he was trying to form the right words and I waited, as we clip-clopped down the road. "I know I am of lowly birth, my lord. By rights, I should have died in the bandit camp, my lord, but I was saved and saved by you, my lord. I do not know my place in the world. I do not know if I am meant to be a warrior, an archer or a man at arms, or stay a servant. Perhaps I was reborn at Houghton Regis and my life started again."

Robbie said, "You are too old to begin training as an archer, Jack." He smiled, "Yet there is too much in you to be a servant. You can use a sword?"

"I have one and I can swash it about, but I have had no training."

Robbie said, "My lord, David, John, or Dick could give him skills. Another man at arms is always handy and, to tell the truth, your men are

The Knight's Tale

old. Most of us served Sir William. The aches when I wake in the morning are getting worse and I know that the others feel the same. It is more than twenty years since we young men stood at Agincourt and slaughtered the French."

I shook my head, "Is it that long?"

"Aye, it is, my lord. The snow and frost on our thinning pates are a testament to our age."

His words touched a nerve. He was right. I had not hired new men and, thinking about it, most of the men were now married and had families. They served me as archers and men at arms but they also spent more time farming their smallholdings on my estate than practising for war. I had chosen Robbie for he was still unmarried. If we had to go to war once more there would be a sea of salt tears from the wives and families left behind. I had to hope that this was not a call for me to go to France and join Sir John Talbot. If I was ordered then I would go, I had no choice in the matter, but it would be with a heavy heart.

"Well, my lord, what shall it be?" Robbie knew me well enough for this degree of familiarity.

I realised that I had still to answer Jack. I smiled, "If you wish to learn sword skills then I shall be your teacher and as for your future…you may be whatever you choose. Let us take baby steps, Jack. These two days away from Houghton Regis will be a taste of a life you might not enjoy."

We rode in silence until Robbie said, "I remember, my lord, a boy plucked from a cell and raised by Sir William who became a great warrior."

"And I am grateful that Sir William did that but Jack is not me."

The journey changed after that. It was nothing to do with us but the road became busier. The king's presence at Windsor drew many people there. Some would go to sell their wares while others would seek favour. I had been invited to court but others would simply turn up and wait, sometimes for days, just with the hope that they might be able to speak to the king. They would have requests for favours or land or money. We passed many clumps of riders as we rode south. We had good horses and I was keen to reach the castle in the early afternoon. The messenger had just said that the king desired a conference with me. Neither time nor date was mentioned. My early departure had been to ensure that neither he nor whoever advised him would be upset.

I did not recognise any of the guards at the gates. That was no surprise really. It had been many years since I had ridden with the warriors of the king. My livery was, however, recognised and I was expected. When the captain of the guard was summoned and I was identified he nodded, "You have made good time, Sir Michael, and you are expected." He glanced at Robbie and said, "Archer, you will be housed in the warrior hall. It is in the Lower Ward and the stables are there. Your horses can be well housed and cared for." Robbie nodded. "Sir Michael, you and your," he seemed to see Jack for the first time and he frowned, "servant, will be housed in the Round Tower in the Upper Ward." He waved over a man at arms, "Hob, take his lordship to the Tower."

"Aye, Captain."

I realised that we were going to have a bed for the night and I would not be riding back to Houghton Regis. Out of courtesy to the man at arms, we dismounted and walked through the gate. He pointed to the left and said to Robbie, "You will smell the stables and the ostler will direct you to the hall." He smiled, "I shall see you there when we dine. From your grey hairs, you will have tales to tell."

Robbie, nodded, "And so long as the ale flows then I shall regale you with them." I was not worried about Robbie.

We handed our reins to him and Jack took our bags. I would have been quite happy to carry my own but there was a protocol. I knew I would be judged from the moment we entered the fortress. I was not of noble birth. It was one of the reasons the Duke of Gloucester had dispensed with my services. His brother, the late king, valued the man while the Duke of Gloucester valued the title and the blood.

We had been seen walking from the gatehouse and at the door to the tower, we were greeted by a liveried servant. Hob said, "Sir Michael of Weedon."

The servant had a wax tablet and he glanced down at it. He nodded, "Come with me, my lord." He said not a word to Hob. Servants in such places thought themselves above soldiers.

I said, "Thank you, Hob."

The man at arms looked surprised but smiled and said, "I was happy, my lord, to leave the gatehouse. I wish you well."

I had learned that it did no harm to be polite. Sir William had always done so. Like me, his beginnings were humble. It had been the Black Prince himself who had spotted the potential in the man at arms.

We were taken up a narrow stairway. Our room was clearly not one of the better ones. We would be close to the top of the tower and the room would be unheated. I was proved right. There was a bed and a paillasse. A single chair and a table with a jug and bowl of water completed the furniture and a simple rail fixed between two arrow slits was the only thing that passed for a wardrobe.

"Is there light?"

The Knight's Tale

The man looked around and said, "I will fetch one, my lord."

"Fetch two, eh? I think that the king can afford it."

He nodded and left. There were shutters by the arrow slits and, unless we wished to freeze, then they would need to be closed. I knew that one candle would not suffice.

"And now, Jack, we change. Comb your hair and use the water to clean your hands. We will be under inspection the moment we leave this room."

I went to do as I had advised. I would stink of horses until I changed my clothes but I was also aware that, despite wearing gloves, my hands and face were grimier than was acceptable. That done I stripped and changed into the clothes my wife had packed. She had used lavender and rosemary. The clothes were pleasant to the nose and the lavender and rosemary would mask my stink somewhat. I would not have thought of that. I was lucky to have a lady for my wife.

I was changed by the time another servant, a boy this time, fetched the two candles. They were not of the best quality, but I deemed that the light would last all night. The room faced the west and that meant we would have light longer than if we were on the other side of the tower. We would only light one candle when we left, after closing the shutters.

Jack had washed, changed and combed his hair. He asked, "When do we descend, my lord?"

I smiled, "Now."

He looked at my sword, "Will you not need your sword, my lord?"

"No, and the only knives we shall need will be for eating. Do not forget to bring the cloth for my hands and a spare."

"Cloths, my lord?"

"Lady Isabelle packed them. Search in my bag."

He found them and we descended. There would, I knew, be a Great Hall. During the day it would be where the king held court. The tables and the chairs used for dining would have been pushed to the side. Now, I knew, servants would be moving the tables and preparing for the evening meal. When we reached the hall, I was proved correct. A pursuivant approached, "Sir Michael of Weedon?" I nodded. "I am Walter of Tamworth and the king said that he will speak with you on the morrow." He pointed to the table being laid with goblets and jugs. There were platters with food on them. "You will dine tonight with the king and his closest knights. Until then he asks that you entertain yourself."

It was clear to me that there would not be many at the feast for they laid out just one table. A servant brought over a goblet of wine for me. I saw Jack's face as he was ignored. In my hall, he would have been offered some. I pointed to the tapestries hanging from the walls. They were of the battle of Agincourt, the king's father's great victory. I said to Jack, "That is inspiring as well as being practical."

"Practical, my lord?"

"Aye, it keeps the walls warm." He walked around looking at the detail on the wall covering. It was clear to me that the representation bore no resemblance to the actual battle. For one thing, the English knights were mounted. In the real battle they had all fought on foot and, for another, there were no English dead. We lost some good men and boys that day. Having said that, I recognised some of the faces. The ladies who had sewn it must have known some of them.

"I envy you, Sir Michael, you were there."

I turned around and saw the Earl of Suffolk, Sir William de la Pole. I bowed and said, "Aye, my lord. This is a spirited representation."

He smiled. I knew him from the battle of Verneuil where he had fought bravely. "But it is not the battle you remember?"

I shook my head, "The horses were all at the rear, my lord, and we lost men that day."

He said, sadly, "I know. I have seen the tapestry that was made of Hastings and I wonder how much of that is true. I wish I had been there but I was fighting for my life after Harfleur. That was a bloody siege."

"It was, my lord, and a pestilential one too."

He waved over a servant for more wine, "It is good to see you, Sir Michael, and, without giving too much away, you are here at not only the king's but my behest. You and I share, I think, the same opinion of his uncle."

I was wary. Was I being tempted to an indiscretion that might result in a sojourn in the tower? "I am too lowly a warrior to have an opinion of my betters, of which there are many."

"And you are discreet, I like that. You are here because you, like Sir William Strongstaff, are both loyal as well as quick-witted. Both those skills will be tested." He saw, from my face, that I wished for enlightenment and he smiled, "I have said enough. The king will tell you all." He looked at Jack who had moved a few paces away to allow us a modicum of privacy, "This fellow looks young to be a squire."

"He is not a squire, my lord, but I needed a servant and did not think that this visit would necessitate a fight."

"Yet, you brought an archer."

"Robbie is a guarantee that, whilst on the road, we will have protection."

"He was there on Crispin's Day?"

"That he was and many other of Sir William's men."

The Knight's Tale

"Then I will send a flagon of ale for him to the warrior hall. Those men deserve more praise than they received at the time."

Other knights arrived and sought the attention of the earl. In the short time I had spoken to him, my hopes that King Henry had a good advisor were raised. He was a soldier, and whereas the Duke of Gloucester had fought at Agincourt, he had no empathy with the men alongside whom he had fought. The earl did. He did, however, have an unfortunate nickname. He was known as jackanapes, or Jack of Naples. It was the name given to a monkey. It had begun to be used by his enemies to insult him. It was unfortunate as the nape had arisen because of the monkey's tail on his coat of arms. A man like the earl always had enemies. His were the dukes of Norfolk and Gloucester.

When the king arrived he was applauded by the young knights. The earl and I followed but, in my case, it was just to avoid standing out. I had dined with his father and his mother and such acclamation was not needed then. Another difference was that the king allowed a fight for places at the table. The earl and the bishop flanked the king but the rest raced to get the seats closest to the king. He did nothing to interfere. I found myself at the end of the table opposite a young knight who was clearly disappointed not to have the ear of the king.

It had been some years since I had trained the king and I saw the differences that time and ill health had wrought. They were not the simple physical differences of a boy who had become a man, but there were other differences. King Henry prominently wore a cross and he constantly deferred to the Bishop of Salisbury who was at his side. The king seemed nervous and looked to the bishop for comfort often. Grace was a long affair.

My position at the end of the table meant I was assiduously avoided, even by the knight who sat opposite. I was unimportant and I was much older than were they. No one asked my name or the reason for my attendance. These knights sought positions in the king's household. His decision to relinquish the regency and rule himself was a recent one. I studied everyone as I ate. The clothes that the knights wore were expensive. They were trying to impress the king. Mine were well made and suited the occasion but they had none of the fashionable elements shown by the young knights. Even their eating knives and spoons were flamboyantly decorated. Mine were simple ones. Indeed, the spoon was a wooden one and my eating knife had been given to me by Sir William when he had first taken me under his wing. The ones I saw were inlaid with ivory, ebony and filigreed with silver. The other thing I noticed, for my nose was assaulted, was that they were all perfumed. My clothes had a faint aroma of rosemary and lavender but their bodies reeked of perfume.

Jack had to have his wits about him for all was new and the squires of the knights, whilst also young, were also keen to impress. There would be no kindly soul to offer advice. He was fast on his feet and the food I was brought was all hot. As he held the leg of hogget for me to carve some slices, I said, "How goes it, Jack?"

He grinned, "The cook likes me. I say please and thank you while the others just grab and run. I have already had a taste of the sweetmeats that you will eat later and they are delicious. I am happy, my lord."

I remembered when I had been a squire. I had met other squires who thought that cooks and servants were to be looked down upon and despised. My humble beginnings, like Jack's, ensured that I was kind to such people. The food was delicious, as was the wine, but I did not do as many of the other knights did and overindulge. Some became drunk and with that drunkenness came loud and boisterous behaviour. The king did not like it. Although the behaviour which would lead to such trouble later in his life was not there that night, I saw in the king two men. I saw the pious one who looked at peace talking to the bishop and I also saw the angry raging beast that he could become.

We had just eaten the sweetmeats, which were delicious as Jack had said, when one of the knights facing the king fell backwards from his chair at which the other knights laughed uproariously. The king stood and screamed, "This is unseemly behaviour. Leave my hall and go to your bedchambers." We all stood except for the earl and the bishop. The king said, "Not you, Sir Michael. You know how to behave and I would speak with you."

For the first time the other knights, as they dragged their feet from the hall, paid a little more attention to me.

When the last one had gone and the guard had closed the double doors, King Henry said, "Come and sit closer to me, Sir Michael, and tell your man that he may now eat in the kitchen. He will not be needed."

I nodded and Jack left. I took my spoon, knife, cloth and goblet to move opposite to the king. I cleared the detritus left by the previous occupant and sat. I saw that the three men were studying me. I wanted a drink now but I had to wait until they had finished scrutinising me.

It was the bishop who spoke first, "You have a good reputation, Sir Michael. Perhaps that is no surprise considering that you were trained by Sir William Strongstaff, and the king's late mother could not speak highly enough of you and your service to her. Your cleansing of the forests of bandits was also well noted. The king has a task for you."

I was always wary when I received such fulsome praise because, inevitably, there would be a demand associated with it.

"You have four manors, do you not, Sir Michael?" I nodded and before I could answer in more detail he continued, "The one my mother gave you at Houghton Regis, Iden, Weedon and one in Normandy, Les Pérets."

"Yes, King Henry, I have been generously rewarded for my service to England."

"Yes, you have been one of our more loyal servants and I would have you perform another such service for me."

My heart sank. Was I to be sent to France to fight alongside Sir John Talbot? I knew that my capture of the Maid had made my name and when I had returned to England Sir John had been disappointed.

The king gestured to the Bishop of Salisbury. William Ayscough had been the king's confessor and, as I subsequently discovered, was only recently elevated

He smiled, "The king is a devout man. You should know that his mother, the late Queen, was also devout." He spread his hands, "Of course you know that for you were the defender of the Queen. She was given, many years ago, a cross. Originally, it had belonged to the great queen, Eleanor of Aquitaine, and came to her from her father which, it is claimed, came to him from Charlemagne. The king would have that cross."

I was confused and I said so, "My lord, I can see why the cross is so important but what have I to do with this?"

"The cross lies in a church in Pontoise. It was placed there while Pontoise was still Norman. It was buried in secret beneath the altar in a box. Few men know where it lies. I learned of it from Father Bertrand who, as you know, was the late queen's confessor. We would have you retrieve the cross."

I was stumped and to give myself thinking time I drank some wine. I asked the obvious question, "How will I retrieve the cross if it lies in French lands and in a church? If I managed to get there and take it I could be hanged as a thief. Surely, my lord, taking the cross from a church is not only a crime but a mortal sin?"

The bishop had an oily tongue, "You are absolved of any crime by both the church and the king. The cross belongs to the king and, as such, its retrieval would be neither a sin nor a crime."

I looked at the king, "You are asking a great deal of me, Your Majesty."

He nodded, "As I recall, Sir Michael, you swore an oath to protect me and another to protect my mother. I know I am asking a great deal of you but this matters to me. The cross represents more than being a mere memento. The links to Charlemagne and Eleanor of Aquitaine can be used by me in the furtherance of our claims to France."

I did not think I would survive such a quest but he was right, I had sworn an oath. I nodded. "I will need to speak to Father Bertrand."

William de la Pole nodded, "Of course. He and Owen Tudor are in Newgate. I will take you thence on the morrow."

I took a deep breath, "There is another oath you should know about and if I am to go to my death for you, King Henry, then I need to unburden myself first."

The young king smiled, "You will not die, Sir Michael. God will watch over you."

I shook my head, "The earl and I have both seen too many good men slain while doing good works to believe that, King Henry. I swore an oath to your mother that I would be a protector for her sons, your half brothers, Edmund and Jasper. I beg you to consider giving them your protection. They are of your blood."

His eyes narrowed, "They could be used by my enemies to rally support against me."

It had been his uncle who had tried to capture the boys and I saw now that William de la Pole felt differently, "Perhaps Sir Michael is right. If the boys were housed close to you, my lord, then we could ensure that they become loyal to you. They could be allies. Owen Tudor is very popular in Wales. Glendower might be dead but there are others who seek to cause unrest in Wales. With the Tudor family on our side, think of the political benefits. I think that Sir Michael has made a sound suggestion."

The king played with his cross and looked at his two advisors. The bishop was noncommittal. Eventually, the king said, "It would be a Christian thing to do but what about the father? Would they not resent his imprisonment?"

Silence descended. Apart from the guard on the door we four were alone. The earl said, "Guard, stand without. Prevent any from entering." The guard obeyed and William de la Pole continued, "Release him, King Henry. It would be seen as a most Christian act. As far as I am aware he never tried to ferment rebellion and was only imprisoned because the Duke of Gloucester deemed him to be a threat. If you keep him close, too…he escaped from prison once. If he were to do so again…"

"I could have him executed."

The bishop said, "And Father Bertrand? If he were alive and Owen Tudor killed, then that might spoil your plans for the cross."

The king chewed his lip as he played with his cross, "I need to sleep on this." He looked at me, "No matter what happens to Tudor and his family, I would have that cross."

I nodded, "And I will hold my oath even though it might bring me my death."

He smiled, "Then all is well. Tomorrow, you and the earl will ride to Newgate and speak to Father Bertrand."

As Jack and I went to our chamber at the top of the tower, I reflected that I had behaved with honour and kept my word to the queen. For the rest, it was in the hands of the king and I could do nothing about that.

The Knight's Tale

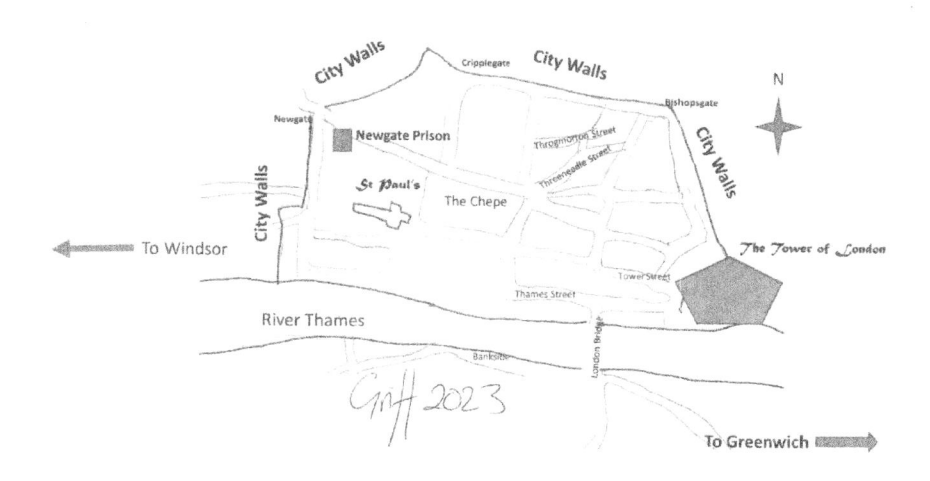

Chapter 2

I did not speak to Jack about the quest. For one thing, I needed to talk to my wife first and, for the second, he was too full of his experience. His polite behaviour and manner had made him popular in the kitchens and he had dined as well as I had. The king's kitchen was far larger than mine and he regaled me, as we undressed, with tales of the equipment and foods that they had. It was as though he had found a treasure trove. It helped me for it distracted me from the thoughts I harboured. They were thoughts of my own mortality.

We were awoken by a knock on the door from the earl's squire, "My master would leave early, my lord."

"We will be down promptly."

We dressed quickly and headed down to the hall which was, unsurprisingly empty save for the earl. He smiled, "Tell your man to eat while he can. I have sent word to your archer that we ride early."

Jack needed no further urging. I went to the table which the servants were filling with the food that would be consumed by the others in the castle. As we were the first, the fried ham was still hot and the bread had barely begun to cool. The butter melted as I spread it. We drank ale. It was too early for wine.

The earl had finished and he spoke as I ate, "I am pleased that you were sent for. Your coming is like the first roll of a stone down a mountain. It is insignificant in itself but you may well have started an avalanche. I think your words about his half-brothers sparked something in the king. He is a religious man and on reflection will realise that his siblings cannot hurt him and, indeed, may well help him strengthen his kingdom. You can be proud that you have kept your oath."

"And yet I fear that this quest to find a cross is doomed to failure."

"Were it any other man then I might agree, but you have skills and a history that suggests you can achieve the impossible." He smiled, "You spirited away the sons of Owen Tudor from beneath the Duke of Gloucester's nose. He is still angry about that."

I could tell from the way that he spoke that it had pleased the earl. Clearly, the two men were far from being friends.

"I still do not know how it will be achieved."

He pushed a small parchment towards me, "This is from the king. He wrote it last night after you had retired. It grants you authority to act on his behalf. Where you are able you can ask for shelter and aid from any of his subjects."

The Knight's Tale

I took it and saw that it was sealed. I would not break the seal until I needed to. "Yet how much of Normandy remains in English hands, my lord?"

"Not as much as we might like. Harfleur is still French as is the Pay de Caux and that means you will have to land at Calais. It means a long ride through lands which are still disputed." He studied me, "You know that you cannot travel with a company?" I nodded, "And the archer you brought here would draw Frenchmen to you like flies on a dead body."

"I know, my lord. I am still wrestling with the needs of the quest. I hope that our visit with Father Bertrand will help me to formulate my plans." A thought suddenly struck me, "Is that another reason for my selection?"

"It is. You were one of the few men that Father Bertrand said he trusted. He only told the tale to the bishop and he refused to speak to me."

I smiled, "Father Bertrand is a hard man. He would have made a good warrior."

"That he would." He saw that I had finished and said, "And now let us leave."

"Should I not bid farewell to the king?"

"He will be at prayer. He trusts you, Sir Michael. Do not let him down."

I shook my head, "I have done many things in my life of which I am not proud, my lord, but breaking an oath and letting someone down are not amongst them. I will go and while I may not return, it will not be because of lack of resolve."

The earl had, apart from his squire, eight mounted men at arms waiting for us. I was surprised he had no knights but I said nothing. He greeted Robbie like an old friend and clasped his arm proclaiming English archers as the rock upon which England was built. Poor Robbie was taken aback by the praise from such an important noble. We left the castle and headed east towards London. We would be riding along the north bank of the Thames and would not have to cross London Bridge.

I did not know London but I knew that Sir William hated both it and the populace. Their vagaries had cost King Richard dear and the old knight had been fond of the son of the Black Prince. He had been entrusted with his care and he felt that that misunderstood king was let down by all. Consequently, I had rarely visited the city and when I had, I ensured I stayed as short a time as I could.

"My lord, when we have spoken to Father Bertrand do I need to stay?"

He gave me a surprised look, "I thought to entertain you in my home just north of the city. Must you leave so soon?"

"I have much to plan and I would spend as much time with my wife as I could."

"You are a strange man. Many knights I know would relish time away from their wives."

"Perhaps they did not do as I did and marry for love, my lord."

"That may well be true and I envy you. Of course, you may leave."

The prison which had been built almost two hundred and fifty years earlier was close to the Newgate but within the walls of the city. It was a grim place. When we arrived the earl was greeted with great deference as his position demanded. The gaoler, however, studied me with suspicion. We left the earl's men and mine with the horses and entered. I was relieved to see that Owen Tudor and the priest were not in the cesspit where ordinary folk languished but had a cell to themselves, and they had not only beds but a table, chairs and even a light. It was, however, still a prison.

The earl said to the gaoler, "You may leave us."

"I am supposed to keep the door locked, my lord."

The earl turned and his tone was venomous. He was not a man to be crossed, "I care not what you are supposed to do, I command you to leave and stand well away from the door. You will leave the door unlocked and Sir Michael and I will ensure that your charges do not flee. Is that clear?"

"Yes, my lord." The man could not get out quickly enough.

Father Bertrand ignored the earl and said, "It is good to see you, Michael. Your family is well? Father John?"

"They are, Father."

He studied the earl, "And this, I am guessing, has to do with Charlemagne's Cross?"

"It is. King Henry is sending Sir Michael to retrieve it."

Owen Tudor remained silent but Father Bertrand snapped, "Sending a brave and honest man to risk his life for a relic. King Henry is not the man that was his father. I wish I had not told the bishop of the existence of the cross."

"Peace priest!" The commanding voice of the earl rang out.

Father Bertrand, however, was no gaoler and he laughed, "Why? Will you put me with the other unfortunates? Do so for I care not. I have not been charged with a crime nor has Owen here, and yet we languish in this prison on the whim of a noble. Is this fair? Is this just?"

I knew that there had been a chance that the two men might be released but if the priest continued his tirade, then that opportunity would be lost. I implored, "Father Bertrand, I have given my word that I will do as the king asks. You will be aiding me if you give me as much information as you can."

He shook his head, "You are too good for these people, Michael." He sighed, "The queen, before she died, told me of the treasure. She wanted it for her son, Henry. I think she believed it might make him a good king. Who knows, perhaps it may? The church in Pontoise is called Saint-Ouen-L'Aumône. It lies on the east bank of the river close to the Abbaye de Maubuisson. The priests there do not know of the box which is to be found beneath the altar. It was placed there by King Henry. You will have to clear away the detritus of the church and the last twenty years to find the stone which can be lifted. There is the mark of a cross upon it."

"Thank you."

"I do not know how you will manage to get into the church unseen and lift the stone without being found, and if you are discovered…"

"I know the risks."

"And do you know how you will do this?"

I shook my head, "Not yet but it is many miles to Pontoise and maybe the idea will come to me. If not, then I shall just have to watch and wait."

"In a land in which you are seen as an enemy." Father Bertrand made the sign of the cross. "I pray that God will watch over a true and noble knight who serves others and not himself."

The earl said, "Thank you, Father Bertrand. I have to tell you that Sir Michael here spoke eloquently to the king about your release and I am hopeful that his words will result in a happy outcome."

Owen Tudor's face lit up in delight, but Father Bertrand put his arms around my shoulders, "And the price of that release is this quest. The queen spoke highly of you, Michael, even in her last confession. She will be in heaven and I know that her spirit will be there with you."

"Gaoler!"

I grasped Father Bertrand's arm, "Farewell to you both. I hope that when I return you are free men."

We did not speak until we were back with our men. "You still wish to leave and return home?"

"I do."

The earl took out a purse, "The king has provided you with these funds. Whatever expense you incur will be borne by the crown."

"Thank you and I shall seek you out when…if I return."

I saw the curious looks given to me by Jack and Robbie. Our diversion had come as a complete surprise to them. We mounted our horses and headed out through the gate and then towards the Roman Road that led north to my home. They were both curious but, equally, knew better than to question me while there were others around. The road was busy until we had passed St Albans. We had bought pies in the market there and watered our horses. As we left and found ourselves on a deserted road, Robbie asked, "My lord, what is it that you do? The earl's men spoke of a secret mission to which they were not privy. I pray you to tell us."

I shook my head, "I cannot tell you all but I can say that I have to return to Normandy on a mission for the king."

"Then I shall come with you."

"I fear not, Robbie. You are an archer. Even without your bow, you are too easily identified as one of those who slaughtered the French at Agincourt. Your misshapen body marks you as an archer."

"Then if you will not take an archer who will you take? You cannot go alone. Take some of the men at arms." Even as he said the words I saw him realise that, like him, they were largely old men.

"Until I can speak to Lady Isabelle and put my thoughts in some sort of order then I do not know. Do not speak of this to another, even fellow archers at the manor. If the French know that I am going to France then there could be a hot welcome awaiting me."

"We will be silent, my lord, you know that."

It was a sombre ride home. Both men had been both flattered and happy with their treatment at Windsor. My words had changed that joy. It was as though I had showered them with ice water. As for me, my thoughts were on how I would manage to get to Pontoise and pull off this seemingly impossible trick. Even my Norman manor would be hard to reach for Pays de Caux was now in the hands of the French. I would have to travel further east and approach my manor from that direction. I had to get to Les Pérets for I knew that Charles, Isabelle's uncle who managed the manor for me, had been a French soldier and he knew his way around such places as Pontoise. I needed his advice.

There were watchers seeking our return and word reached Houghton Regis of our return. The warm welcoming light from the widening door to my manor was comforting. Once within its sturdy walls, I felt happy and safe. That feeling would not last long this time.

I knew that my two companions would say nothing but Isabelle knew me well. She could read my face much as a sea captain could read the weather or a chart. She knew that something was amiss but, as my children chattered and sent question after question at me, she just watched me. Margaret, the queen's daughter, had become one of my children. She had come to us as a baby and now seemed just like one of my own. She asked questions, too, and was just as innocent as my son and daughter. When we had dined and the three of them were sent, complaining, to bed, Isabelle sat with me before the fire.

"You know, husband, even before you came through the door, I knew that there was something amiss. Your face, your slumped shoulders and the fact that you have not once mentioned the king or the reason for his summons tell me that something dire has occurred."

I took her hand in mine and stroked the back of it with my finger, "You are right and, to confess, I know not how to begin. Not all the news is good but for us, as a family, it is." I told her everything that had been said and done in the time I was away.

She forced a smile, "You are right that there is good news. You have kept your oath to the queen and her husband and children will be safe but I do not like stealing from a church."

I sighed, "I suppose that it is not stealing. King Henry had it placed there for safekeeping before the marriage to Catherine of Valois. The king told her of it when he was hale and hearty. Neither could foresee the future and the queen did not know that her home and heart would lie in England."

"She would not have wanted you to do this. We both know that."

She was right. This was the whim of a king who sought a relic to help him to… I honestly did not know what. The coming of Owen Tudor into her life had changed Queen Catherine. When she had confessed to Father Bertrand, Pontoise had still been in English hands. Now it was French once more. The situation had changed since she had spoken to her confessor.

We watched fire flicker and sparks dance along the logs for a while. We could be silent in each other's company and did not need to fill the silence. My wife was clever and she was putting her mind to the problem at hand. I, too, was wracking my brain for a solution.

"When do you have to travel?"

"There was no time given but I am constricted by the weather. Soon it will be winter and sailing will be perilous. In addition, we do not know the situation in Normandy. If Rouen and Les Pérets fall then my task will be all but impossible."

"You have said you cannot take an archer but could you take a couple of men at arms?"

I shook my head, "The fewer men with whom I travel the better my chances are of escaping scrutiny. My old squire Jack would have been perfect but I cannot drag him away from your sister and his family."

She smiled, "It is strange that one Jack left your life and another came."

The Knight's Tale

It was my turn to smile, "This Jack is not the same as the one who was my squire. My squire was resourceful and a good warrior. Young Jack is like raw clay. He may turn out to be a worthy successor but I doubt it. My squire was tempered in war and we served together for a long time. No, I have a problem about who I shall take but, in talking to you, I have an idea how I can escape close scrutiny. I will wear old mail and ride the poorest of hackneys. I will play a knight who seeks to make a pilgrimage to Rome. It might explain why I have no squire and travel alone. It will explain my interest in churches. If I wear no livery and allow my beard and hair to grow then I might not be recognised." Her smile told me that she approved. "I have told Robbie and Jack to keep their counsel. I know that if word was spread then many of my men would wish to come with me."

She stood and took my hand, "Come, husband, let us retire. Perhaps sleep can give you the inspiration that I cannot."

I kissed the back of her hand, "You do inspire me, but this task would tax Hercules and I am no Hercules."

That night I had dreams and they were not pleasant ones. In each of them, I was alone and descending down a dark tunnel which became narrower and narrower until I could neither move nor breathe. When I woke it was with relief. No succour had come in the night but only more despair.

My wife said, "You woke me in the night, with your screams."

"I am sorry."

"You could do nothing about them for it was the task you have been given. You should know that if you choose not to do this then…"

I shook my head, "I have to do this for the king commands it. He is young and he is unpredictable. When he emptied the hall at Windsor it was a shock. Even King Richard did not have such behaviour. I promised both his father and his mother that I would be there as his protector. I may not want to do this but I have no choice. What I will do is spend the day preparing what I need for the journey. I know there will be comments about the growing of a beard but that cannot be helped. We will tell people that I have a skin complaint and that shaving irritates my skin. When I am gone then you can tell the others what I do but until then it is our secret."

Of course, young Jack and Robbie knew and the two of them watched me like hawks. They said nothing but it seemed to me that they had decided to be my guardian angels.

I had old clothes and mail. I found them and spent some time cleaning the mail. I was now used to wearing plate armour over mail and when I donned the hauberk I felt almost naked. I also chose a simpler helmet than the one I normally used. The arming cap was the same one. I could not use my good sword but I had an old one that had a good blade and kept its edge. The shield I would take was a simple one with no design on it. Swords for hire would adopt the livery of whoever paid them. The horse was easy. There were older animals that I often used to ride around my lands and I chose Mary. She was a good mare and not too old. She was clearly not a courser and would draw no attention to me. By the end of three days, I had prepared what I would need. I knew that my behaviour was attracting comments but I could do nothing about that save maintaining my stoic silence.

It was on Sunday, after my archers had practised at the mark, that Elizabeth and her son Jack approached me. Isabelle and the children had returned to our hall and I was alone, watching my archers as they bantered with each other.

"My lord, may I speak?"

"Of course, Mistress Elizabeth."

"Jack has told me of your quest." I cast a glare at Jack but before I could speak she went on, "Do not blame my son. He woke screaming two nights after your return and I dragged from him the reason. He wishes to come with you. He knows, as I do, that he is both young and unskilled in martial matters. I confess that, in my heart, I do not wish him to go but we both realise that we would not have a decent life without you. We are grateful for the home that you have given us. We had nothing and you gave us all. Jack has his mind and his wit. He is clever and resourceful. He learned those skills when we lived with the bandits. Take him, my lord, for with him you will have a chance to return. I have not spoken of this to another. Your secret is safe." She bobbed her head and curtsied, "And now, Jack, let us go home for Sir Michael has much to occupy his mind,"

She was right. I watched the arrows as they slammed into targets. Any one of my archers would be better than Jack but I could not take them. It would be the same with my men at arms. They were also all married men now or old. There might have been a couple of younger men but they would be as inexperienced as Jack. The advantage of Jack was that he had already played the part of a servant-squire and he fitted the illusion I was creating. I had to give the image of a poor knight and I knew that Jack would add to that deception. He was young but not too young. He had shown that he could play the part of a squire at Windsor. What he did not have were the language skills. He could not speak French but, that apart, he was as good a companion as I could hope for. After the practice, I walked home, lost in my thoughts. I would use Isabelle and see if she approved.

I suspected that Elizabeth, who worked in our kitchens, had spoken to Isabelle for there was no surprise when I broached the subject. Indeed, she nodded, "He is a clever boy and would fit the part of a squire for a poor knight."

"But he is young."

"From what I have been told you were little older when Sir William took you under his wing. Elizabeth and Jack both wish this to happen. It is meant to be and, in all honesty, I cannot think of another who could travel with you. It would be Jack or you would go alone and I do not want that. Father John and I will pray that Jack will not come to harm and I know you, Michael, you are a survivor. If anyone can do this then it is you."

She had made the decision for me. I summoned Jack so that I could confirm it was his decision and I was not surprised when Robbie came with him.

"Yes, my lord, I would travel to France with you. I know that there will be danger and Robbie has prepared me for what is needed on the road."

Robbie gave me a smile that was tinged with guilt, "I know you cannot take this misshapen lump of an archer but Jack here is the best that remains. We have a good leather jack he can wear and, in the days before you leave, we can make him into a swordsman. He is good with horses and he has skills that he acquired when he lived with the bandits. That is what you will need, my lord, for this task, a boy who has his wits about him. Jack will do."

"I can see that this conspiracy is a powerful one." Jack beamed at my acceptance of the inevitable. "Robbie, choose him a horse that will match Mary. He will need boots and a good cloak."

My men at arms knew something was going on when they were asked to train Jack, but Robbie ensured that no one knew our true intention. He was trusted by all. Once we had left, word would gradually seep out but, by then, I hoped we would be in France and beyond the rumours back in England.

The night before we left I relished every moment with my family. My son and Margaret were now close and enjoyed each other's company. They fussed and played with Maud. My wife had to chastise them now and then for their exuberant play but I did not mind. That night the two of them seemed subdued. They knew, it seemed, that something different was to happen. The last time I had left my manor had been to rescue Edmund and Jasper Tudor. Since that time I had been able to stay at home and my children were used to it. Normally

The Knight's Tale

Elizabeth, along with Sarah, served at our table but that night they both joined us at my wife's behest.

I tried to make light of the evening but the spectre of our imminent departure hung over the table like a ghost of the past. When it came time to bid them all goodnight, Elizabeth and Sarah ignored protocol and hugged me. I saw my wife smile.

"You take care, my lord, and come home safe with my son."

"Aye, Sir Michael, little Margaret views you as her father. Return to us."

I was a little choked at the show of emotion and I nodded, "You know that I shall."

My wife and I ascended the stairs. The goodbyes had to be given after the meal for Jack and I would be on the road before the sun had risen. I did not want us seen riding, as we would be in our old clothes and on old horses. Even if we were not recognised there might be comments and we wanted nothing to disturb the pond. The last thing we needed were ripples to reach either the Duke of Gloucester or the French.

"I know you cannot tell me how long you will be away, husband, but promise me that if you can, you will let me know you are still alive."

I kissed her, in the dark and said, "Each night I will say a prayer and send my thoughts to you."

She sighed, "When this is done, I pray that your service to the crown is ended. You have a life to live that is yours."

"I fear, my sweet, that Fate has determined otherwise. Sir William was chosen by the Black Prince and his life and that of the royal family became entangled, binding him for life."

The Knight's Tale

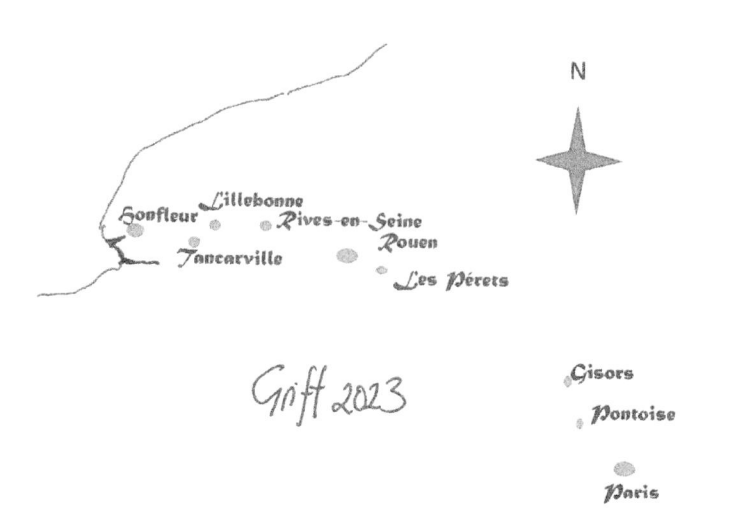

N

Honfleur Lillebonne
         Rives-en-Seine
         Rouen
Tancarville
         Les Pérets

Griff 2023

Gisors
Pontoise

Paris

10 Miles

Chapter 3

As we left the hall and crossed the yard to the stable, my land was silent except for the sounds of foxes moving in the night and the night creatures that flew in the air. When we reached the stable my hand went to my dagger for there was someone already there.

"Peace, my lord, it is just I, Robbie." My archer stepped from the stall where he had been saddling Mary.

"I thought to leave unseen."

"And I guarantee that you shall. There is gossip about your behaviour, my lord, but no one has an inkling of either your destination or your quest. Poor Lady Isabelle will have to endure a storm of questions when the others know you are gone."

I fastened my bags on the back of the saddle, "If we have a week before the truth is known then I shall be happy. Once we are in France we can disappear."

"Your men will tell no one."

I shook my head as I fixed my shield to the cantle, "I trust every man in the manor but there are those who pass through. It is they I worry about." I hung my helmet from the saddle. "I know that you will do so without being asked but watch over my family, eh Robbie?"

He nodded, "They will be safe when you return or I will have a place in the graveyard."

We led our horses from the stable and went to the barred gates. I realised that had Robbie not come then the gates would have been left open and that would have invited comment. I saw alarming flaws in my plans already. Robbie stayed at the gate as we continued to walk awhile. I raised my hand in farewell and the gates were swung shut. We were on the road. We walked four hundred paces beyond the last house in the village and then mounted. We let our horses walk for we had a long journey ahead of us. We said nothing until the sun rose and we were able to let our horses trot. The road was empty and we could talk.

I knew that Jack was excited and nervous in equal measure. I explained to him, once more, our plan and our names. He needed to have them embedded in his mind. "So I am Sir Ralph of Stoney Stratford and you are my squire, Jack. You will not have to worry about remembering another name and if you just use 'my lord' when addressing me, then all will be well."

He nodded, "Why Stoney Stratford, my lord?"

"It was Sir William's first manor but there is no knight who hails from there now and as Sir William's sons have shunned the sword and become merchants and farmers, there is little likelihood that the name will draw any attention to us. I intend to head for the ferry at Tilbury. London Bridge has watchers and we would have to pass the home of the Duke of Gloucester. My beard, hair and clothes make me look different but I am sure that the duke would see through the disguise."

"Do you know the road we take, my lord?"

"No, and that is a good thing. If I have never travelled it then it is unlikely that we would be recognised."

I had thought to take a ship from Rye for that would have meant I could have stayed with Edgar White Streak at my manor of Iden. I had dismissed the idea almost as soon as it had reared its head. Edgar and I had served together and not only would it attract attention to me, but it would also put the old man in danger. This route, whilst new, was our best plan.

We had planned, or rather I had planned, a two-day journey. It was more than forty miles to the ferry and whilst Storm or Shadow could have easily made that in one day, Mary could not. There was a small town, Enfield, some thirty miles from my home. Walden Abbey had endowed the church of St Andrew there and I knew that they had a small dormitory. It had become crown property forty years earlier. I had never passed it and I hoped I would not be recognised but it would provide us with shelter and food.

It was as we neared it that Jack showed that he was thinking about things, "My lord, why not use your passport from the king?"

"I am not sure how much use that will be. If I use it, then it will draw attention to us. As far as I am concerned it is there as an emergency guarantee for us, but if I have to use it, then our mission will have failed. The purse the earl gave me is of more use. Once we reach France then the passport will be redundant."

The prior welcomed us into the tiny dormitory that lay close to the church. He was surprised at our arrival, "We have few visitors, my lord."

"But do you have a chamber for us?"

The prior nodded, "We have six cells and there are just four of us here but our fare is not the same as you might enjoy at the Abbey."

I smiled, "Prior, I am a poor knight set to make a pilgrimage to Rome. Whatever you have will be more than adequate."

"There is, I fear, no stable."

"But there is grass and the weather is clement."

The priests were happy to have us as they saw few people. Their purpose was to grow crops that were sold at the local market and to provide extra accommodation when the Abbey was overcrowded. Prior Peter was an old man, "Ah, it has been many years since that was needed. The four of us are all that is required. We rarely see any visitors but it affords the opportunity to reflect on our mortality." It was then I noticed that all four were old men. "We have dedicated our lives to God and soon we shall all see him." He smiled, "I envy you, Sir Ralph, for you shall see Rome. I would have liked to do that but…"

I felt guilty for he was envious of something that would never happen. I was giving him a lie.

The cells were small and cold but Jack and I each had our own cell and bed. Even though it was a small community they observed all the services of the mother abbey. It meant we were ready to ride at dawn having been woken by the movement of the priests for their services. The handful of coins that the prior accepted made scarcely a dent in my purse and we headed to the ferry at Tilbury.

The last forty years had seen the port grow as the banks of the river were strengthened and the river bottom dredged. The ferry was on its way back when we arrived. The wife of the ferryman was there to take our coins. The crossing cost four times what we had paid thus far for food and shelter. The woman had an ill manner about her and Jack did not like her. Once we were aboard the ferry and heading for Gravesham he said, quietly, "That woman was like some of those at the bandit camp, my lord."

The ferryman also had an evil look about him and I nodded, "Not all bandits hide in forests, Jack. This is a necessary evil and it will save us a whole day."

Whilst there was a chantry in Gravesham, we did not stay there for it was connected to the leper hospital. Instead, we bought bread from a baker and found a place six miles from the river. We would camp for Rochester lay just a mile or so away and we could cross the bridge there. It was pleasant to camp beneath the trees. It was many years since I had done so. Jack was at home in the wood we used. He had lived that way until he had come to my manor.

The bridge at Rochester was busy and traffic was crossing both ways. That suited us and we were anonymous. Our poor clothes, my old armour, added to my beard and hair, made us look like others. The odd lord we saw, with brightly coloured clothes and a fine horse was noticed and the cause of debate. We were not.

We made Dover late in the afternoon and I headed for the port that lay beneath the magnificent Dover Castle. Calais was in the Pale, the part of France that was England and there were many ships crossing. The problem we had was finding one that could and would take two horses. Leaving Jack to watch our animals on the quay, I sought a captain in one of the many inns that lay close to the sea. The sea captains used the inns much as a merchant might use an office. They were places where they could conduct their business both legally and, I suspect, illegally. The inns profited from contraband brought in that was not taxed. It took a number of conversations to find a captain willing to take us. One Eyed Peter had the look of a pirate but he was more honest than most. He did not overcharge me for the horses and said that he would be leaving on the morning tide. For an extra couple of coppers, he allowed us to sleep aboard his ship. Each day my story was becoming more believable. I was seen as a poor knight on a pilgrimage. The real test would come in France. The voyage was a short one but, for Jack, exciting. We would not need to sleep on the six-hour crossing and he was happy to be sprayed by the salt water and the wind.

It was almost as soon as we landed that my plan began to unravel. Calais and the Pale of Calais were regarded as The Staple. These were unique laws and practices for Calais. It meant that it had specific laws and powers that might be denied to ordinary towns. As soon as I landed, I was greeted by a port official. He saw my horse and my mail and came over to me.

"What is your name and the purpose of your visit to the Pale of Calais?"

I had my story ready. I had used it three times already and it felt believable, "I am Sir Ralph of Stoney Stratford and my squire and I are headed on a pilgrimage to Rome."

He smiled and I felt relief. That relief was shattered when he spoke, "Good, then you have no military obligations, come with me and we will visit with the Captain of Calais, Sir Thomas Rempston."

"But…"

I saw that the official was one of those who enjoyed his power, "That was not a request, it was a command. You are now in the Pale and subject to the laws of The Staple."

I nodded. We were defeated before we began.

Calais had a castle and the Captain of Calais, effectively the man who commanded for the king, ruled his fiefdom. I left Jack with the horses hoping that I could persuade Sir Thomas to let us go on our way. The castle was filled and there were many mailed men. It did not bode well. My guardian approached a Sergeant at Arms and spoke with him. The grizzled veteran nodded and came over as the port official left to return to the port.

"Sir Ralph?" I nodded. "Sir Thomas will see you soon. Wait here."

There was a threat in his voice which implied that if I did not do as he said then force might be used to restrain me. I knew when I was defeated and I went to a table where there was wine. I took my coistrel from my belt and poured myself some wine.

I did not have long to wait. A liveried officer emerged and the sergeant approached him. I was waved into the chamber. I drained my coistrel and hung it from my belt. Every action was intended to show that I was a poor knight and not a lord with four manors on the service of the king. The captain was at a table and there was a younger knight next to him.

The sergeant said, "My lords, this is Sir Ralph of Stoney Stratford recently landed from England." He glanced at me, "He says he is on a pilgrimage to Rome."

"Thank you, Sergeant." The captain looked up at me, "I am Sir Thomas Rempston, Captain of Calais and this is my deputy Sir John Sutton, Baron Dudley. We have not heard of you."

"And there is no reason why you should, my lord. I have neither land nor family."

"Yet you are a knight," I said nothing. "Sir John Talbot has need of knights in Normandy. You shall serve England."

"But my pilgrimage…"

He smiled, "Rome will still be there when you have served England."

Baron Dudley said, "And you will be paid scutage." He smiled, "I will be leading the men and we leave for the Pays de Caux in three days' time."

I was defeated and I knew it. I bowed, "Of course, my lord. I will be delighted to serve England once more. Where will my squire and I sleep? Should I find an inn?"

Sir Thomas smiled but it was the smile of a wolf. He did not want me to leave the castle and continue my journey, "We shall find a chamber for you both. The men at arms are in the warrior hall but there are some chambers for knights. Even ones so poorly attired as you appear to be."

It was an insult, but I swallowed it, "Thank you, my lord."

The captain waved over the liveried official, "Show Sir Ralph to his chamber."

As I followed the man I realised that it was not a disaster, not yet anyway. The journey to join Sir John would take me closer to Pontoise. Of course, it might involve fighting and the risk of death but that was an accepted outcome for this whole quest. It would also mean I had to desert and that brought its own problems. I would have to adapt and change my plans. The room we had been allocated was at the top of a tower and just below the fighting platform. There was a bed but no fire. "Is there a paillasse for my squire?"

Had I not asked then there would not have been one but having made the request he had to accede, "I will have one sent up, my lord."

I followed him down and went to the outer bailey and Jack. "We will be staying for a while. Let us stable the horses and head to our room."

What I liked about Jack was that he was quick-witted. He merely smiled and said, "Yes, my lord," knowing that any questions or comments might hurt our deception.

When we reached the room there was a mattress for Jack. It was thinner than one might have hoped but a knight like Sir Ralph could expect nothing more. I said nothing to Jack for I was unsure who might be listening. I told him what we had been commanded to do and he asked the right questions so that if one of the guards heading up to the fighting platform overheard he would not be suspicious.

"Where is Sir John campaigning, my lord?"

"The Pays de Caux. It is to the west of Rouen."

"And when we are done we can go to Rome?"

"God willing, aye."

Most of the other knights were, like me, almost forced into military action. Sir John was the lieutenant-general but the wars had taken a heavy toll on his army. The Burgundians had sued for peace with France and the burden of retaking France fell to the charismatic Sir John Talbot. It was not easy to maintain the deception. I had to constantly remember that I was not Sir Michael but Sir Ralph. Most of those who were conscripted were English. There were fifteen or so knights and the rest were men at arms and archers. There was also a handful of Flemish warriors; three knights and men at arms. They were unlucky for Flanders was their home and they were closer to it than any. However, the men of Flanders often hired out their swords. The problem with the Flemish was that they served anyone, French, English or Burgundian. I did not trust them.

The day before we left a messenger arrived from Sir John with the news that he had defeated La Hire and Xaintrailles at the battle of Ry. It meant we set off in high spirits. There were just two hundred of us and that included archers and men at arms. As there was a Burgundian army at Crotoy, we had to take a detour and cross the Somme at Abbeville. The dissolution of the alliance was a problem. It added two days to our journey. I think the other knights thought me surly for I did not engage much in conversation nor did I show any interest in them. There was a simple reason. I did not want my web of lies to trip me up and I endured their hostility with my stoic silence.

The Knight's Tale

We reached Rouen and joined Sir John and the rest of the army. Winning a battle meant more than killing the enemy. There was always plunder after a battle and the army had done well. There were hostages and that meant ransom as well as captured horses, armour, weapons and jewellery taken from the dead. The men at arms and archers who had marched from Calais with us were mercenaries. They were soldiers for hire. I doubted that the archers would fight for France but they needed to be paid and with the Welsh and Scottish borders quiet then the only place they could earn a crust was in France.

I kept my head down when we were introduced to the lieutenant-general. It was just the twenty knights who were accorded that honour and I made sure that I was as far to the back as I was able. Even so, I am certain that Sir John saw me. I hoped he would not recognise me. It was many years since I had escorted the Maid for trial, but I had been a prominent knight. I prayed that my disguise was working. When we were sent to the camp, I was relieved. He had not recognised me.

There were tents and Jack and I found ourselves with the meanest of the ones that were left. Others shared but I was shunned by my new comrades. The tent, as we discovered, leaked. I wondered if I might have to desert this army if I was to complete my quest. The people of Rouen fed us. The battle meant that Rouen was free from the privations of the French raiders. It was peasant fare but delicious and filling. It was just as we were about to retire when a knight approached our fire, "Sir Ralph?" I nodded. "Sir John would like to speak to you."

Jack looked startled and I smiled, "I will return forthwith. Try to do something with the leak."

The knight said, "I am Sir Thomas Kyriell, recently made a knight banneret. I do not know you."

I said, "I am a lowly knight, barely that. I have neither land nor warhorse and, as you can see, my mail is so poor that I fear it was worn at the Battle of Hastings."

"It is what lies beneath the mail that counts and not the quality of the armour. Fear not. Sir John's star is on the rise and soon you shall wear French plate taken in battle."

Sir John had been given a house and I was taken within. Two mailed men stood guard on the door. "You may leave us, Sir Thomas." There was an unsheathed sword on the table and Sir John had a serious expression on his face. I was not offered wine or refreshments.

"Who are you, Sir?" I was startled. "I seem to recognise your face but your name evades me. You are not a knight of Stoney Stratford for Sir William Strongstaff's sons are lords of that manor and unlike him, they do not fight." Perhaps it was the mention of Sir William that struck the memory for before I could answer he suddenly took the candle and held it close to me. "You are the young knight charged with guarding the king, you are Sir Michael of Weedon. You served Sir William and served him well. You were the one who took the Maid."

There was little point in my denials and I nodded.

"Wherefore are you in disguise?"

I sighed and shook my head, "I am on a quest, my lord, and I swore an oath."

"To the king?" I said nothing. He stood and took the sword from the table. He sheathed it. "You were always an honourable knight." He took his cross from around his neck and said, "Put your hands on this and swear that you serve the king."

I did as he asked, "I swear and also that I am a true knight of England and that I am on the service of the king."

He replaced the cross and sat. "You know that men have spoken to me about you. Some say you are a French spy. It means that I cannot let you leave the army and carry on with your quest. If my men thought I had let a French spy leave it would undo all the work that we have done. You will have to stay with me."

There was no rush but there would be danger. "Of course, my lord."

He smiled, "To be truthful, Sir Michael, I am happy to have a knight such as you serving with us. Many of those who came with you are not the best." He nodded at my mail, "I can furnish you with better armour if you wish."

Shaking my head I said, "I chose this disguise to help me accomplish my quest. If I were to suddenly sprout good armour then it would draw attention to me."

"You are a clever man."

"And where is it that we fight, my lord?"

"First, we retake the Pays de Caux and then I intend to threaten Paris. I have no chance of taking that city but I can, at least, make them fear that they might lose it."

As I left to return to my tent my spirits were lifted. Pontoise lay on the road to Paris and I now had the means to get there. If I survived the retaking of the Pays de Caux!

Chapter 4

We left two days later. I still rode with what I considered was the rag-tag end of the army, the pressed mercenaries from Calais. Baron Dudley had joined the staff of Sir John and we were led by Sir Walter Wolsey of Masham. He was an older knight and had not come with us from Calais. I could tell that he was disappointed with the men he had been given to command. We camped just twenty miles from Rouen at Rives-en-Seine. There was a small Anglo-Norman garrison that held the bridge and crossing of the Seine. They were relieved when we arrived. Sir Walter was summoned to a council of war and when he returned, he had our orders.

"Sir John intends to drive towards Tancarville and Lillebonne. The French have men in both towns. We are heading for Lillebonne and it is the Lieutenant General's intention for us to mislead the French into believing that we are the main army. He hopes that they will empty Tancarville and he can fall upon that town with his main force."

One of the Flemish knights who had come from Calais shouted, "Are we the sacrificial lamb, my lord? Is it that we are meanly attired and newly arrived?"

Sir Walter shook his head, "We have to make a show of an attack. We will make noise. We will raid outposts but when the full force of the French army falls upon us then we will retire in good order, drawing the French behind us."

He had assuaged their fears but there was still resentment. Falling back meant we would not reap the rewards of a successful battle. We left and headed west along the narrow Norman roads. Sir John led the bulk of the army to follow the river south and west to Tancarville. His own knights and men at arms showed their disappointment in the men with whom they had to fight. It did not bode well that there was no harmony in this warband.

We had no light cavalry and it would have been foolish to use our most valuable weapon, the archers, as scouts. Instead, Sir Walter wisely used the knights. There was a little grumbling for, if we were ambushed, then it would be us who took casualties. Most knights had a belief that they were the most important part of the army. Sir William Strongstaff had taught me differently.

After half a mile of enduring a slow pace and grumbles from most, Sir Walter turned to me, "Sir Ralph, you have not complained. I would have you and my son, Sir Marmaduke, as the scouts. Ride just twenty paces ahead of us. That way the knights who have yet to earn the coin paid by Sir John Talbot will have a little warning."

The Knight's Tale

We were such a small band that others heard it and the archers laughed. I knew that it would annoy the other knights.

"Of course, my lord. Jack, my spear."

I had not brought a lance but a long spear. It was an old-fashioned weapon and a lance would outrange me, but I had been on a chevauchée before and knew that the spear would be a better weapon as it could be thrown. Jack handed me my spear and I said, quietly, "Stay at the back near the baggage. No heroics."

He nodded, "Yes, my lord." He was sensible enough to know that he did not yet have the skills needed to survive on the battlefield. He had come with me not as a warrior but as a thief.

Sir Marmaduke was the son of Sir Walter and he had a lance. His livery had a red bar above the three game birds showing that he was Sir Walter's heir. Nodding to him, I urged Mary forward. The knight was young. I took him to be little more than twenty years old. I hoped that his father had chosen him wisely and not out of favouritism. Sir William had always chosen the best man for the job at hand and I hoped that Sir Walter was the same. Sir Marmaduke had a visor on his helmet and it was raised but, in keeping with my disguise as a poor knight, I had an old-fashioned open-faced sallet. I had good vision but no protection for my eyes, nose and mouth. The coif around my head and neck was, however, the best piece of armour I had brought and I hoped it would protect me a little. We rode silently for a scout used his ears. I sniffed the air occasionally and after a mile or so the knight asked, "Why do you sniff, Sir Ralph? Are you unwell?"

I had been trained by the best scouts and knew that they always explained what they did, "No, Sir Marmaduke, I seek enemies. The French do not eat the same food as we do. The wind is coming into our faces and will bring their stink with it. If we smell the sweat and the stench of last night's food then we know there are enemies ahead. When we smell woodsmoke but see no houses, then we know that there is a camp ahead. Your nose gives a warning. The high hedges of this bocage country hide an enemy from our eyes." He nodded and I stroked Mary's head, "The other thing is to use your horse. Mary may be old and she might not be a war horse, but when her ears prick or she raises her head then I will be wary, for she might sense danger."

I came to know Sir Marmaduke quite well on this raid and learned that, whilst young, he was not arrogant and he heeded my advice. He changed after my words, and I saw him using more of his senses and not just some of them.

The Knight's Tale

I smelled the woodsmoke a short while before I saw the roof of a building. I reined in, "You had better tell your father that we have found a settlement. I will wait here."

He wheeled and headed back to his father. The tardy knights had allowed the gap between us to increase. I heard the hooves from ahead and my instincts took over. I pulled up my shield and couched my spear. Four riders appeared. All were mailed and plated and they filled the road. They had their visors up and behind them, I saw the gonfanons of more mounted men. Seeing me, they shouted the alarm and then galloped at me, expecting me to flee. There was no point. They rode war horses and I would be caught and killed even before I had turned and taken five strides. Instead, I hefted my spear and rode at them. The leader, who rode in the middle, thought he had time and he turned to shout something to those behind. His shield was not at the fore and I had too good a target not to try to take advantage. I hurled the spear at him. He was not expecting me to do so and the spear caught him in the chest. The spear had a sharpened head and was thrown with power. It knocked him from his horse and as he fell, he failed to release the reins of his horse. The animal was pulled down towards the man on his right. I drew my sword and headed for the man to his left. Behind me, I heard the horns of Sir Walter. He realised the danger and was ordering the attack. I would not be alone for long. The man with the lance lunged at me but I had my shield across my cantle and the unwieldy lance slid, scraped and scratched along it. I swept my sword at his unprotected middle. I struck the place where the breastplate ended and my sword swept through mail links, gambeson and flesh to draw blood.

I saw, ahead, the column of Frenchmen and the village where they had clearly stopped, and knew that if I continued I would be dead or captured quickly. I wheeled Mary and rode at the two knights who had been disordered by the falling of the leading knight. I could now see Sir Walter, his son and the other knights charging down the road. The two Frenchmen were caught in two minds and I was not. I rode between them. I hacked with my sword across the back of one of them and, as he had no backplate, managed to cut through to flesh. As I withdrew my sword I punched with my shield at the other man. He had already been banged and buffeted by the falling knight and my blow unhorsed him. I saw that Sir Walter had, with him, the men at arms but I could not see the archers.

I wheeled Mary to ride alongside the knight and I shouted, "A column of French knights ahead, my lord."

He nodded but I saw no expression as he had his visor down. He and his son had lances couched and I rode next to them, aware that I just had my sword. The French were disorganised. While Sir Walter had the time to charge down the lane the French were just ambling. It meant that we hit them hard. I wondered at the wisdom of such a foolhardy attack as the French outnumbered us, but when arrows began to fall from our left I saw the wisdom of Sir Walter. He had sent the mounted archers alongside the road, hidden by the hedgerows, and they were doing what they did best; raining death from the skies. The range was so close that their bodkins easily penetrated most of the plate. Only those wearing the most expensively made plate armour survived.

I blocked the blow from a lance with my shield and used my sword to hack off the end. The knight was slow to discard the now useless weapon and draw his sword. It afforded me the opportunity to use the blow taught to me by Sir William Strongstaff. I swung my sword at his plated arm but used the flat of the blade so as not to blunt it. I heard the cry from behind the boar's head snout and when his arm dropped, I knew that I had broken it.

"Yield, my lord."

Instead of yielding, he wheeled his horse and rode away. He further disrupted the already disordered line of horsemen and Sir Walter took advantage, urging his men on. The French horn that sounded a moment later told us that we had won. Even as the French fled west to Lillebonne, our archers reaped a fine harvest as they emerged from the hedges and sent arrows into the backs of the fleeing men. Some of our knights were keen to chase after them but Sir Walter was too wise a warrior for that.

He lifted his visor and shouted, "Hold! We have a victory and we have recovered Saint-Arnoult. Let us enjoy the moment." He turned to his son, "Send some men at arms to secure the far end of the village and have our archers as piquets."

"Yes, my lord." Sir Marmaduke had raised his visor and he was grinning as he said to me, "Bravely done, Sir Ralph. I wonder that you have such poor mail and horse when you fight so well."

Sir Walter nodded his agreement, "That was courageously done. Sir John said that there was more to you than meets the eye." He pointed back down the road. "You shall have the first choice of the plate, horses and prisoners from those you attacked." His squire had arrived, "Edward, go with Sir Ralph. If any other tries to take booty from those first men killed, then tell them they will incur my wrath."

"Yes, my lord."

As I rode back with Edward to the scene of my first encounter, I reflected that even Sir Walter's squire was better equipped than I was.

When we reached the place where I had charged, we saw men at arms and squires milling around the bodies and the horses.

Edward had a commanding voice, "Hold, those belong to Sir Ralph and that is the command of Sir Walter. Touch them at your peril." He waved an arm towards the village. "There are more ahead of you."

I saw Jack and he was smiling. I think it was with relief for we had both survived. I dismounted and saw that one of the horses had been hurt badly, it was dying. I took my dagger and said, "You fought well. I shall give you a warrior's death." I sank my dagger into the horse's ear and it died.

The wounded Frenchman said to me, in French, "Thank you, Sir, Charles was a brave horse, he did not deserve to suffer. I am your prisoner although I am not sure how long I have to live for your blow was a mortal one."

I realised that he was the second man I had struck. The leader lay dead beneath the horse that had been called Charles. I knelt next to the wounded man and saw that my sword had cut through to his stomach. I shouted, "Jack, fetch a healer."

"Aye, my lord."

Jack ran off but the Frenchman shook his head, "I am undone by the poorest knight I have ever met. When I saw you on the hackney with the open sallet and the ancient mail I thought that the English were scraping the bottom of the barrel." He suddenly winced and I saw that despite his efforts to hold in the contents of his stomach, blood was pooling and puddling beneath him.

"Save your strength until the priest comes."

"Aye, he can hear my last confession." His horse had wandered over and nudged him with his muzzle. "You will have no ransom from me but I can see that you are a horseman. I give you Gilles, freely. I would rather a real warrior rode him."

Just then the priest arrived. He took one look at the man and shook his head. I said, "He would confess, Father."

The priest nodded and knelt. I stood and took off my helmet. I stroked Gilles' muzzle, "You have a new master, Gilles. I shall try to be kind to you."

Jack said, "The men are all speaking of the mad charge of Sir Ralph. What would Lady Isabelle think?"

"As you will never speak of this, Jack, it matters not. The horse that was slain will be butchered. Help me to pull the dead knight from beneath it. The armour, purse and sword are mine, as are those worn by the knight who is about to receive the last rites."

The Knight's Tale

I did not need the purses, weapons and armour but if I did not take them then the other knights would be suspicious. As we stripped the mail and plate from the first knight I had slain I realised that it had been his horse, Charles, that had killed him. My spear had knocked him from his saddle and he was crushed by the horse.

The priest stood, "It is done, my lord, and he is dead. His name was Sir Jean de Béthancourt. He has lands in the Hauts-de-France." He shook his head and gave me a sad smile, "He said that in addition to his horse, you should have his mail but he wished his sword and rings to go to his son."

I nodded, "You know where he is?"

"In Lillebonne. I said I would deliver them to him. I will do so." The priest was an honourable man.

By the time the bodies had been stripped and buried it was dark. The smell of roasting horsemeat filled the air. It was a hot meal but I did not eat any. It was not that I had any objection to eating horsemeat but the horse was, to me, a warrior. I left Jack to clean the newly acquired armour and mail and to sharpen the weapons when I went to a council of war with Sir Walter. He was in a house that had been occupied by a Frenchman. The man had fled with the others for he had been given the house when the French had captured the village. It was the largest house.

I was the last to arrive, having cared for both Mary and Gilles, and when I entered I was greeted with a cheer. The men with whom I had travelled from Calais now saw me as a hero. I was still the same man I had always been but people's perceptions had changed. The exceptions were the Flemish knights. From them I had scowls.

Sir Walter put his arm around my shoulders and walked me to the table where there was food prepared and wine to be drunk, "Today, Sir Ralph showed us what we can achieve. I do not think that we will enjoy such a complete victory again for they will be wary of us, but we have done that which Sir John wished. The French have had their nose bloodied and will have to send men to shift us. Tomorrow we will leave ten men at arms to guard this, our new home, while we push on down the road. My hope is that we can relieve and recover more Norman properties taken by the French, but even if we just draw their eye upon us then we will have done all that Sir John wished." He held up his goblet, "Here is to Sir Ralph, the darkest horse in the whole army."

Everyone raised their coistrels and goblets to toast me.

Sir Marmaduke said, "And Sir Ralph and I will lead on the morrow as we did today."

There was a clamour from other knights who wished to ride with us. A simple victory had effected a major change. All that I had done was to obey my natural instincts and to fight as Sir William and his men had trained me.

Before I left for a well-earned rest, I had a word with Sir Walter. I told him of the request from the dead knight. "If the priest takes the sword and rings to Lillebonne then his mission and his priestly robes should afford protection. He can tell us what he sees."

"It is a risk to the priest."

"He wishes to honour the request of a dying man; I can understand that."

"As can I. Ask him if he will do this thing and he can leave before we do on the morrow. I have no intention of galloping around the land. I would rather be conservative and take few chances."

I liked Sir Walter. He was not reckless. I had served with Sir John and knew that, good soldier though he was, he could be a little too much of a risk-taker.

A farmer had offered the use of his barn to some of us, although Sir Walter wished me to stay in the large house with him and his son. I declined for the barn afforded Jack, me and our three horses, comfort and, most importantly, privacy. The first thing we did, after we had attended to the three horses was to examine the mail and armour. There was little damage to either set. Jack was too small for the plate and, in any case, it would have been inappropriate for him to wear it. There was, however, a mail shirt that fitted beneath his leather jack. We put the spare armour and my old mail in a hessian sack. Mary would be ridden by Jack and his hackney would become our pack animal. The one sword I had taken was a good one and I gave the older one to Jack. The shields were also good but would need the covering changed. A knight did not fight using the livery of another. Jack would do that when he had the time. I decided against wearing either of the two visored helmets. I was comfortable with the open sallet. The purses we had taken were full and I divided the coins within equally. Jack did not want to take them as he felt he had not earned them.

"Jack, you and I are as one; I may be the warrior but you also have a part to play and I am more than happy to share. You share the dangers and you should reap the rewards."

Gilles was a fine warhorse. I was keenly aware that he was a French mount and I spoke to him in French. Jack heard me talking to him and that was the day he began to learn to speak French. His first words were all equine related but as his audience was a horse, then any mistakes he made were excusable. He and Mary already got on and when he mounted her there was no problem. We left our war gear in the barn. I had recovered my spear and discovered that it was undamaged. After a breakfast of horsemeat fried on the fire of the night watch, we set off. Horsemeat needs long cooking and Sir Marmaduke and I were still chewing as we rode towards Lillebonne.

The Normans we passed greeted us as liberators but I thought it was a little premature. We had recovered one village and that was all. Anquetierville was a small village and we stopped there to water and rest our horses. The French had not quartered anyone there for it was a tiny place and the largest building was a small church. They told us that the French had passed through on their way to Lillebonne and were most dispirited.

We were about to mount when one of the piquets on the road rode back to tell us that a rider approached. It was with some relief that we realised it was Father John who was on his way back from Lillebonne.

Sir Walter, his son and I spoke to him. "You had no trouble?"

He shook his head, "The knight's son, Philippe, was but a boy of twelve and he was grateful that we had returned his sword as well as the rings and that his father had received absolution. I was allowed to leave unhindered." He smiled, "There is an air of fear in the town, my lord. I do not think that they will be sending out men any time soon. The gates were barred and the walls were well manned."

Sir Walter nodded, "They did not count us and they think we are in a greater number than is true. Sir John was right. Now if his plan works, they will send men from Tancarville and Sir John will have his opportunity to take that town."

Sir William had taught me to think and I did, "My lord, if they come from Tancarville then they will approach from the south and west. We need to watch that road. If the men of Lillebonne described us as a large force then they will send enough men to do the job."

"You are right. We will head back to Saint-Arnoult and use our archers to keep watch on the road from Tancarville."

He gave orders and we mounted. As we rode back with the knight I said, "We should quit the buildings we use, my lord."

He frowned, "Why?"

"We do not want reprisals taken out on the villagers. Let us camp in their fields. It is better to have a few nights of discomfort rather than risk the villagers suffering. This is Normandy, my lord."

"You are right and I now see what Sir John meant. You are surely more than a poor knight, Sir Ralph."

I smiled, "I am what I am, my lord. The knight you see before you is the same now as the day he won his spurs."

The Knight's Tale

It was an enigmatic answer but it seemed to satisfy the older knight.

We moved into fields and used hovels. The two cloaks we had taken from the dead knights were good ones and oiled. Jack and I used those as improvised tents. We found trees that afforded shelter for our three horses and we made our own camp. We were invited to join the fires of many others but I declined. I wanted as little contact with them as possible for, when we left to head to Pontoise, I wanted to be able to slip silently away and we could not do that if we shared a camp with others. I know we disappointed many and they thought less of me as a result but it could not be helped. I had a task to perform for the king.

The sentries and scouts we kept out proved their worth. They reported enemy scouts approaching from the south as well as the west. They looked to be combining their forces from Tancarville and Lillebonne. We were preparing to leave and head back to Rives-en-Seine when a rider galloped in. It was a messenger from Sir John Talbot. We saw him speak to Sir Walter for a while and then he turned and rode back whence he had come. Sir Walter's squire, Edward, sought me out.

"Sir Ralph, Sir Walter would have a word with you. We have orders."

Sir Walter had a happy look on his face when I approached along with his son. The scouts had said that the two enemy forces were less than a day away and the men were becoming nervous. We were like washing hanging out to dry with a storm approaching. A wise woman would take in the washing.

"Great news, Sir John has taken Tancarville. The French emptied it and he took it without a fight. He is heading north for word did not get to the rest of the French army of his victory. He hopes to take the French in their rear."

Sir Marmaduke looked confused, "Then…"

I answered, "We are bait, Sir Marmaduke. We hold the attention of the French and while they try to gobble us up they will be turned by an attack in their rear."

"Sir Ralph is right, Marmaduke, we are ordered to hold."

I said, "But not here, my lord." Sir Walter frowned and I explained my thinking, "There are too few houses here for us to use as a defence. When we rode here I noticed a wooded hillock to the north of the road. The road is within bow range and we could deny the French passage down the road and force them to assault the hillock. If we used that then our archers would have elevation and we could dismount our knights and men at arms and make them bleed as they attacked. Remember, my lord, we have seen no French scouts. They do not know our numbers and will think that there are more of us than we are. If we have to flee then we can move across country. We are horsed and they are not." Our scouts had reported that the men coming for us had foot soldiers as well as mounted men.

"It is a risk, Sir Ralph."

"There is another consideration. This village would be destroyed in the fighting. Houses would be burned and people killed." I was thinking of my own manor that lay a few miles east of Rouen. "If we are here to liberate Normandy from the French, we should not sacrifice the very people we are sent to save to do so."

"You are right, Sir Ralph."

It was my last argument that won the day and we headed out to travel the few miles to the hillock. We reached it not long before dark and Sir Walter forbade fires. Instead, men were set to take stakes and embed them on the slope of the hillock. It was not particularly steep but they would not be able to rise hard at us. Sir Walter had not been at Agincourt but he had heard of King Henry's defences. He bowed to my knowledge.

"You were at Agincourt then?"

I nodded, "I was young and more of a witness than anything. It was a great victory."

"Aye, it was, and would that King Henry had not succumbed to disease, France would be ours now."

This was the reason that the war with France continued. Since the Burgundians had left the alliance, I knew that it was a war we could not win. Sir John Talbot was the lone candle burning in a French night. He was too reckless to win. King Henry Vth had not been reckless, he had been ruthless and calculating yet the most courageous of kings. Those attributes had brought us victory. Sir William had told me of the wound that the king had received at the battle of Shrewsbury. How he had fought for six hours with an arrow embedded in his skull I will never know, but he had and Shrewsbury was as much his victory as his father's. It was a measure of the man whom I knew to be the greatest king that England had seen.

The horses were tethered on the north side of the woods. The squires were left as horse guards. Jack now had three mounts in his charge but he seemed happy enough. He had become completely accepted by the other, older squires and his happy approach to life endeared him to the men at arms. The rest of us, once we had eaten, slept in the eaves, behind the stakes. I took off my mail and newly acquired plate. I knew how to dress quickly and, wrapped in my cloak, I slept as well as possible. I rose before dawn with a mist still covering the road.

The Knight's Tale

As I stood, the sentry close to me nodded and said, "All quiet, my lord, save for the foxes and the owls."

I went to make water and then returned to dress. I had to ask the sentry to help me fasten some of the straps as Jack would normally have done that for me but he was guarding the horses. I saw the sentry shifting from foot to foot and I said, "If you wish to make water then I am happy to stand a watch for you."

His relief was clear, "Thank you, my lord."

I rested my hands on my spear as I stared at the mist. It would have been a perfect time to attack us if the French had been in position. I thanked God that they were not. It would be hard enough to face them in broad daylight but an attack in the mist would have destroyed us. The sentry returned and we watched the sky in the east begin to become lighter until the first rays of the sun blossomed. There was little heat in the sun and the mist would remain. I said, "Rouse the camp, sentry."

He went around and shook awake, first the knights, and then the rest of the camp. We wanted no horn to alert an enemy who might be within hearing of our position. We needed surprise.

Sir Walter smiled, "Up first and dressed for war. You are a warrior and yet you came to us poorly attired."

He was like a dog with a bone and I hated deceiving the old man but I could not divulge my quest. I shrugged, "Bad luck sometimes strikes, my lord, and there is nothing a man can do about it except pick himself up and begin again at the bottom."

"And that is a good philosophy, Sir Ralph. Many men who had fallen would have sunk into melancholy. I will make water and then dress." He nodded at the mist, "When the sun becomes warmer the mist will disappear."

Jack appeared shortly before Sir Walter returned. He had food with him, "How are the horses?"

"They are well. Gilles thinks that the other two are there to serve him. Mary had to put him in his place."

I smiled as I took the stale bread, ham and cheese from my squire. Mary had been the perfect choice but I was glad that I now had another horse.

"Will we have to fight today, my lord?"

"We will have to fight but I know not when. That all depends on the French. They have foot soldiers with them and that will slow down their approach. If they knew how few we were then they could simply use their horsemen and we would be fighting for our lives already. Keep your weapons handy and, if they have not attacked by noon, then saddle the horses. As soon as you hear the horns then saddle them in any case."

"I will, my lord. Good luck."

I nodded towards the archers who were organising their arrows, "Success or failure will depend upon those men and their bodkins, Jack. No matter how well we fight, we will be outnumbered and our archers will have to have a good harvest of Frenchmen if we are to walk away."

"And Sir John?"

"Oh, he will come, of that I have no doubt. It is the timing of which I am uncertain. Now go."

By the time the road was clearly visible, we were all armed and in place. None of us wore our helmets for they were restricting. We would don them when the French appeared. More than half of our men were archers and they were the ones, dressed in dun-coloured clothes, who waited close to the stakes. Their bows were yet to be strung and they all squatted. Some played dice, others used their knives to whittle wood. The knights and men at arms stood in clusters chatting quietly.

We had two sentries closer to the western end of the wood and it was almost noon when they scurried through the trees towards us. They knuckled their heads, "The French come, Sir Walter. There are more than fifteen hundred of them. We counted at least fifty banners."

Sir Walter nodded, "Go and join your comrades." He turned to me, "That means at least one hundred knights or more."

"Then surprise is even more important."

Sir Walter said, loudly so that all could hear, "The French come. They will not expect us here. We could simply hide away but Sir John needs us to draw the French to us so that they are committed. I will give the command for the archers to loose their arrows." He nodded to the priests who were with us and they moved along the line offering the chance for a last confession. Some men just wanted the priests to make the sign of the cross over them. Such small comforts helped men who knew that before the day was out they could be dead. They had all chosen this life but I knew, from talking to men like Robbie Red Fletch, that it was just before a battle that they thought of other lives they might have led.

The French had a group of light horsemen leading the column. Sir Walter let them pass and the archers strung their bows. It meant when the knights rode along the road, their shields covering their left legs, they were unaware of the ambush about to be sprung. Some had their helmets hung from their cantles, while the rest had their visors raised and I could see that they were chatting. The mounted men at arms could be seen coming on behind and that meant the men who could hurt our archers, their infantry and crossbows, were at the rear. Our archers selected the bodkins that they would use.

The Knight's Tale

Sir Walter shouted, "Loose!"

This was not the hail of arrows that had destroyed the cream of the French nobility at Agincourt, but the archers we had were as good as the five thousand who had fought on Crispin's Day. The flights descended and struck knights and horses in equal measure. Even those horses that had protection for their heads suffered. A bodkin crashing into a metal chamfron could hurt and would certainly upset a horse. It took two flights for the French to react. Horns sounded and those who had not worn helmets donned them. Shields were raised and horses were turned to face the threat. The light horsemen returned, but by then our archers had further thinned the enemy ranks with another five flights.

The crossbowmen and men at arms raced to present themselves before the horsemen. Our archers did not like crossbows. They called them the devil's machines. Changing from bodkins to war arrows, they shifted their targets and that allowed the knights and men at arms some respite. I saw that at least fifty mailed men had fallen and others had horses that were clearly wounded.

Sir Walter shouted, "When they are within forty paces, archers retire and we shall set about the French."

There was a cheer. The corpses by the road raised the spirits of our men as we all knew the French did not have the antidote to the poison of the arrow. The problem with a crossbow was that not only was it slow to set up, it needed a solid base and while the crossbowmen sought a comfortable stance and loaded a bolt, our archers slew them. The dismounted infantry, largely spearmen, reaped the benefit and they formed up. Another horn sounded and the infantry began to move up the slope while the knights and mounted men at arms reformed their ranks ready to take advantage of any lack of resolve in our defence.

Sir Marmaduke came to stand next to me. The lance he had brought on the raid was of little use here for it was too long and unwieldy. Instead, he drew his sword. I had my spear held overhand. I would be able to jab and poke at the spearmen who would ascend. Sir Marmaduke and the rest of the knights would have to use their swords to whittle away the spears. Our men at arms were armed as I was. With Sir Walter's banner behind us and the knights in a knot in the centre of our pitifully short line, the enemy would be drawn to us. The advantages we held were that we were well protected by armour, while the spearmen were not and we would be above them. Our survival, however, did not depend upon either us or our skill but on the arrival of Sir John.

The Knight's Tale

The spearmen knew their business and held their shields before them to deflect both arrows and spears that were thrust at them. They were confident in their use of the spear and I saw that, in anticipation of attacking from below, they were holding their spears underarm. There were weaknesses in both mail and plate when a blow came from below and these spearmen hoped to exploit that weakness.

Sir Walter shouted, "Archers, take out the spearmen." The spearmen had good helmets with coifs and each of them wore a leather brigandine over a mail hauberk. The archers would need bodkin arrows to ensure success.

When the spearmen were just over eighty paces from us, the archers began to pick out their targets. Archers did not like to waste arrows and they sent them at faces and legs. The Frenchmen brought up their shields when they saw an arrow coming at them. Sometimes they succeeded and stopped the arrow. At other times they failed. Few of them stopped the arrows to the legs. These men were brave and kept on coming but an arrow in the leg lost a man's blood and weakened him. The numbers were thinned but, as they had three ranks ascending, any gaps were soon filled.

"God is with us this day! Hold them!" Sir Walter had as much courage as the men who were climbing steadily towards us.

The problem the spearmen had was that they had to negotiate the stakes. Had they all been able to lock their shields then it might have made a difference Their shields were ready for the blows that would come at them. I saw that some knights had changed from a sword to an axe and a few of the men at arms wielded poleaxes, halberds and war hammers. They would rely on the fact that a blow from their weapon, even to a man wearing plate, could break limbs, while a spear striking plate and mail would merely cause a wound.

I saw the man I would strike. His moustache, which I could see above his coif, was flecked with grey. That meant he was a veteran and I would not underestimate him. I saw in his eyes that he was about to thrust and I took my chance. I was younger and quicker than the veteran and my spear darted out. He saw it coming but as his mind was on the thrust of his own spear, the raising of the shield was tardy and my spearhead drove through his cheek and into his brain. As deaths go, it was a quick one. I withdrew the spear and rammed it at the man facing Sir Marmaduke. His attention was on the young knight and he never saw my spear heading for him. I drove it through the links on his coif and into his neck. When the blood spurted and arced like a fountain, we knew he was dead.

The Knight's Tale

I had no time for complacency. The dead veteran had been replaced and the man behind stepped on the body of his dead comrade. His spear drove at my chest but as I had been pulling back my spear after my second strike, my spear deflected his and I took my chance and punched at his head with my shield. The dead body had given him height but it had also made him unstable and he tumbled backwards. We were now engaged along the line. Their superior numbers meant we were in danger of having our flanks turned.

I shouted, "Archers, to the flanks."

Sir Walter should have given the command but he was so busy fighting two spearmen that his attention was elsewhere. I saw that men at arms and knights were down. The priests had dragged them from the line and were busy tending to their wounds in the trees. Someone on the French side realised that the stakes were the problem and I heard an order shouted from the rear to pull them out. The first men who tried were easily speared or stabbed and so they had to resort to two men protecting one man while he removed a stake. It eased the pressure on our line and some knights and men at arms took the opportunity to pick up their second weapon from behind. I was comfortable with my spear, knowing that I was handy with a sword, too. I heard horns from below as the French leaders prepared another attack. I deduced that they had worked out how few we were, and I suspected a charge of horsemen was about to take place. With the stakes removed, then we were vulnerable.

I saw that one of the three men before me was not concentrating on me but on his work. I stabbed at the knee of one guard and when my spearhead was pulled out it was covered in blood. The man screamed and I rammed my spear at another guard. This time I tore through the man's calf. I then took a risk. Had Edgar White Streak seen me do it then he would have shouted at me. I stepped from the line to drive my spear into the chest of the man wrestling with the stake. He fell back but in his falling pulled the spear from my grasp. I drew my sword and stabbed both of the men I had previously wounded.

It was then that the French horn sounded and it heralded a retreat. Many men cheered. I said to Sir Walter, "They will attack with horses."

"Aye, and we have bled already. Archers, form lines behind us. Knights and men at arms, close in and make two lines." He shook his head. "I hoped for relief but..."

"Do not give up, hope, Sir Walter. We can always run for our horses if we need to." I knelt and picked up three spears dropped by men I had driven off. The one with my spear embedded in him had rolled down the hill. I rammed them, shaft first, into the bloody soil. They would not be as good as stakes but they might make horses veer. Some other knights and men at arms saw what I had done and emulated me.

When the spearmen and crossbowmen had vacated the field, I saw the two hundred horsemen form up in two ranks. They had lances. One comforting thought was that they did not have a long ride to build up speed and the slope would slow them, too. They would not simply crash into us and sweep through our pathetically thin lines. However, that thought was replaced by the certainty that their numbers meant they could simply walk over us. We were English and we did not cow to the French until we lay dead and, as the bodkins of the archers now began to strike horsemen, I held my shield before me. There was no reassuring shield in my back and when the first lance hit me I knew that it would drive me back, as it would with the rest of our line. It would herald the end of our foray. Sir Walter had eliminated the chance for us to escape when he had brought up our archers. The time to run would have been then.

Sir John Talbot, I know not if by design or luck, timed his attack to perfection. The battered French infantry and shattered crossbowmen were watching the inevitable slaughter of the *'rost beefs'* when Sir John's horns sounded the charge. The horsemen charging us did not hear it quite as quickly but when they did, their natural reaction was to slow and turn to look. The English horse, unlike our warband, all carried banners and it was a clear sign that knights were charging. It caused such confusion that our archers were able to bring down more horsemen. Some of their knights did charge us but it was piecemeal and they did not push back the men that they attacked.

When Sir Walter issued the unexpected command, "Charge!" then the matter was decided. Our tiny wall of men at arms, archers and knights ran at the horsemen. I hacked with my sword at the plated knee of one knight. The metal held but there was no padding beneath and I must have broken something, for he screamed in pain and then whirled his horse to ride down the slope. I lunged with my sword at the lower end of the breastplate of the next knight. It found no resistance as it slipped between the metal and into flesh. He turned and fled. All along our line, I saw the rippling effect of our attack and the retreat of the French. As the men before me cleared, I caught a glimpse of French infantry being speared by knights and men at arms. The French knights and men at arms who were retreating were not heading south but east. The French infantry would be sacrificed.

The French knights who were unwounded, surrendered. There would be a ransom for their captors. I had no such reward but I was alive and that was the most unlikely outcome of the battle. I kissed the crosspiece of my sword and thanked God. Now I had to find a way to leave the army and continue my quest for the king.

Chapter 5

The Pays de Caux was ours. Sir John himself rode up to congratulate Sir Walter on the success of our chevauchée. Sir Walter was a chivalrous old knight and he waved me over, "We would have failed but for this young man's insights into war. Sir Ralph needs to be rewarded, my lord."

"Does he, by God? Sir Ralph, you and your squire shall ride with me when we return to Rouen. Perhaps the ride will enlighten both of us, eh?"

Inwardly I sighed. I would not be simply slipping away and heading for Pontoise as I had planned. "It would be an honour, my lord."

We had more than a week to wait before we left. There were ransoms to be collected and wounded men to recover sufficiently to make the short journey to Rouen. The rest helped our three horses who were able to graze and fatten up. We dined well, for the two captured towns of Lillebonne and Tancarville had full granaries. Garrisons were left in both towns before we left and, as he had indicated, I rode close to Sir John. Baron Dudley had returned to Calais and we were a much smaller column than the one that had beaten the French.

Sir John was now governor and lieutenant general of France. In many ways, it was a meaningless title but he had come far. I wondered if Sir William, had he survived, would have held that office in his place. Sir John ensured that we could talk without being overheard.

"I see that your old skills have not left you. You may be in disguise, but your qualities and skills cannot be hidden."

"Yet, as I told you before, my lord, I have sworn an oath to the king and I have a delicate quest to make."

"And I have thought on your words, too. Let me make a proposal to you that will not compromise your oath. Will you listen to me?"

"Of course, my lord."

"It seems to me that your quest lies in France, the France ruled by the French, hence your disguise. Would that be correct?"

"It would, my lord."

"Then I ask you to stay with the army and me until we are close enough to the place you seek before you leave." He saw my hesitation, "You are an honourable man. You were chosen to train the young king. All I seek is your word that you will stay with us for as long as possible. Will you give me that promise? Then you can leave without any hindrance."

"My lord, why me? I am but a single knight."

"Sir Walter told me the effect you had on the men he led. You must know that I recognised the knights I gave Sir Walter as being the weaker men in my command. I expected them to run before the French. It would still have served my purpose but Sir Walter told me that your actions put steel in his men. Since I have joined you the name of Sir Ralph of Stoney Stratford has been bandied around all the campfires. Your success in defeating four knights in your first combat has inspired many. I now have knights who clamour to be the vanguard. You have become more than a sword for hire seeking mercenary pay and the longer you stay with me the more chance I have of creating that spirit King Henry enjoyed with his band of brothers."

I did not agree with his arguments but I saw that there was little point in my riding off ahead of the English army. Part of my disguise was now in tatters. I had a warhorse and well-made plate armour. I nodded my agreement, "I will stay with you until we reach…until I am in sight of my quest."

"Good. Then you should know that I plan on surprising the French. If they think that we will rest on our laurels in Rouen then they are wrong. We will replenish the men that we left as garrisons and we will strike in the heart of France. Who knows, perhaps I can make the whole of Paris tremble."

He was an infectiously enthusiastic man. He reminded me of Sir William. If I was not on my quest for the king then I would have happily followed him.

That was the only time I was alone with the lieutenant general but I rode just behind him. Jack was at the rear with the other squires. I felt guilty that he was alone but there was no need for my guilt. He thrived. The other squires wanted to know more about me and Jack became popular by association. For a boy who had spent much time hiding in the forest with bandits, the elevation to one whose opinion was sought by the sons of nobles was nothing less than miraculous. He was now a young man and unrecognisable from the urchin who had crawled from the forest.

We entered Rouen as conquering heroes and Sir John as a veritable Caesar. We rode to the castle and my new position ensured that we were accommodated in the castle. The room was not a large one but the horses would be safely stabled and we would be comfortable. The problem was that I was known. My manor lay close to Rouen and I had often visited the castle. I was lucky that the governor and castellan were both new men and did not know me and while some of the sentries thought that there was something familiar about me, they were deceived

The Knight's Tale

by the hair, beard and the name, Sir Ralph. Even so, I did not risk walking Rouen's streets.

Jack's French was improving all the time and, after five days in the castle, I acceded to his request to go with some of the other squires to Rouen's market. Jack, like the other squires who had fought on the hillock, had purses fattened by the French. When he returned he was flushed. The squires had enjoyed the hostelries. The story of our success in the Pays de Caux had resulted in generosity from locals who wished to reward them. He was not drunk but he could not wait to tell me all that he had heard.

Your name, Sir John's and Sir Walter, were spoken as if they were Achilles, Ajax, Caesar or Alexander."

"My name?"

He giggled, "Sir Ralph. That none had heard of you was the talk of many." He saw my face, "I kept silent even when they pushed me for more information. I was, what is the word Lady Isabelle uses? Ah yes, enigmatic. I tapped my nose a lot and implied that there was some dark deed in your past."

I shook my head, "You have missed your vocation, Jack, you should be a jongleur and make up songs to amuse people."

He became serious, "No, my lord. In this disguise, I see hope for me. Sir Ralph is a fiction but his story is of someone who is obscure and rises to fame and honour. There is no one more obscure than me but I can see that if I work hard to be a squire and then a warrior, who knows where I may end up? When I lived in the forest, all that my mother and I hoped and wished for was a roof, food and safety. We thought our lives would be mean ones and we would have to scrape a living. You and Lady Isabelle gave us all that we hoped for but by serving with you, I see that I can aspire to more. I just need to stay alive and learn. Do not worry, my lord, I will do both."

When we left Rouen, we would have to pass through my manor. I did not want to be recognised as it might cause problems. I rode with my newly acquired helmet with a visor. Without my livery, my normal squire or horse, I hoped to be anonymous. It proved to be as well that I adopted the disguise, for those with farms close to the road we used turned out to cheer us as we headed east. I recognised many faces and without the helmet, I would have been identified. Sir John had not told us of our destination while we were in Rouen. I understood that for there were spies everywhere. Once we were on the road there were many different choices he could make. That we had not taken the river road was significant. The French controlled the river and if we had taken that route, our progress would have been marked and our destination signalled.

When we reached Les Thilliers-en-Vexin he held a council of war and, along with Sir Walter, I was invited. "We shall head to Gisors. The castle is still in our hands and the lord, although absent, still supports King Henry."

I was sceptical. Many Norman nobles did not want to risk the anger of the English mercenaries and so they said that they were loyal. Their absence, however, meant that they could be absolved by the French king of any wrongdoing. It was the same in England on the borders where nobles held land on both sides. They were often absent from their manors, especially if there was war in the air. The good news was that we would not have to assault the castle at Gisors. It lay on the border between Normandy and the traditional French border. If we were seen there, then the French would know that an attack across their border was imminent. What they would not know was the direction of that attack.

Sir John said no more, and the rest were dismissed. An equerry restrained me, "Sir John would have a word with you, Sir Ralph."

The lieutenant general was alone, and he waved me to a seat, "I have not told the others our ultimate destination, but your delicate mission and your unique position mean that I will give you more insight into my plans." I waited and he stretched the moment of suspense by pouring us both a beaker of wine. "We will head for the bridge at Pontoise. If we hold that bridge then we threaten Paris itself. I would go on the offensive." I had not expected to be handed such a gift and my face showed it. He stopped, the beaker halfway to his mouth, "I can see that I have struck at the heart of your quest. Pontoise, that is where you are headed?"

My face had given me away and I nodded, "It is, my lord."

He beamed, "Sometimes we are gifted opportunities and it would be rash to reject them." He tapped the side of his head, "I had plans here but you are a God-given chance to make them better. I will select twenty knights. I will choose men who, like you, are French speakers. You still have the shield from the French noble you slew?" I nodded, "Then all the better. With French mail, a French horse and French livery you can surprise the men at the gates of Pontoise."

Sir John Talbot was a clever and quick-thinking man, many said reckless. He saw opportunities and he seized them. He came up with a plan there and then. It would involve danger for me and for Jack but no more than had we tried to complete my mission. If anything, the odds of success were increased. We refined the plan and finished the jug of wine.

"Until we leave Gisors all of this remains a secret, even from your squire." I nodded. He beamed and placed an arm around my shoulder, "And when Pontoise is taken and the people of Paris begin to fill their breeks then you may leave my army and return to the king. I will announce that you are returning to give England the news of our victory."

He was the most confident man I had ever met and that confidence was infectious. There were still many things that could go wrong but I knew that even if we failed to take Pontoise, I had a greater chance of finding the cross and returning to England.

Although I did not tell Jack of the plan, on the ride to Gisors I prepared him for the last part of the journey. He would have as hard a job as I would even though he would not be expected to put himself in danger. While I rode Gilles and did what Sir John had asked of me, he would be with the two horses and all my war gear. He would need to ensure that all the horse furniture was perfect and that the three animals were in the best of condition.

"When we leave Gisors you will need to be armed and armoured. It will help your old horse as you will wear the mail. I want you to have my shield. I will use the one we took on the road to Lillebonne."

"You will use the shield of the dead knight, my lord? I thought that was not done."

I lied, "You need protection, for once we leave Gisors then we will be in French land. An enemy will not discriminate between a knight or a squire. I want you to be protected." I am not sure that he believed my words, but he nodded.

When we entered Gisors there was no welcome from the people there. This was the Vexin and the traditional border between Normandy and France. They had seen more war than anyone and our arrival meant that they would be in danger. We spent the evening in the castle, and there the lieutenant general had the doors of the Great Hall barred and guarded as he gave the rest of his leaders the plan we had concocted back in Les Thilliers-en-Vexin. Heads swivelled to look at me as my part in the plan was explained. It was good that I would soon be leaving the army, for my disguise was now as thin as a piece of parchment.

"So, Sir Ralph and his twenty chosen knights and their squires will leave at dawn to ride the twenty-one miles to Pontoise. Timing will be all. Sir Walter, you and the men who raided towards Lillebonne showed me that you have the skills that are needed. It is you and your men who will follow Sir Ralph closely, but not too closely. You understand what is needed of you?"

"We do, my lord, and we are honoured to be chosen. We will let neither you nor my friend, Sir Ralph, down."

I was touched by the old knight's words, but I felt guilty that I was deceiving him. I wondered if I would ever be able to tell him the truth.

After the meeting ended, I gathered the twenty knights who would accompany me. I gave them detailed instructions. If they wondered at the change from the ragged knight who had left Calais all those many weeks earlier, they said nothing and I saw, in their eyes, that they accepted me as their leader. Sir John had chosen me and he was the one Englishman who had the beating of the French.

Sir Walter and his son clasped my arm as we left the castle. "You need not look for us, Sir Ralph. You should know that we will have you in sight and that we will play our part."

I smiled, "And I did not doubt it for a moment. God-willing, this deception will save lives and win a great victory."

The small column of men left Gisors at dawn and headed down the road to Pontoise. We were all helmed in the French manner. The twenty had been chosen for their language skills and their armour. Jack rode with the squires at the rear. His defence would be my spear. Our plan depended upon we knights looking as though we were seeking solace. Riding with lances and spears would make the men at the gate of Pontoise suspicious.

We reined in just as I spied the towers of Pontoise in the distance. There was a wall around the town, but it was the keep and its towers that we saw along with the spire of the Cathédrale Saint-Maclou de Pontoise. I turned to my knights. "This is where we adopt our disguise. Don your helmets and lower your visors. We ride to Pontoise as though the devil himself is behind us. Those at the rear, keep turning to look for enemies. Squires, do not keep order but ride pell-mell. From now on, until we either succeed or lie dead before the walls of Pontoise, we speak French. You have all been chosen for your language skills as well as your knightly courage. Today, we need both." I did as I had ordered them to do and tightened Gilles' girths. I mounted and said, in French, "Are you ready, my friends?" They cheered and I said, "Let us ride."

The rest had helped our horses and we galloped down the road.

We were spied when we were half a mile from the gates and our martial dress and speed made the guards slam the gates in our faces. I reined in and shouted, "I am Sir Bertrand de Béthancourt and we are fleeing from the English. Let us in or we will be slaughtered."

The sergeant shouted, "I know of a Sir Jean de Béthancourt, who are you?"

"I am his brother. Sir Jean died fighting the English. Do you not recognise the livery? Now open the gates or I will soon join him."

Sir John Talbot had thought this plan out well. It was based on some truths and some lies. When the sergeant shouted, "Open the gates!" Then we knew that the lies had worked.

As the gates opened, Sir Walter and his pursuers were seen. A voice from within the town shouted, "For the love of God, hasten or we will all be slaughtered."

I drew my sword and rode at the men holding the gates open. Already horns were sounding the alarm as men ran to the fighting platform. The outcome of this bold strategy hung in the balance. I struck two of the sentries. I used the flat of my sword on their helmets and rendered both unconscious. The other knights had also spread out and were clearing the gateway for Sir Walter and his men. Sir John would be hard on their heels with the bulk of the army but we one hundred had to hold the gate.

The squires galloped in and I wheeled Gilles to seek more threats. A French knight led twenty or so men at arms, not towards the stairs but us. They had pikes and spears. I had not yet learned all of Gilles' skills but I gambled that the knight who had owned him had trained him well. I pulled back on his reins and stood in the stirrups to make him rear. It takes a brave man to face flailing hooves and the men approaching me halted. It bought time for Sir Walter and Sir Marmaduke to gain the gateway. We were outnumbered and as bolts began to fall from the walls, men were hit. I rode Gilles directly at the French knight. I had but a few horse paces between us but it was enough. As the knight swung his poleaxe, I jinked Gilles to my right and the poleaxe hit the shield that covered my left leg. I stood and brought down the edge of my sword. It was a hurried blow but I managed to strike between the shoulder and the neck. The knight sank to his knees.

The bolt that hit me struck my helmet. It did not penetrate but it rocked my head and rang like a bell. It confused me. I was slow to turn but, as I did so, I saw the pikeman racing at me, swinging his weapon. I knew that my sword would not stop the blow in time and I was a dead man. The spear that struck him was thrown but it was a good strike and caught him in the neck. The pike fell at his feet and I turned to see who had saved my life. It was Jack. He had ridden Mary to get as close to me as he could. I raised my sword in salute.

It was at that moment that Sir John led his household knights to clatter across the cobbles and into the town. As Sir Walter and his men raced up the stairs to secure the walls, I knew that we had won. It was a most unlikely victory but Sir John Talbot had managed to take the town that lay just fifteen miles from Saint-Denis and Paris. More importantly, I was within touching distance of the church, the cross of Charlemagne and the end of my quest.

Chapter 6

As much as I wanted to get on with my mission I could not, at least not immediately. We had taken the gate but we had a town to secure. I followed Sir John as he galloped towards the bridge end of the town. His ruse had succeeded and we rode through a town filled with terrified citizens trying to avoid the wrath of the English and escape across the Seine. They would head to Paris. It was their flight that helped us to take the town without too great a loss of life. They thronged the bridge and before the sun had set, we were in control of the gates, the bridge and the town gate to the south of the river. I knew that the church I sought was on the far side of the bridge, the southern end of the town. As much as I wanted to ride to the church while there was confusion, retrieve the cross and be done with my task, I knew that such action would draw attention to me. Our army had Frenchmen as well as Flemish, Swabians and Italians. Sir John could not be choosy about the men he hired to fight for England. A priceless heirloom such as Charlemagne's Cross would be a draw that would make such men change sides quickly. I had to bide my time.

Sir John had the gates secured and the prisoners disarmed. Oaths were taken and arrangements were made for ransom. The lieutenant-general allowed us to commandeer our own rooms. I found a small house, close to the bridge, that had been abandoned. From its size, it had not been occupied by a family. Since I had married I had known how to detect a woman's touch. The house had no evidence that a woman had lived there. It had a stable that was secured by a gate and that was perfect. I also chose it because it lay just a few hundred paces from Saint-Ouen-L'Aumône, the church we sought.

Sir John sent a messenger to ask his lieutenants to gather at the Hôtel de Ville just after matins. I had planned on visiting Saint-Ouen-L'Aumône to scout out the layout. Father Bertrand's description was a starting point only. I resigned myself to having to wait at least another day before I could complete my quest. I knew that luck had played a part in my search for the cross and I should be grateful for that.

There was a euphoric air to the meeting. The victory had been sudden, surprising and successful. No one had expected it except, perhaps, Sir John himself. It was not a feast we enjoyed, but food gathered from the town and served on platters. Sir John spoke to us as we ate, "We have achieved more in these last two months than since I came to France." He waved an arm at the gathered knights, "And it is you that I have to thank. The ransoms you take are well-earned and you should know that we will stay here in Pontoise until they are delivered.

The Knight's Tale

The town walls are strong and but for the efforts of Sir Ralph and his brave knights, we would not have breached them."

He meant well but I could have done without the attention of every eye in the room. Their cheers and congratulations were flattering but I did not need them. The Flemish knights had still not warmed to me and they glared.

"Those who had no opportunity to take ransom, fear not. For the next week, I intend for those men to raid the lands around Pontoise and take from men who thought that they were safe. Paris itself will be threatened." There was a cheer and then he raised his hands, "I do not want the populace of Pontoise angered. Make sure your people do not abuse them. I want no mischief within these walls as we seek to hurt those who live closer to Paris." He smiled, "Enjoy this food and once more, well done to you all." He caught my eye and, as he sat, gestured for me to approach.

I had eaten enough and I stood. Jack hovered at my shoulder, "Take some food and return to our new lodgings. I will follow soon enough."

"Yes, my lord, I have scouted out the kitchens already." Jack was nothing if not resourceful.

My back was slapped so many times on my way to speak to Sir John that, had I not still been wearing mail, I should have been black and blue. The level of noise was such that I had to put my head down close to Sir John so that he could speak directly into my ear. "You have kept your word and more. I will keep mine. You may leave the army when you have… I hoped that you would stay but you, like Sir William, are an honourable man All that I ask is that before you leave, you come to me so that I can give you authority to return to England. If nothing else, you can carry my report of this great victory."

"I will do so, Sir John."

I bowed and left his side, Sir Marmaduke's hand arrested my arm, "Will you not join us, Sir Ralph? My father and I would like to enjoy your company."

As much as I wanted to join such good warriors, there were plans I had to make. I shook my head, "I am sorry, my lord, but I must join Jack. The house we have secured is in a rough part of the town. Unlike you and your father, I have no men serving me who can guard it."

"We can loan you some."

"I have done well out of this chevauchée and, when time allows, I shall hire more men. I have spoken with Sir John and he has a task for me and Jack. I fear that I will not be continuing with you and your father but I promise that before we part we shall talk."

The Knight's Tale

He looked disappointed but nodded, "You are a deep one, Sir Ralph, and I will honour your request. I know that my father would have you as a household knight in a heartbeat."

"And I like him too. He is a throwback to...well, let us say a great knight whom I once served."

With my cloak about me, I left the building. Sir John had patrols in the town to keep order and I had been given the password. It meant I reached the house quickly. I found Jack there and I said, "Let us go to the church."

"We go to recover the cross?"

I shook my head, "No, we need to be circumspect. Sir John's patrols do not know our quest and we might be apprehended as looters. It would not do to be hanged on the brink of success."

The bridge was guarded and we were stopped. Luckily, I was recognised, "Sir Ralph, what is your business south of the river?"

"I spied a church there. The cathedral has many men praying within. I seek a quiet place to thank God for his help in our victory."

"Pass then."

We walked over the wooden bridge. The Seine was not as wide as it had been downstream but it was still wide enough. I had left Sir John while it was still early and I could hear, from within the church, the sound of voices. There was a service. We entered and in the candlelit interior, I saw less than twelve people knelt in prayer. The priest was intoning Latin. I saw, as Jack and I knelt that he had noticed us. We bowed our heads. When he said, "Amen," we raised our heads and that allowed me to study the altar.

It was a simple church. Unlike the cathedral there were no golden candlesticks, they were made of pewter. The altar itself had a white cloth and it was unadorned. This was a church of the people. The women and old men who stood at the end of the service were meanly attired. We were studied as they left. The priest came up to us and spoke. His English was heavily accented, "What brings two English soldiers to my little church?"

I answered him in French, "I am a soldier, Father, but a pious one. I killed men this day and I would pray for their souls."

He nodded and this time spoke more easily in French, "Better that you put down your sword, my son."

We stood and I shook my head, "It is my trade, Father, but you should know that I do not use my sword indiscriminately."

"This is a church. Words spoken here are heard directly by God and all lies will be punished."

"I know it is a church and you should know that I will visit again. I hope that it does not offend you, but I will be here on the morrow for your first service and again tomorrow evening."

"God welcomes all to his church." He made the sign of the cross. "You seem to be genuine, Englishman. We shall see."

We did not speak until we were back in the house. I shook my head as Jack took off my mail, "I thought that simply getting to Pontoise would be the hard part of this, but I cannot see how we can do what we must. The priest will watch us."

Jack smiled, "You forget, my lord, that you have brought a thief. The priest never looked at me once. If you can give me instructions and keep the priest distracted, then I can find the cross."

I looked at him with new eyes, "You are sure?"

He shrugged, "It will be easier for me than for you, my lord. What did Father Bertrand tell you?"

"That it was beneath the altar and the stone that covers it has a cross carved upon it. He said that you would need a knife to clear away the dust that will have gathered there."

"There was a man in the forest, a thief called Will the Fingers. He was not an archer but he was known to have stolen from churches. He told us, one night when he was drunk, how churches all had a secret place beneath the altar. He boasted of how easy it is to get at them. He said you needed two knives and you slide the knives between the stone at two sides and lift. I have two knives."

"Then tomorrow morning we can see the altar and then, at the evening service, I will distract the priest. It is a plan and I am glad that I chose you."

"I am happy to repay you, my lord."

The first service of the day would be at Prime and so we rose when the Abbey close to the church sounded its bells for Lauds. We ate and dressed. This time we did not bother with my mail and, with cloaks about us, we headed to the bridge. There was a different set of guards on the bridge but the password worked and we crossed. The door to the church was open and a couple of candles dimly lit the church. I did not see the priest but we made the sign of the cross and headed to the altar rail. We knelt in prayer but both of us studied the floor. At first, I saw nothing, but when the priest arrived carrying a freshly lit candle, its illumination showed us the cross and the stone.

"You are a pious knight and I may have misjudged you."

After the service, I did not speak to the priest, but we left and returned to our home. "You saw it?"

The Knight's Tale

Jack nodded, "And there seemed to be less dirt between the stones than I would have expected. If I might suggest, my lord?"

"Go ahead, as you say, you are the thief."

"I will not go with you. The priest entered from a door to the rear of the church. I will gain entry that way and, when the service is over, if you can distract him then I will do the rest."

"Perhaps we should return when the church is empty."

He shook his head, "The priest will probably lock it. We cannot take that chance, my lord, and trust me, I can do this."

We ate and then went towards the cathedral. We enjoyed the fact that we had no tasks to perform. We had seen men crossing the bridge to leave the town and raid when we had returned from the church. Others were on guard duty and there were many waiting for ransom. I had allowed the knights who had accompanied me on the attack on the gates to claim the ransom. I sought out Sir Walter. If we were going to retrieve the cross that night then I would be leaving on the morrow and I wanted to say a proper farewell to the old knight.

Such was the fame of Sir Ralph of Stoney Stratford that I was greeted warmly by every English knight as I sought out the house commandeered by Sir Walter and his household. When Jack and I entered they fetched us wine and ham.

"You left early last night, Sir Ralph. You are an enigma."

I smiled, "I am anything but. I am a simple knight with lowly ambitions."

"My son told you, last night, that I would happily have you as a household knight. I have a large manor in Yorkshire and as a bachelor knight you would be comfortable."

"When I was ordered to come on this raid I told the Captain of Calais that I was on a pilgrimage to Rome. I still intend to make that journey, although I have also promised Sir John that I will take news of our victory back to England first. Thanks to our success I am no longer a poor knight and my journey to Rome will be easier. When I have the time and I have obeyed Sir John's commands as well as finishing my pilgrimage, then I might consider your offer but, as you and Sir John have much to do here in France, I do not think that the matter is an urgent one."

"You are wise and nothing you have said changes my opinion of you, but I will honour your wishes and you should know that my offer will still stand whenever you are in a position to choose your new life."

We spent the rest of the day preparing our horses and for our flight. Once we had the cross, I wanted to leave as quickly and quietly as I could. Already the army was preparing to move off and for Sir John to continue his raid. Jack and I gathered the food we would need. We also procured some oats for the horses. We would be riding hard and it was a long way to Calais. With Harfleur still in French hands then we would have to make the journey north.

Jack and I crossed the bridge together. It made life easier. We were now known by the guards and they saw nothing amiss in our mission. Jack disappeared when we neared the church. The priest was at the door earl to greet the congregation when they arrived. He smiled at me, "It may be that I was wrong for you seem to be truly virtuous." Just then a group of Flemish mercenaries, all of them drunk, passed us on their way to the bridge. The French who were approaching the church for the service, pushed themselves into the walls. "Would that others were of the same mind."

"Then, Father, there is more work for you to save their souls."

"I fear that some men's souls are so mired in mischief that they are beyond redemption. I have enough to do with my people who live here on the poorer side of Pontoise." He shook his head, "You may enter." He gestured with his arm and the people moved. Some dipped their fingers in the holy water as they passed.

We watched the people pass and then went into the dimly lit church. The candles were not of the best quality. It was a poor parish. There were more people than there had been on the previous evening. It was not yet crowded but it showed that Sir John's patrols, the Flemish excepted, were working and the people felt safer. The priest began to speak. We responded and the service followed its normal pattern. When Jack ghosted next to me, I was surprised, not to say shocked, but I said nothing. At the end of the service, we rose and walked to the door. I was desperate to speak to my squire but I dared not. I had to trust him. What had happened? Were we to spend another day in Pontoise?

When we reached the house and he took off his cloak I said, "What happened?"

He grinned and said, "Nothing." Then like a conjuror, he produced the cross from the folds of his tunic. "While you spoke outside the church, I took advantage of the absence of the priest. I left the box in the aperture. I did not think we needed it for it was a plain box and, this way, should someone lift the stone the box will still be in place."

I shook my head, "You are a wonder, Jack."

He held out the cross, "It seems plain for the cross of an emperor."

I examined it and he was right, for it was made of silver and not gold and there were no jewels inlaid but I saw writing on the reverse. It was beautifully etched.

Jack could not read and certainly not Latin, "What does it say, my lord?"

"Charlemagne had me made."

"Then it is the right cross." I nodded. "And now we leave for England?"

Putting the cross around my neck I said, "Aye, and until we see the king, it will stay around my neck."

I said prayers that night to thank God for Jack and to ask forgiveness for the theft. I knew that it was not technically a theft, as it had belonged to Queen Catherine, but it felt like a theft and I wanted no more sins on my conscience.

We rose before dawn and were at the Hôtel de Ville while Sir John was at breakfast. My name afforded me entry and Sir John gave me a shrewd look, "You have completed your quest?" I nodded. "And as I have not heard of any crime, then you are to be commended." He gestured for me to sit and eat, "I confess that I feared it would be some blood feud that brought you here. I am glad that it was not." He ate some bread with ham and mustard on it. He chewed and I ate some too. When he wiped his mouth and washed down the food he said, "I take it that I cannot persuade you to stay."

"My quest is only half done, my lord."

He nodded and waved over his squire, "Fetch me the document." As the man left us, he leaned in and said, "When first you were brought to my attention you said that you were on the service of the king." I nodded. "Then this parchment." His squire handed it to him. "This shall be your passport and a message for King Henry. He will have heard of our victory but this will let him know that I am not done yet. Guard it well, for I would not have our good work undone."

I knew that he had not meant to, but he was doubling my work and the danger we might face. I nodded, "I shall guard it with my life."

"Do not throw your life away. If you think you are in danger, then destroy the parchment. The king will have to hear my words from your lips." He handed me the parchment and then his arm. "God Speed."

I was aware, as I left the hall, that all eyes were on me. Sir John was an honest and honourable knight, were all the other men in the hall?

Chapter 7

Jack was already mounted on Mary and holding the reins of Gilles when I left Sir John. We headed for the gate. The sentries there must have been warned of our departure for we were allowed to pass unhindered. As we left the town, we had an open road. The guards ensured that no one was leaving Pontoise and the presence of our army would deter those who might normally visit the town.

I reined in half a mile from the town at a crossroads. I pointed north and west, "We could go to Gisors and head directly for Calais. We could avoid the French castle at Beauvais, but we would have a one-hundred-and-fifty-mile journey through lands that might harbour enemies."

"You know this land, my lord, and I do not. What is the alternative?"

"We head for Rouen and travel through the land that is Norman. It adds thirty miles or so to our journey but…"

He nodded and I wheeled Gilles to head for the road that led west. As we rode, I reflected that the dangers of war apart, the acquisition of the cross had been relatively easy.

The first night we slept less than thirty miles from Pontoise. The small abbey had been founded by Empress Matilda and we were welcomed. The fare was plain and the room was a cell, but our horses were stabled and I enjoyed the silence of the abbey and the chance to think about my future. As I lay on the simple bed I thought about what we had done. The retrieval of the cross had been but a part of it. Jack had shown skills that were admirable and his attitude had been exemplary. If I had not brought him, I would never have known the skills that he possessed. I also thought about myself. For the first time in a long time, it was my skills that had been needed and not the name of Sir Michael of Weedon. I knew that often men saw me as an extension of Sir William Strongstaff. I was not the same but in his mould. In the battle for the Pays de Caux and Pontoise, I had shown that I was a good warrior with natural skills.

The next day, as we took the road west, I said, "Jack, you have done well on this quest. How do you see your future?"

"My lord?"

"Do you wish to return to the life you had in my hall at Houghton Regis, or would you continue to train as my squire?"

He beamed, "Me, a squire? My lord, it would be a dream come true."

"But there are risks. You saw some of them. A life at Houghton Regis would be safer."

"If you will have me, my lord, then I will work hard and smooth off the edges that I know are still rough. I will acquire the skills that I need. I have other talents that are not needed by a squire, but they will help me, I am sure."

I was intrigued, "What things?"

He laughed, "I can make a trap to catch an animal or a man. I know how to throw a knife and hit that at which I aim."

I suddenly noticed that he had not only a knife in a scabbard on his belt but another tucked in the back and one in each boot, "Is that why you have acquired so many?"

He nodded, "Those who searched the corpses on the battlefield left these. There were more that I could have taken but these were the best-balanced ones. I am still learning how to use a sword but the use of a knife and dagger comes naturally to me."

"What else?"

"I can climb. When we lived in the forest and I was much younger than I am today, men called me a squirrel, for I could clamber up a tree as easily as most men walk a road."

I laughed, "I can see that there is much about you that I do not know."

He nodded, seriously, "And you, my lord, have shown me that there is more to you than I thought. When I served at the table the name of Sir Ralph was spoken often. Men respected and liked you. It was not for your name, they did not know that, but for what you did."

It was strange that the youth had come to the same conclusion that I had. We were meant to be knight and squire for our minds were attuned together.

"If we push on, we might be able to make Fleury-sur-Andelle before dark." He had no idea of the geography of the land but I did. The small village was close to my manor of Les Pérets. I had passed through the village and knew that there was an inn. Often merchants stopped there before heading to Rouen. I had liked the solitude of the abbey but I wanted a comfortable bed and a richer meal. Once we crossed the river we would head north and I would avoid my manor.

We had husbanded our horses and, as we had oats, they were happy to be pushed.

Not far from the village, the road zig-zagged through the forest above the river. Carts often took many hours to negotiate the steep bank. It was there that our speed and Jack's lack of experience brought us almost to disaster. Mary lost her footing and, in trying to keep his saddle, Jack lost control of the spare. The animal took off, not down the road but through the trees.

The Knight's Tale

Poor Jack was mortified, "My lord, I am sorry."

I smiled, "No matter. We are but a short way from the village. If we arrive after dark it will not be a problem. Come, let us find the horse."

He shook his head, "It was my mistake, my lord. You wait here and I will find it." He took off through the trees. There was still enough light to see where the horse had gone. I dismounted and tied Gilles to a branch. I took some oats from the bag and let the animal eat them from my palm. I spoke to the horse as I did so. "The boy has much to learn but he has the ability to learn. He will get better." Gilles neighed and snorted. I laughed and ruffled his mane, "You are a good horse and no mistake,"

I heard hooves on the road behind me. I was turning, thinking that Jack had managed to find the horse quicker than I anticipated when a Flemish voice said, "Sir Michael, we thought to take you at your manor but this is better."

I saw one of the Flemish knights who had been conscripted at Calais. He had with him two men at arms. He had almost caught me out, but I recovered my composure and said, "You have me confused with another. I am Sir Ralph of Stoney Stratford." As the knight and one of the men at arms dismounted, I realised that they had both drawn their swords. This was becoming more sinister.

"I served in France when you were with the army. I remember you with the Maid. I am not mistaken. The beard and the hair did not fool me. I kept my counsel for I wondered at the disguise, and we followed you. It was clear you were up to something. I watched you in Pontoise and we saw you go to the church often. You took something from there. I know not what it was, a pyx perhaps, but it must be worth gold for you left Pontoise as soon as you had it in your possession."

"I do not know what you mean."

He smiled, "Then when we have searched your horse, we will search you and find it. If not, then the gold in your purse, your armour and your horse will have to compensate."

I looked at the three men. I had seen the knight often. He was a surly and solitary man. I suddenly realised that his squire had died in our first fight on the road to Lillebonne. I had offered him sympathy for his loss and he had seemed indifferent. He wore simple mail while his men had leather jacks. The three of them looked like dangerous men. I knew then that they intended to kill me and I was just glad that Jack was not there. He would survive. Nor was I willing to simply let these three robbers kill me. I had to choose my moment. I still had my left hand on Gilles' mane. As the man at arms approached Gilles, I pulled my left hand away. He reacted to the movement of my hand as a threat and had his sword pointed at me. "Keep your hand where I can see it."

I nodded but he was not watching my right hand and, as I held up the palm of my left hand, I took the dagger from my belt and I hid it up the sleeve of my right.

"And your right hand."

I held up both palms. Night had fallen and while the knight searched my bags, the man at arms kept his sword pointed at my chest. It took time for the knight to complete the search. He discarded the two parchments, the message from Sir John and the passport from the king. They were not the treasure he sought. His joy at finding my purse was short-lived when he realised that there was no religious relic with it.

"So, Sir Michael, you have it on your person. Strip."

I laughed and shook my head, "If you think that I will take off my clothes here then you are mistaken. You will have to kill me in cold blood."

"And you think that is a problem? Killing men who are unarmed is something we have done before. Albert…"

The order was for the man at arms to kill me. Even as he pulled back his arm I was slipping the dagger into my palm. I am still not sure if I would have been able to kill all three men but it did not matter. The man at arms who had remained on his horse suddenly arched his back and screamed. The Flemish knight and the man at arms turned at the sound. I used my left arm to knock aside the sword and I rammed my dagger under the arm of the man at arms. The Flemish knight reacted quickly and he lunged at me. I turned the body of the man at arms. I think he was dying already but the sword of his knight completed the process. I switched my dagger to my left hand and drew my sword. I had to block the next blow from the knight with my dagger but it allowed me to swing my sword at his side. He was mailed but my sword was sharp and heavy. I broke links and ribs. He reeled and I flicked my dagger at his face. It raked across his nose and he took another step back. I was still unsure if the man at arms on the horse was dead or alive and I dared not take a chance. I lunged with my sword and struck the knight in the throat. His sword dropped and he gurgled his life away.

I turned to look at the man at arms who had been mounted. I saw he was on the ground and Jack was wiping his dagger on the dead man's tunic. I saw that he had slit the man's throat. He shook his head, "I am sorry, my lord. I almost got you killed."

I sheathed my sword and said, "You were the one who took out the man at arms?"

The Knight's Tale

"Aye, my lord, I soon found our horse and heard the voices. I told you that I could use a knife and was quiet. I tethered the horses in the trees and came up. I saw you with the sword at your body and I threw my dagger at the man's back. It did not kill him. By the time I had reached him, you were fighting the knight and I could not take a chance that the wounded man would go to his aid. I killed him."

"And I am grateful. Go and fetch our horses."

He disappeared into the dark forest and I manhandled the three bodies onto the backs of their horses. By the time he returned, I had mounted Gilles. "A change of plans, Jack. We will ride to Les Pérets. I want safety this night. The road is too dangerous. If there was one enemy who knows what we did there may be others."

We descended the road to the river slowly. We passed over the bridge and through the village like ghosts. If any peered out they would have taken us for merchants with laden horses. They would not know that they were covered with bloody corpses.

The manor was barred as I knew it would be. The war was ever close in this part of the world and Isabelle's uncle, Charles, my castellan, was an old soldier who knew his business. He would keep the gates barred and guarded at night.

I banged on the gate, "I crave entry. Open the gates."

The gate had a wooden aperture that slid open and a voice said, "Who comes at this late hour? State your name and business."

"I am Sir Michael of Weedon, and this is my manor."

The face stared up at me, "I do not recognise you."

"Then fetch the castellan, Charles." I heard him shout something and faces appeared on the gatehouse. I saw Charles, the old soldier to whom I had given custody of the manor. He peered down and I said, "Charles, it is I, Michael."

He recognised my voice and shouted, "Jean, you imbecile, it is Sir Michael. Open the gate and do not leave him out in the dark."

Brands were fetched as we clattered across the cobbles. I said, "These are three men who tried to kill us."

Charles was an old soldier and he nodded, "Jean, take the bodies and remove their mail. Bury them by the hogbog. The pigs will enjoy rooting there. Murderers do not deserve a sanctified grave." He nodded and waved to two others to help him. "Henri, take the animals to the stables." He beamed, "It is good to see you, Sir Michael and this must be your new squire. Come in, come in. Marie, food!"

We stepped into the hall that had been my home when I had first married Isabelle. The deaths of her parents had made the place haunted for her and now we lived in England. It felt familiar as I stepped through the door and entered the comforting warmth of the manor.

Charles was an old soldier and he organised wine and poured the two of us beakers of wine. "It is good to see you and to meet your new squire."

"His name is Jack and he has just saved my life."

I saw Charles' eyes widen in surprise, "Here is a tale. While Marie heats up some food, regale me with the story for life is dull here."

I told the story and watched Jack squirm with embarrassment when the old soldier heaped praise upon him. "Many squires go through their lives without such a momentous event. It bodes well, young Jack, for the future." He pointed his beaker at my face, "And there has to be a reason you are so disguised. I now see why Jean did not recognise you."

I smiled, "The mission was a secret one but you should know that I was acting for the King of England. I can say no more for I am bound by an oath." I shrugged, "The plan was for me to enter France, complete my task and return home. That did not happen and I ended up fighting in the Pays de Caux and the taking of Pontoise."

"You were in the battle for The Pays de Caux?"

I nodded, "And at Pontoise where Sir John took the town."

"I had heard rumours."

Jack boasted, "And more than that, my lord, it was Sir Michael who ensured that we took the town."

Just then the food arrived, and Charles said, "Eat and then I will hear the rest of this fine tale."

The telling of the tale, the lateness of our arrival and the relief of arriving at a safe house meant we did not get to bed at what my wife would have said was a Christian time. It was Jack and I who hogged the tale-telling. Charles wished me to use the master's bedroom as this was my hall, but I was having none of it and Jack and I shared the second chamber.

A Norman manor smells different from an English one. Isabelle had noticed that first. As I woke and sniffed the air, I knew that I was in Normandy. Food was being cooked and the smell wafted upstairs. It was an inducement to rise and we did. I would not need my mail and it was good to walk unhindered by the heavy hauberk. While I was in the manor, I would be safe. Charles had risen and I smiled as I saw him fussing over the laying of the table and the presentation of the food. He had no need to do so but it would do me little good to tell him so.

Satisfied, he said, "I pray you sit. This morning it will be my turn to give you the news of the manor and those men you left behind."

Not all of my men had returned to England. A handful of men at arms and archers had chosen to stay in Normandy and make it their home. Most were younger men. The veterans like Robbie, Will, David of Denbigh and Richard, had chosen to come home.

As he spoke, I realised that the younger men had made homes and now had families in Normandy. No matter what happened to Normandy, they would stay. A family gives you roots.

"There is one, however, who has not settled. You remember Will Willow Tree?"

"He was the youngest of the archers was he not?"

"That he was. The newest of your archers and, when you left, one who had yet to grow into an archer's body. He has now done so but he yearns for England. I had intended to write to you and ask if he could come back but…"

"Of course, he can. The others, they are settled?"

"Settled and with families. I am not sure that the archers' children will become archers for it is not a Norman tradition, but time will tell."

"And yourself, Charles, how do you find the manor? Has the wanderlust left you?"

"It has and I have found peace. I am just sad that my brother and I did not have the time together that I would have wished."

The mention of the dead cast a sombre mood over the table and we were silent as we ate and drank. When he spoke again Charles ensured that it was on safer ground than the raking over of graves. "It was good that Sir John took the Pays de Caux, although the French still hold Harfleur. Still, the taking of Pontoise gives us hope that this war might be won."

"I had hoped that I might be able to take a ship from Rouen to sail back to England."

He shook his head, "The French have a chain across the river. King Henry bled at Harfleur when first he came. It is a hard town to take. It may be that Sir John can take it. He is a bold man."

"Bold, but I must caution you, he can be reckless. Thus far he has ridden his luck and it has been on his side. You were a soldier and know that such luck cannot be relied upon."

"And you, Sir Michael, what now? You return to the king and then…?"

"I swore an oath to Queen Catherine to watch over her sons and ensure that they are safe. They can never have the crown but they deserve lives. I still have work to do."

"An oath is a powerful thing. At least your oath to protect the king is no longer a sword hanging over you. The king's uncle absolved you of that."

I tapped my chest, "I am still, and always will be, the king's man."

We spent the day visiting the men I had left behind. They were all keen to show me their families and their homes. Each had a small holding where they raised the food they needed to feed their families. The manor paid them as warriors. The last one that we met was Will Willow Tree. Charles was right, he had grown. Jack had asked me why he was called Willow Tree and I had said it was because he was tall and gangly like a willow. Older now, I saw him he was misnamed. He should have been called Will Oak Tree, for he was tall and broad. The food and the life in Normandy suited him and he had prospered.

"Charles tells me that you would return home, Will?"

He nodded, "I like Normandy, but I miss England. The others found Norman brides, but I seek one that is English."

"Then when I return to England, in a day or so, you shall come with me. You have until then to say your goodbyes."

He looked both relieved and pleased.

We next visited the horses. "Charles, I will not need all the horses we took from our attackers. Will can ride Mary and I would give Jack the courser ridden by the Flemish knight. If he is to train as a squire then he should be appropriately mounted. The horse we brought from England suffered an injury when she slipped from the road. I will leave her here to heal and take, instead, one of those we captured from the Flems."

"That is generous of you, my lord."

I looked around at the manor, "I miss this place but it is in good hands. My wife, your niece, is happy in the palatial Houghton Regis. Regard this as your home. I will make no demands on you. We have profit enough from my three manors in England. A man can only spend so much coin."

I no longer needed my disguise, so I shaved and Jack cut my hair. It felt good to be clean again. I would be Sir Michael of Weedon once more. We stayed for three days in total and then left to head north to Calais. That Will was popular was clear from the gifts he was given by his comrades: a dagger in a good scabbard, a decorated arrow bag, a spare bow and a beaver hat sporting an eagle's feather. We had a long ride ahead of us but I did not leave at dawn. Instead, we made a leisurely twenty-mile journey north for I had wanted a decent farewell from my Norman manor and village.

Chapter 8

The journey to Calais was uneventful and the peace helped Jack to get to know Will. The two got on well and I was pleased. It also allowed Jack to get to know the courser taken from the Flemish mercenary. It was a stallion but I think that the Flemish warrior had mistreated it. The horse was thinner than it should have been and a little nervous. Jack lavished attention on the animal he called Prince. He chose the name for he thought the horse had a noble quality. Whatever the reason, the horse liked the name and responded well to Jack's kind treatment. They bonded on the road north.

When we reached Calais, rather than risking a visit to the castellan which might result in further military service, I went to the port. I had not used my mandate from the king but I did so at the port. I secured berths for us and our horses on a ship travelling to Tilbury. From there it was a short ride to London. I was anxious to deliver my prize as well as the parchment from the lieutenant-general and then get home.

We did not discover where the king was until we reached the Tower. I asked for him there and was told that he was in the castle at Windsor. He was holding court there. It meant we had to stay for a night in London and I never enjoyed that. My passport gained us rooms and stabling in the tower. The soldiers there had heard rumours about Pontoise and when Jack let slip that we had been involved, then we had the tale to tell again.

We reached Windsor by noon. The king and his guests were out hunting but we were granted a room in the main castle for Jack and me, and Will was given a bed in the warrior hall. Sir William de la Pole was on the hunt with the others and I sat in the great hall awaiting their return. The noisy arrival was in the afternoon and, to my surprise and delight, I saw that Owen Tudor was with the courtiers along with his sons. The king had released them from Newgate.

When I was seen there was delight from all five men although for different reasons. The king and the earl came over and the king said, "You have it?"

I nodded but first I handed over the parchment, "This is the report from Sir John Talbot. It tells of his victory at Pontoise."

"And the other?"

"Should I give it here?"

The king looked at the earl who shook his head, "No, come to the solar. The earl and I will work out the best way to use this prize."

The Knight's Tale

The earl said, "The king would have conference with his most loyal knight, Sir Michael. For the rest, you may occupy yourselves until it is time for the feast."

I turned to Jack, "I shall not need you."

We went through a corridor to the room that faced west and was bathed in late afternoon sun. The earl closed the door and the king had the look of a child at Christmas upon his face, "Give it to me." I took the cross from my purse. The king looked disappointed. "Was there no jewel-encrusted box?"

I shook my head, "It was a plain box and nothing else was within. We left the box there. If anyone seeks the cross they will assume it still resides beneath the altar."

The earl beamed, "You are the best of fellows. We will have a box made for this treasure, King Henry."

He smiled, "You are right." He held the report from Sir John in his hand, "We heard rumours of Sir John's success but I have learned to dismiss half the stories we hear."

"Sir John trapped the French in the Pays de Caux and we used a ruse to take Pontoise. The lieutenant-general lost few men and the army is in good heart."

"You shall be rewarded. There is a manor in Yorkshire, Easingwold, and the lord there died childless. It is a royal manor and so I give it to you. Once it was a hunting lodge but none have used it for many years."

"That is generous, my lord, but there is no need."

His face adopted a petulant look and he snapped, "I decide where there is a need. Loyalty must be rewarded." Just as quickly the pout was replaced by a beaming smile and he said, "Now go and join the others. The earl and I have things to plan."

Sometimes the young king seemed to be two people who occupied the same body. I did not envy the earl his task of guiding him.

When I re-entered the hall Owen Tudor, his sons and Jack pounced on me. The husband of Queen Catherine said, "Thank you, Sir Michael."

"For what?"

"Do not be so modest. The earl told us that you made the plea to the king and he heard it. We were released and I am given a pension of £40 a year and my sons are to be raised at court. Our lives are safe and it is down to you."

I smiled at the boys, "I promised your mother that I would watch over you and I never break a promise."

Edmund took my hand and kissed the back of it. "You saved us once when men tried to kill us and you have saved us a second time. We are indebted to you, Sir Michael, and if we can ever do anything to help you…"

Their father shook his head, "We have our lives and our freedom. I think we enjoy what we have and do not seek any more. Father Bertrand has told us that you are a true knight, Sir Michael, and he is right."

I was seated next to the Tudors at the feast. I did not recognise many of the other courtiers who sought positions on the table close to the king, but I was a curiosity that drew the gaze of everyone. I was not helped by the fulsome praise heaped upon me by the king and the earl. Sir John had reported my part in the taking of Pontoise and I was toasted by all. I did not like the attention, not least because I did not know the lords who stared at me. I had learned that not all smiles were welcome ones. I enjoyed, however, the company of Edmund and Jasper. Both were fine young men and I saw the queen in them. For their part, they were keen to be soldiers and bombarded me with questions. When Jack brought the food, he was also interrogated. I think it amused him.

"So, Sir Michael, what next? Back to France to fight with Sir John?"

I shook my head, "No, Master Tudor. I have manors to manage, a family to raise and a squire to train."

"Train us, my lord."

I looked at Edmund and Jasper and shook my head, "The king will keep you here at court. You are his half-brothers and that means he will keep you safe."

What I did not say was that they would be kept close so that they could not be used by others who wished for the crown. Until the king married and had children, the two half-brothers could be used.

I enjoyed the feast for the two young men were very personable and I liked them. They had survived and I hoped that their experience would make them stronger. The pension given to their father by the king was not a fortune but as the boys would be brought up at court, it did not matter.

The next morning I sought out the earl and begged leave to depart for my home. He nodded, "You are a good servant to the crown and you deserve to enjoy time with your family, but know that there will be other times when the king needs you. You must come as soon as you are called."

"Of course, my lord."

"And before you leave, I will have the deeds for your new manor prepared."

I knew that would delay my departure but it could not be helped. I was not even sure I would manage to visit the manor. Yorkshire lay

The Knight's Tale

many leagues to the north. The document was fetched within the hour and, after collecting Will Willow Tree, we headed north riding as fast as our horses would allow. I wanted to be home before dark.

As we neared the manor Will began to sing. "Are you happy, Will?"

"I am, my lord. I enjoyed my time in Normandy but it was not home, it was not England. When you and Jack arrived and spoke English it was like honey to my ears."

I knew what he meant. Edgar White Streak and many other of my men felt the same. They were happy to fight for England and the crown, but England was their home. Jack and I were looked for but the arrival of a face from the past brought out more of my men to greet us than I would have expected. My mission had been a secret but the length of time I had been away meant that there had been much speculation. The return of Will Willow Tree would fuel that speculation. I could not help but smile when I saw Jack's mother, Elizabeth, examining her son for wounds and injuries.

Even before Isabelle had come outside to speak to me, Robbie Red Fletch was at my side, "So you did not take an archer with you, yet you return with one. Did you need one, my lord?"

"I always need archers, Robbie, but Will has not had to draw bowstring in my defence. All is well."

He nodded towards Jack who was being smothered by his mother's hugs, "And Jack?"

"Grew into the man. He will now be a squire. He acquitted himself more than well. He has tales for you, Robbie." On the way home, Jack had asked if he could still live with his mother. I had, of course, agreed. I did not need him to serve at the table. We had servants for that. However, I would expect him to eat in the warrior hall where the bachelors lived. It was a small one and there were just five who lived there. Will would make it six.

Isabelle gave me the warm welcome I had been anticipating for the last ten miles. After she had kissed me she said, "You need a bath for you reek of horses." She stroked my face with the back of her hand, "But I am glad you have shed your beard and cut your hair. They made you look like a bear."

I put my arm around her and guided her towards the door. Jack and the others would see to the horses and the bags. "And John and the girls?"

She laughed, "Maud has grown and thinks she rules the roost. Margaret is both tender and tolerant but Jean," she always pronounced our son's name the French way, "finds it tiresome."

"It will be good for him."

The Knight's Tale

My son had not bothered to greet me. I knew what he would be doing. He was with Jack and the men outside unloading the bags. He would be seeking presents and treasure. Robbie and Jack would ensure that he did not appropriate anything untoward. I had gifts for him, but I would choose when he would have them. I had taken weapons, sheaths and belts from the battlefield in the Pays de Caux, as well as Pontoise. The men I had slain were rich men and whilst I had not enjoyed a ransom, I could benefit from the things they had with them. I also had gifts for my wife and the girls. They had been purchased.

I did as my wife asked and bathed. The manor at Houghton had enjoyed, being a former royal residence, a bathhouse. Sadly, it was unheated and, unless it was summer, was not a place in which to luxuriate. I bathed as quickly as I could and then dried myself before I shivered with the cold. My wife always stored my better clothes, the ones I did not use on campaign, with lavender and rosemary. It meant that for the first days of wearing them, I smelled more sweetly than I would normally. She combed my hair. Since the haircut at my manor in France, it was more manageable.

I had no Jack at the table and I was able to give my version of the trip to Pontoise. I made it just exciting enough so that John was animated and yet palatable enough for the girls and my wife. I did not mention the taking of the cross from the church. I might tell Isabelle but the children did not need to know. When I mentioned the new manor, John became quite excited.

"When do we go to see it, Father?"

I shook my head, "I have no need of it, and it lies many miles north of here. If I do go to visit then it shall be in high summer. There is a steward there and it was the king's. I think it will be well run."

"Is it a castle?"

John was desperate for me to own a castle. I shook my head, "It is an ancient hunting lodge and will be similar to this one but less grand." I saw the disappointment on his face. "Castles are only needed where there is danger. They are not built for comfort but for defence. This is more comfortable."

"But if it is north of York then it is close to the Scottish border."

I smiled, "The Scots are not a threat these days. Robert the Bruce was the last Scot who terrorised the border and even he never got as far south as York." I could see that he was deflated. "England is, at the moment, at peace and I for one am happy that is so."

There was a brief silence until Isabelle said, "But not so my home, Normandy."

"No, my love. Sir John Talbot has stopped the crumbling of the king's lands across the sea but I fear that it will be but temporary. The French will rally and they will try to take back what we gained."

I did not say it, but I knew that unless we had a king such as King Henry's father leading English and Welshmen, then Normandy and the French lands would be lost.

Later that night, after the children had been put to bed, we spoke of my wife's home and I told how we had secured the cross. She sighed and took my hand in hers, "It belonged to the queen and it is right that her son has it, but what will he use it for?"

"Perhaps nothing. He was crowned King of France and England. He was but a child when that happened yet I think it left its mark on his mind. The cross is a link to Charlemagne and, as such, is a link to the crown. I wish he would put France from his thoughts and look to England."

"But the land is secure?"

I shook my head, "There are men who see a boy with the crown on his head and vie to be both advisor and manipulator to him. The earl is a good man and has no claim to the crown but there are others that do."

"I do not understand English politics."

I smiled, "I will try to explain. King Edward III had four sons. The Black Prince who was his heir was never king but his son Richard was. He died childless and as Lionel, Duke of Clarence, had a daughter and no son and heir then the next king was from the house of Lancaster, King Henry IVth. There is another branch, the York side. Prince Edmund was the Duke of York, and his son married the granddaughter of the Duke of Clarence. Their son, Richard, Duke of York has a strong claim to the crown should the current King Henry be like King Richard and die childless."

"You think that might happen?"

"It has ever been that a king must have sons. The first King Richard died childless and that led to a bad king, King John. There was a civil war at that time. No, until the king marries and his wife bears him a son, then there will be those in England who seek to put another in power."

I had put unwelcome thoughts in both of our heads but we took comfort in cuddles in the bedchamber that made them briefly disappear. I knew that they were not dispelled forever. As with Sir William before me, my fate was entwined with the royal family. What happened to King Henry VIth would affect me directly.

It was the next day that I gave the presents to Isabelle, Margaret and Maud. Maud's was just a poppet I had bought in Calais, while my wife and the queen's daughter were given fine lace. John was the one who appreciated his presents most of all. I gave him his in the yard where Jack had presented himself, ready to be trained as a squire. My son was given a fine knife in a scabbard as well as a short sword. He could barely lift the sword but that did not stop him from swashing it about with two hands.

"It is not a toy, John. Jack is to be trained as my squire. His skills with a sword need to be improved. You will be my page and you, too, will learn to use the sword, but as a weapon and not a toy. Do you understand?"

He nodded contritely, "Yes, Father."

"Neither your sword nor Jack's will be sharpened. Until we go to war there will be no need. Thomas of Chester will work with me to make the two of you into swordsmen."

Jack nodded. I knew he was eager to learn. He was older than John who was still a boy. John said, "And when do I learn to be a horseman?"

I laughed, "First, you need to learn how to ride. It will be many years before you are either big enough or skilled enough to ride even a horse like Mary. But what you can learn to do is to groom horses. Go with Jack and meet my new warhorse, Gilles."

Jack said, "And my courser, Prince."

The horse taken on the road now looked twice the horse we had first found. Jack had ensured that the horse ate before he did and he was always seeking treats for him. While they headed to the stables I sought out Thomas of Chester. He had married Sarah, the former nurse of Margaret. She now ran the kitchen with Elizabeth, and Thomas acted as a sort of steward and bailiff. He had been one of the best men at arms I had ever known. He had skills. His predecessor as steward and wife were old and I had given them a cottage by the gatehouse. They were all happy with the new arrangement.

"Thomas, in addition to your duties as steward, I would have you help me to train both Jack and John. Jack is my squire and while John is but a boy, you and I know that a knight can never begin training too early."

His beaming smile gave me his answer before his words, "I would deem it an honour my lord. I hope that Sarah and I will have children and that one will be a boy, but I should like to pass on my skills while I still have hair on my pate that is not white."

"Good."

And with that, we settled into a new routine. Each morning we would train in the yard, first with wooden swords and then with blunt weapons. In the afternoon, while I saw to manorial matters, Isabelle would help Father John to improve the education of the two boys. Jack's French was better than it had been but I wanted him to be fluent. Our priest would teach them to read well in both English and Latin. I know the two preferred their mornings but I was rigid in my rules and, unless they worked hard in the afternoon, then they would not be given the weapon training in the mornings. That time of peace was priceless.

Chapter 9

We did receive news, for the road north lay close to our home, and we had visitors who passed through. It was from one such visitor that I learned of the success of Sir John Talbot. He had retaken Harfleur. We began to hope that he might hold onto the king's possessions in Normandy, Aquitaine and France. I had feared that the new residence of the queen's sons might be another kind of incarceration but the news we had was that King Henry lavished gifts upon them and treated them well. I had kept my promise to a dying queen. Of course, it did not mean I could forget about the promise. The king had enemies and who knew what a pretender to the throne might do? Months passed and both my son and Jack improved their skills. I was enjoying my life as the lord of the manor. Sir William had rarely enjoyed such times.

The peace I had meant my lands and my family prospered. The time after I returned from my quest was a glorious one. Such was the joy in my life that I did not even bother to visit my new manor at Easingwold. My children and my ward grew. The manor prospered under the peace and I was contented. I might have stayed at Houghton Regis, oblivious to the manor, but for a messenger who arrived from the Earl of Suffolk, Sir William de la Pole. I recognised the seal and I asked the messenger, "Will you stay the night?"

He shook his head, "No, my lord, for I am ordered to ride back to his lordship with your answer."

My heart sank. I was going to be used once more. I used my knife to slice through the wax and read the missive:

Sir Michael,
You have not yet visited the manor of Easingwold and the king and I wonder at this oversight. The king is a little insulted that you treat his gift in such a way. If you do not wish the manor then tell my messenger so that the king may favour another with the honour. If you do wish to be lord of that manor then you should visit it forthwith.

Suffolk

My procrastination had been a mistake. I could see that now. If I gave the message that I did not wish the manor then I would be marking myself as someone who did not care for the favour of the king. As the king had shown me, he was unpredictable. I still remembered the raging outburst at that first feast. As much as I did not want the manor, I could not afford to make an enemy of the Earl of Suffolk. He now controlled the king.

The Knight's Tale

I folded the letter, "Tell the earl I will ride to Yorkshire by the end of the week." I took a chance for the messenger looked familiar. "What do you know of Easingwold?"

The messenger was a man at arms who was about my age. I think I had served with him but I could not be sure. His smile told me that he did know me, "I know, my lord, that the lands around your manor belong to two branches of the Neville family and that there is a feud between Ralph and Richard Neville. Your presence might calm matters down."

It made sense, "Thank you."

"It is nothing. You may not remember me for I was young when we served in France. I am Henry of Oxford. You are a good knight as was Sir William. It is good to speak to an honest man. The court is full of those you cannot trust. Take care my lord and tread carefully." With those words, he left.

I thought I had remembered him. The wars in France had not always been successful but those of us who had fought in them enjoyed a bond. I looked up as my wife came in, followed by Sarah with a tray of food and drink.

"Did our guest not wish to stay?"

"He had to return to the earl. I have been given orders to visit my manor at Easingwold."

She frowned, "Why?"

"Politics. It was a royal manor but it is surrounded by feuding families who seek power. I will have to visit and stay for a while."

"Do you need me to come?"

I had learned to read my wife and knew from both her face and tone that she did not wish to come.

I shook my head, "I will take Jack, John and Will Willow Tree. That will suffice. It might do our son good to see other squires and pages. Houghton is a little quiet."

She smiled, "Yes, my husband, he has grown in the last couple of years and wants more than this little haven of peace."

She was right and my son threw himself into the organisation of the trip. Will was courting a young woman but he was also keen to thank me for his return to England. Jack had also changed since our return from France. In the time since then, he had developed good sword skills and now spoke like a well-educated man. He had responded well to his promotion to squire.

We left and headed up the Great North Road. It would be a one-hundred-and-eighty-mile ride. We had good horses but, even so, it would take us at least five days to make the journey. My son was full of questions from the start.

"Why have you not visited the manor before, Father? It has been some years since you were gifted the land."

I shrugged, "I am not a man who needs great riches. We are comfortable and I did not think I would enjoy the ride north. I have spent enough time away from your mother."

"Then why now?"

I saw a wry smile from Jack. He said, "Master John, a page does not ask so many questions. That is your father's business."

"No, Jack, you should all know the reason. We are going not to a place of peace but of contention." I told them of the rivalry between the Nevilles. "And now one of the children of the old Ralph Neville has married the Duke of York."

"And how does that affect us, Father?"

"The Duke of York is in line of succession to the crown. He is related to King Edward III through both his mother's and his father's line. The branch of the Neville family into which he has married is also descended from John of Gaunt. I now see that this gift was not as generous as I thought. The king, or perhaps the earl of Suffolk, wants a loyal knight close by to the heartland of the Neville family."

My honesty was, perhaps, misplaced for John became animated, "We are like spies then?"

"No, we are not although, as Jack will tell you, when you serve at the table, you keep your ears open and your mouth closed." I would have to rely on Jack to manage my son. I was anticipating that my arrival would prompt a request to visit with at least one branch of the family. My service to the crown had not gone unnoticed.

It was as we travelled through England that I learned of the unpopularity of both the earl of Suffolk and the king. I did not see it in my manors for they were loyal to me and I was loyal to the king, but in the inns in which we stayed, we heard the name jackanapes spoken with derision. The king was not accorded any honour. Part of the problem was the stalemate in France and the king was still unmarried. The war cost money as well as lives. The land was taxed to pay for the war. When the king's father had led the army then we had enjoyed success. Since then England had endured defeat after defeat. There was resentment in the land as a result. It worried me and explained the letter from the earl. This was not to do with an insult to the king by me, rather he was sending me into the Neville heartland to gather information.

We stopped in York briefly for I had to visit with the Sheriff, Sir Robert Waterton. It was a necessary courtesy. He looked relieved at my arrival. "It is good that you have come, Sir Michael. The manor has suffered from a lack of a lord. It has been many years since it was used as a hunting lodge."

"I fear that my visit will be a brief one, my lord, as I have other manors that demand both my time and attention."

"I understand that, Sir Michael, but the people need to know that there is a lord who cares for them." He smiled, "I am a Yorkshireman, my lord. My lands and my family are here in the north. London is another world."

I got the impression that he did not care much for the South. "I rarely get to visit London and I agree with your sentiments. I promise that I will ensure that all is well before I return to my manor."

"And you will visit with me before you return home?"

"Of course, my lord."

"It was a short ride to the manor that lay just twelve miles north of the great city of the north. As we approached, in the late afternoon, I saw that it was a run-down manor. The gates lay open and one had broken hinges which meant it could not be closed in any case. There looked to have been a wall and a palisade but they had fallen into disrepair. The hall itself looked large, however, it, too, was a little dilapidated. As we reined in, I realised that I might have to stay longer than I had intended. The Sheriff had been right. I owed it to the people to see that they were served by their lord of the manor. Sir William had taught me that.

No one emerged from the hall as we clattered on the cobbles. Jack frowned as he dismounted. He strode purposefully to the door and banged upon it, "Ho, within, your new lord has arrived."

I dismounted and said, "Will, go with John and see if you can find stables."

He said, "This is hardly a warm welcome, my lord."

"We shall see."

"Come, Master John." The two of them led the horses around the side of the manor towards the cluster of buildings that were visible there.

I joined Jack. I shouted, "I am Sir Michael of Weedon. Open the door."

I heard voices within and eventually the door creaked open. An older woman, her shoulders draped in a shawl appeared. She had the emaciated look of one who does not eat regularly. She gave a sort of bow and said, "I am sorry, my lord, we have illness within."

The plague had once devastated the land and still made appearances. I said, "The plague?"

The Knight's Tale

She gave me a smile that showed more gaps than teeth and shook her head, "Old age, my lord. I am Alice the wife of Edgar, the steward of this manor. He lies in bed coughing. He has not risen this week and I fear he will not do so again."

The situation was getting worse by the moment. "Jack, fetch our bags."

She opened the door to let me in, "The beds are not aired, my lord. None have used them..." She shook her head, "I cannot remember the last time but then I am not sure what I ate yesterday. Old age is a terrible thing." She held a tallow candle in her hand and it showed that we were in a corridor and a stairway led to the first floor.

"Go to your husband. My men and I will find what we need. Are there any servants?"

"Just me and my husband, my lord. I will take you to your rooms first, my lord." She began to wring her hands, "We have tried, my lord, to keep up the house and grounds but no one seems to care about us and we could not write to ask for help."

"What happened to the manor?"

"Lord Wreketon died childless twenty years ago, my lord and none has looked after the hall since then."

I smiled at her for I could see that this was not her fault. I worked out that the lord had died a few years after Agincourt. That was the time when King Henry V[th] was on the cusp of grasping the crown of France. His eyes were on France and not the royal manor in Easingwold that was now without a lord. With the death of the king then it would have been forgotten. I remembered the time and the turmoil. That was when I was the protector of the young king. This would be neither an easy nor a quick task. I had learned, over the years, to take difficulties in small bites. The first thing to do was find rooms and then food. There would be no accounts for me to study as neither the steward nor his wife could read. As Alice led us to our chamber I said, "Is there a church? A priest?"

She nodded, "St John and All Saints is the church, my lord, and Father Oswald is the priest."

"Good. Jack, go with this lady and I will wait here for John and Will." I borrowed the candle to light a tallow candle that was in a sconce on the wall. I did not want to be in the dark in a house I did not know.

She left and I walked down the corridor. I found a couple of stubs of candles and I lit them. It gave light to the corridor. My son and archer entered and Will shook his head, "The place is falling apart, my lord. It

The Knight's Tale

will take more than four of us to put this manor in order and I wonder if it is worth it."

I sighed, "Sometimes, Will, a man has to do things he did not plan to do because they are the right things to do. This couple have been loyal and faithful. We cannot simply abandon them." I pointed to the back of the hall, "Find the kitchens. The house is as cold as a field in winter. John, find kindling and light the fires." Will took one of the candle stubs and opened the door ahead.

My son looked deflated, "I do not know what I expected but it was not this."

The two went through the door to the back and Jack rejoined me, "I have Will and John lighting fires. Let you and I explore this ruin. Alice?"

"She and her husband have a room at the back of the hall. She is there with him. I feel sorry for her, my lord."

"As do I, and if nothing else, we owe it to such a loyal couple to do all that we can."

We lit two tallow candles we found, there was nothing better, and we searched the rooms. It was a large hunting lodge. There were four sleeping chambers on the first floor and two servants' rooms as well as the steward's on the ground floor. There was a large feasting hall and it was so big that it could have held a feast for twenty. The furniture was so old, however, that only five chairs functioned. There was a small room just off the door that might have been a guard house and a west-facing room that was probably the solar. It was too dark to explore outside. When we returned to the hall there was a fire blazing in the hearth. John said, "There is no wood store but a storm must have brought down branches, we used those."

"Good. You are learning valuable skills."

He shook his head and swept the dust from a chair so that he could sit, "If these are the duties of a squire then…"

"John, we did not choose this path but let us make the best of it. Will, is there food?"

"We have brought more than they have."

Jack said, "If you had seen the state of the woman then you would not wonder. She was a skeleton with ancient flesh hanging from her bones."

"Then let us make a stew of what we have and what we can find. Tomorrow, we look for hope where there appears, at the moment, to be none. The four of us will have to work as one."

We went to the kitchen and lit the fire there. With water in the pot, we prepared food to put in it. John apart, we knew how to campaign. I

The Knight's Tale

had often prepared food and learned that it mattered not what it looked like but how it tasted. By the time the stew was ready, there was an appealing smell in the kitchen. As Will ladled food into the bowls I said, "Jack, take John and deliver two bowls of food to the steward and his wife. Will and I will take our food to the hall. We will finish off the last of the ale from the ale skin."

John was silent when he returned and sat just staring at his bowl. "Come, John, you must eat."

He turned to Jack, "What was that smell?"

Jack looked at me and shook his head, "It was the smell of death, my lord. The old man has hours, not days, left on this earth. The bowl we took him will be his last."

I made the sign of the cross, "Then the first thing we shall do, on the morrow, is to find the priest. He has work to do here."

We ate in sombre silence. The meal ended, we ensured that the fire was not dangerous and headed for the rooms. The house was like ice and I wondered at how the old couple had managed to survive. There was little point in using four rooms. I made a decision. "We will all sleep in one room. We shall be warmer."

No one argued. I prayed before I slept for I needed God's help. This, to me, seemed the hardest task I had yet been given. When I had saved Edmund and Jasper my enemies had been human and I could use my skills as a swordsman. When I had found the cross for the king it had been well within the skills I possessed but this was something new. I needed my wife and she was many leagues from me.

The cold woke me early and when I rose it woke the others, too. Even John, who liked his bed, was awakened. We went downstairs. Alice was up and in the kitchen. Her cough did not sound healthy, "Mistress Alice, go to your husband. We can see to ourselves."

She shook her head, "That is not right, my lord."

I smiled, "I am the lord here and I say what is right. John, escort Mistress Alice to her room."

I saw a change in my son when he put his arm through the woman's and said, "Come, Mistress, lean on me. I shall not let you fall."

When they had gone, I said, "Jack, find the church and the priest. Tell him that Sir Michael of Weedon needs him."

Will had fed the fire in the kitchen and added water to the stew. He said, "We have a little more food to put in, my lord, but after that..."

I nodded, "Then after what passes for breakfast I would have you and Jack ride to York and buy food. There may be an alewife in the village but you can buy ale there, too."

John returned and shook his head, "The old man is asleep but his breathing sounds like a saw cutting a tree." He went outside to find more wood. I would not have chosen the events that were unfolding before us but they were changing my son and for the better.

It was still dark but I could see the glow in the east where the sun was rising. These were short days and long nights. By the time the sun was up, Jack had returned with the priest. He was an older man and he also looked thinner than I might have expected.

"I am Father Oswald, is this about Edgar?"

"My squire thinks he is close to death. I thought you might give him comfort for his last journey."

He nodded, "It is a week since I saw him last. He was unwell then. I will go to him." He paused, "Not many lords would have thought to do this, Sir Michael."

"Then there are many lords who do not know their duty."

We ate, this time in the kitchen. The fire in the hall had died and the vast space was cheerless. The kitchen was humble but comfortable. We had finished by the time the priest returned. He shook his head, "Your timing was impeccable, my lord. Edgar is dead but I was able to give him the last rites and he is with God now."

"And Alice?"

"She is at his bedside."

"Jack, go to her. When she is ready, bring her here and we shall make sure that she eats. I would not have her follow her husband."

"Aye, my lord."

"Will, take John and find more firewood. Examine the outbuildings and I will speak to Father Oswald."

When they had gone, I ladled food into a bowl. The priest said, "You have no need, Sir Michael."

"This is now my hall and I know how to be a good host. Besides, it looks like you need a good meal, too, and while this is plain fare, it will give you strength. When you have eaten you can tell me about Easingwold."

He cleared his bowl so quickly that I refilled it. When he had finished, he smiled, "You are right, Sir Michael. I have not eaten well. No one in the village has."

"And why is that? There have been no wars to take men from the fields."

"I have been here for thirty years, my lord, and when I came Lord Wreketon was still alive, although he had some worm eating him. He was but thirty years and two when he died. His illness took his eye from the running of the manor but, in any case, the plague of eighty years since took more than half of the village. There were less than fifteen houses. Now there are just ten and fewer than thirty people living in the village. There is no money to buy what they need and too few to grow enough. Seed costs coin."

He glanced at my face nervously and I said, "Speak, Father Oswald, you will learn that I am a patient man, not given to sudden bursts of anger."

He smiled, "I can see that already."

"There was no lord and this is not Neville land. York might be just twelve miles away but it might as well be on the moon. I went to the archbishop but he was preoccupied."

He was being generous. I knew that the church was a political animal and the archbishops plotted as much as they prayed.

"Now I am here and I will do all that I can, but I confess that I had not expected the problem to be as great as it is." He nodded. "You said this was not Neville land. What did you mean by that?"

He studied my face and must have seen something that decided him on honesty, "Sir Richard Neville is the lord of the surrounding land and lives at Middleham. The grandson of the old Lord Neville is Sir Ralph and he seeks the title. It means that they war with each other and Easingwold has no defender against the raids from men who are little more than bandits. We have not suffered deaths, but animals have been taken from the farmers. There is neither kine nor horse to pull a plough. The people live from beans and the greens that they forage. I fear, my lord, that had you not come then within a few years this village would have died." He paused, "It still might."

I smiled, "No, Father Oswald, it will not." Just then Jack brought in Alice. She was not crying but she looked exhausted, "I am sorry for your loss, Mistress Alice, but you need to eat. Jack, fill her bowl." The door opened and my son and archer entered laden with wood. "Light the other fire, Will, and then go with Jack for the task I appointed you." I threw a purse to Jack.

There were just four of us around the table in the kitchen and Alice began to weep, "I am sorry, my lord. My husband and I did our best but…"

I walked over to her and put my arm around what was just skin and bone, "I am here now and I will be the lord of the manor. I will send to my other manors and bring people here. We shall make this a comfortable home once more and, until you are well, you can allow us to care for you."

Father Oswald smiled, "And now that we have a Christian lord who understands both compassion and care, I have hope that this manor will rise like a phoenix from the ashes of despair."

I hoped so too.

Chapter 10

Will and Jack had returned from York when we buried Edgar two days later. It was at the funeral that I saw the other villagers. It looked like a village ravaged by war rather than one that lay in one of the most fertile parts of England. Once the funeral was over we set about making the hall habitable. There were just a handful of mourners at the interment. I still intended to send for people to help but we needed to see the size of the problem first. The hall was well made and had been well furnished but it was run down. There was a hogbog but there were neither pigs nor fowl within it. The fishpond had been neglected and was now just a muddy patch of water. We would have to repair and restock it. Before I sent to Houghton Regis, I wanted to know all.

That night, as we ate in the kitchen once more, the food was better than we had enjoyed since we had come, Will shook his head, "You know, my lord, if we were on a chevauchée and came upon a farm such as this we would have simply passed it by as being worthless."

Jack nodded, "Even the bandits would ignore it."

I had a sudden thought, "And yet if there was a lord here, and we know that there was, then he would have had treasure, would he not?"

John looked confused, "Why do you say that, Father? I can see no sign of a treasure here."

"That is because it is more than twenty years since Lord Wreketon died. He was a relatively young man. He might have had treasure."

Will suddenly banged the table, "And if he did have treasure we know where he would have kept it."

John was still lost and he said, "Do we?"

I beamed, "Aye, we do, and Will is right. Let us move this table."

Three of us were of the same mind and it was just John who was in the dark. When we moved the table the three of us knelt and blew the dust from the floor. Jack took a cloth and dampened it. He began to wipe at the stones. It took some time but we saw the edges of the stones that had been laid there. As we expected, there was one stone with a mark upon it. Will and Jack used their daggers to run around the edge of the stone and scrape away the detritus of years.

"John, bring your dagger and kneel there." With four of us around the square of stone I said, "On my command, we lift." I sank my dagger down as far as it would go. John was the slowest to manage to do so but when I saw that his dagger was as deep as the hilt I said, "Lift."

Had I made a mistake then the attempt to lift the stone would have broken blades, that was all, but as the stone began to rise I knew I was right. The stone was an opening and intended to be lifted.

The Knight's Tale

"Steady now." We worked together as the daggers lifted the stone. It was a narrow one and we soon had it at the level of the floor. Will, Jack and I put our left hands beneath it and lifted it away. There was an opening. "John, a candle." One of the items brought back from York was a quantity of decent candles. When the candle was brought, we saw the chest. Will had archer's arms and he lifted it, but the effort showed that it was not light. He carried it to the table and placed it there. There was a lock.

John asked, "Do we break the lock?"

Jack grinned, "I shall pick it."

We watched in eager anticipation as Jack worked his stiletto in the lock until it clicked open. I lifted the lid and within we saw that there was a cache of coins. Most of them were silver but in the glinting candlelight, I saw a couple of golden ones. Silence filled the kitchen until Jack said, "And this shows, if nothing else, how honest were Edgar and Alice. Had they known of this treasure…"

"And the death of the lord meant its existence died with him. Now we have the means to bring this village back to life. We can use it to buy animals. Will and Jack, I will send you back to Houghton Regis. We need men to work here. Jack, tell Lady Isabelle all and she will know what to do. Tell her that there is at least six months of work here."

"Will you and John manage on your own?"

I looked at John, "What do you say, son?"

"I say that we can do anything, Father." My son was growing into a man.

My two men left early to try to reach Houghton Regis in less than four days. They were both good riders and had sound horses. Alice tried to help John and me but she would keep shaking her head and wringing her hands when we found anything amiss. There was much that was not right. I could have used the villagers to help us but that did not seem right as they had a greater need for their labour than I did. Father Oswald came to help when he could although the parish was so poor that he had his own field to tend. I found it hard to stir myself for this was worse than some of the parts of France and Normandy I had seen, ravaged by war. This land had not seen war for many generations and yet it suffered.

One day as the priest, my son and I toiled to repair the gate on the stable, Alice insisted upon preparing food for us. It allowed me to ask questions of the priest. "Father Oswald, there were few people at the funeral. Why?"

He did not answer immediately. He hauled on the rope that we were using to pull the gate into position and tied it off while he did so. He turned to face me, "People have long memories. When Edgar and Alice were given the stewardship of the manor they were both young. They were also ambitious and saw themselves as better than the rest of the village. They were both favoured, as one would expect, by the lord and when Lord Wreketon died and their families were taken by the plague a year or so later then the two found that they had no friends. Since that time they have become isolated. The two lived alone in the house and did not even stay in the church beyond the time it took for me to hear their confession. I knew that Edgar was ill but not how ill. I was shunned. It seemed to me that Edgar and Alice created their own world in which they lived. They may have been happy," he shrugged, "who can tell, but now Alice is alone and it may well be that her past arrogance is now haunting her. I have given what comfort I can but the disease she has is in her head."

Over the next few days, I tried to speak to the old woman and offer her help but her eyes became veiled almost as though she shunned the contact. John also tried and he enjoyed slightly more success. He was, occasionally, rewarded with a smile. What I also noticed was that she ate like a sparrow. It may have been that she was unused to eating well but I believe she did not want to eat. She wanted to die.

It took ten days for my men to return and when they did Will was not with them. I saw that Jack had brought with him the younger men from Houghton Regis, the ones without families who had lived in my warrior hall. They had sumpters that were laden. He dismounted and nodded approvingly at the small improvements that we had made. He waved a hand, "Lady Isabelle wished to come when she heard of the situation. I persuaded her, my lord, to stay at Houghton. This is not the place for a lady such as your wife."

"I am guessing that she still wished to come even after you used your tongue so well."

He laughed, "She did but my mother and Sarah helped. She sent great quantities of food as well as seeds and tools. There are more clothes for you and Master John."

"And where is Will?"

Jack lowered his voice, "You know that he has been courting Mary, Ned's daughter?"

"Aye, they are a well-matched couple."

"Will spoke on the way south. He said that when he saw the love that Alice and Edgar shared he wanted to begin his own married life as soon as possible. He asked Ned for Mary's hand and it was agreed. They are to be married."

I nodded, "Good, but I would have liked his broad shoulders and wisdom here."

"Oh, he will come, my lord. When they are wed he will bring Mary here." Jack spread his arm around the manor, "When we rode south, we spoke of the desolation we had found. We both know, as do you, my lord, that this will take more than a month of work. He is happy for him and his new wife to shoulder the work."

"He would be my steward?"

"He did not say so in as many words but, aye, I think he would. Since he came to Houghton Regis he has been looking for a place that is his. He knows that this is a challenge but he and Mary are happy to take it on. I spoke with her and with Will. We grew close on the road from Normandy, my lord, and he is a friend. Had you asked me I would have been your steward." It was as though he had suddenly heard his own words and his face became serious, "My lord, we did not mean to be presumptuous. If you have another in mind for the post…"

I shook my head and gave him a reassuring smile, "No, I am happy that Will and Mary are willing to take this on. Indeed, I am humbled that I have people who will make such sacrifices for me but it is a great wrench for Mary."

"She and Will are as one, my lord. Wherever they set up home it will not be with Mary's parents. The land close to Ned's farm is all taken. Twenty miles or two hundred, it would still be a world away."

As we helped my men to unpack, I realised that Jack was right. My wife now lived an ocean away from her home and while her sister lived less than forty miles away, a day of riding, she rarely saw her. The four men that Jack had brought would sleep in one of the rooms in the hall until the servants' quarters were repaired. John and Jack shared one room and I had another. The young men were kind and all helped Alice whenever they could. The extra five pairs of hands made a huge difference and within three days of hard work, the manor had been transformed. Such was the transformation that I was able to visit the village, with John, and distribute the seeds and some of the tools that had been brought. I told them that when the spring came I would buy a pair of oxen to pull the plough and that the villagers would be allowed to have use of the animals. Had I said I was giving them a sack of gold each I could not have had such a warm response. That single visit changed both the mood and the appearance of the village.

As John and I walked back I pointed to some of the buildings. Less than half of the houses were occupied and of the other half, only two houses were habitable. "We will pull down those wrecks of houses that are little better than hovels. If any wish to have the land then we can help them to build. I want the village to look as though it is growing and not dying as it does now."

He nodded, "You know, Father, I thought the work of a knight revolved around a sword and lance. You have shown me that it is not."

"My first squire, your Uncle Jack, had the chance to be dubbed a knight. Indeed, he has great skills with a sword, lance and horse but he chose to be the lord of Weedon. I still use my weapons but it is not my choice to do so. I am bound to both King Henry and Queen Catherine's sons. I may have to draw my sword to protect any of the three of them. I hope I need not do so but …"

Alice slipped away that night. She had visited Father Oswald at the church for confession and when she returned to the house she had a smile upon her face. My men had cooked the food which she pecked at and she went to bed before anyone else. It was John who found her, the next morning. Her wasting away had kindled a kindness in my son that I had not seen before. At Houghton Regis, he had teased both Margaret and his sister, not in a cruel way but in the manner of many youths. The old woman's plight had touched him. He raced to the kitchen, "Father, I think Alice is dead."

When Jack and I went with John to her room we saw that he was right. She had simply given up in the night and was now with Edgar. I could see that John was upset. This was the first death he had witnessed at close hand. I put my arm around him, "See, John, she smiles even in death. She chose to go when she was ready and few people manage to do that. Now go and fetch Father Oswald. She shall be laid in the same grave as her husband."

This time there were more mourners at the funeral. The four young men from my manor swelled the numbers a little but more of the villagers turned out. Perhaps my visit with seeds and hope of prosperity had made them change their minds a little. Whatever the reason, Alice had more respect accorded her than her husband.

Two weeks after she died a wagon came from Houghton Regis. Will and his bride had arrived with all their possessions as well as a boar and a sow. The hogbog we had repaired would be put to good use.

I helped Mary down and said, "This is more than kind, Mary. Are you sure you wish to take this on?"

She smiled, "I go where my husband goes and I am happy, Sir Michael. I have a letter here from Lady Isabelle." She handed me a parchment sealed with wax.

Will came around and said, "I hope that I have not upset you, my lord."

The Knight's Tale

I shook my head, "I would have had to find a steward that I could trust to run this manor for me. You have saved me a difficult task. I trust you but, as I said to Mary, if the task proves too hard then I will bear no ill feelings if you decide to return to Houghton Regis."

"My lord, when I was in Normandy, I wondered what my future would be like. I am an archer but I did not want a life of war. I saw some of my comrades happy with Norman brides and that made me think about a life without my bow. This is perfect. Yes, it will be hard, for Mary and I will be far from our home, but we can build something here. I can repay you and Lady Isabelle for all your kindnesses."

"Good. I wanted clarity and you have given that to me. Now get settled in. You are the new steward. You shall have the room occupied by Jack and John. We have made good the quarters for the other men. When I leave then the hall will be yours."

"And when do you leave, my lord?"

"You and I will need to buy a pair of oxen. We will also need to buy animals for both this manor and the farms. If nothing else the deaths of Edgar and Alice have shown me the pitfalls to avoid. They kept apart from the village and built barriers. You will need to eliminate any such impediments."

Mary proved to be the difference. While we toiled to repair the hall and then demolish the poorer houses, she visited every house in the village. Her winning smile and enthusiasm were infectious. Father Oswald came to me at the end of the first week to tell me how the villagers had taken to her. It was strange. Had Jack and I not been attacked on the road, then we would never have visited my Norman manor and Will Willow Tree would still be languishing in a place he did not wish to be. What would I have done then with King Henry's poisoned chalice?

By the time the first shoots sprouted leaves on the trees, we had bought oxen as well as sheep and a milk cow. We had acquired fowl and stocked the fish pond. The hall was repaired and the village was a different place to the one we had found months earlier. When a young man and his bride came from Shipton, the village that lay closer to York, to ask permission to farm in Easingwold, then I knew we had turned a corner. I let Will make that decision and one of the empty houses now had a new family. It was the first growth in a long time.

I celebrated with a small feast. We all shared in the cooking and with newly repaired tables and chairs we were able to dine in the Great Hall. The hall now felt warm and cosy. When the food was finished, I raised my goblet, "Here is to Will and Mary, the new stewards of

Easingwold." Everyone toasted them and Mary blushed. "We will leave for Houghton Regis at the end of the week."

Hob suddenly burst out, "My lord, I would stay here, if you would give your permission."

Before I could answer Alan Red Hair said, "Me too."

I laughed, "Am I being abandoned?"

Hob shook his head, "No, my lord, but, for my part, I feel that I have put much of me into this hall. I would see it grow. If I was back in Houghton then there would be no challenge. I have spoken to Will and know that he has plans to make this a good manor."

I looked at Will who said, "I am sorry, my lord, if I have spoken out of turn."

"No, Will, and I am pleased. Such ambition is a good thing. And you two? Do you wish to stay also?"

James shook his head, "No, my lord, Absalon and I both have young women we are courting back in Houghton. If Bet is of the same mind as Mary then I may ask you for permission to come north, but I am not sure she would be wrenched from Houghton."

I smiled, "Then all is well."

That night I thanked God, in my prayers, for having helped me with such loyal men.

Chapter 11

Often, we make plans and do not know that others are also making plans. Two days before we were to leave, at noon, a rider wearing the Neville livery rode into my yard. My men and I were all in working clothes and were repairing the bread oven. The liveried man said, "Sir Michael of Weedon?"

I nodded, "I am he."

"I have come from Middleham. Sir Richard Neville requests your company. I am Edward Gilling, gentleman."

I knew that I could not refuse although I had no desire to meet with him. "When?"

He smiled, "Now, my lord."

I frowned, "How far is it?"

"I left this morning, my lord, thirty miles."

A thirty-mile ride did not fill me with joy, but I had no choice. He was the Earl of Salisbury and the Warden of the West March. "Jack, John, prepare the horses and our clothes."

Will said, "If you would come within, my wife will provide you with food, Master Edward."

He dismounted and smiled, "Good, for breakfast seems a long time ago now."

We had no time for farewells. We would be staying overnight so we each had better clothes with us. Had my wife not sent them up with Will and Mary then we would have been forced to wear plainer ones. It would not have worried me but men like the Earl of Salisbury judged men by their apparel.

Our horses had been well rested and that was just as well for Edward Gilling kept up a fast pace. His horse would suffer having ridden sixty miles in one day. While our speed made conversation difficult, I was anxious to know the reasons for our summons. The fact that we were required to be there in one day was ominous.

We stopped to water the horses at Topcliffe, and I took the opportunity to question the gentleman. "Why the haste, Master Edward?"

"I am sorry, Sir Michael, what do you mean?"

"If this was a polite invitation to meet with the earl then we could have left at our leisure. Sir Richard wishes to see me urgently and I ask you why?"

He was clearly ill at ease. He must have been told to keep a close mouth. "You are a new lord in this land and Sir Richard felt it was time that you met."

"Yet Easingwold is not Neville land but belongs to the crown and I have been there for many months."

"You will have to ask the earl, I am merely a messenger."

We mounted our horses who had finished drinking, "And yet you are a gentleman. Why were you chosen?"

We spurred our horses and he turned and smiled, "I am anxious to gain the earl's favour. I am a gentleman but I have no land. I am one of the earl's household, and if I can impress him, I may be given my spurs or land. Perhaps both. You are lucky, Sir Michael, you have many manors."

"And yet I began with nothing and I did not have to bow and scrape to achieve what I have."

I had not meant it to sound barbed but it did and his words showed it, "As I said, Sir Michael, you are lucky."

A squally shower engulfed us and with cloaks and cowls about our ears, it made conversation impossible. It was getting on to dark when the massive keep of Middleham loomed up on the skyline. This was a fortress and a statement of the power of the Neville family. There were armed guards at the gate and men in the towers. There was no war nor the prospect of one so it begged the question why the show of martial might? We had been seen from a distance and when we reached the inner ward there were men to take our horses.

Edward Gilling bowed, "I dare say I will see you again, my lord." He hurried off towards the warrior hall.

The steward said, "If you would come with me, my lord, the earl has a chamber for you. There is a bed and we can find paillasses for your people."

I smiled at the indignant look on John's face.

As I had expected, the room, while large enough, was on the highest floor, just below the fighting platform. It would be cold beyond words. There was water, and cloths on which to dry ourselves. The steward said, apologetically, "The earl is waiting to dine, my lord, so if you would change as soon as possible…"

I sighed, "Of course." When he had gone I said, "Jack, you know to keep your eyes and ears open but John, this is new to you. Dumbness is an admirable quality in this situation."

He gave me a sour smile, "Yes, Father, after all, I am just one of your people."

"Do not take it to heart. Better to be considered unimportant in situations like this. Men often drop their guard."

We headed down the stairs and were guided by the sound of music from the musicians in the minstrels' gallery. This was a castle that showed the power of a family. The Nevilles had benefitted from the fall of the Percy family after the Battle of Shrewsbury and now it was they who controlled the north. One branch of the family was the Warden of the West March, and the other the East. The wall hangings were well made. Brands burned in sconces making it well-lit. As with all castles, it was colder than a hall such as mine but this one had more fires burning than I had seen other than in the king's home. They had money, quite literally, to burn.

Before we entered the hall, I turned to examine John and Jack. Usually, I did not worry about such things as their appearance or hair, even with the king, but Richard Neville was an unknown. Why had I been summoned so hastily? The two saw my gaze and both smoothed their hair and adjusted their doublet and hose. I smiled. "This night will pass."

We entered the hall to a wall of noise. It was not a large gathering but they were noisy. I saw servants waiting with food. Edward Gilling scurried to my side and said, quietly, "Thank you for coming so promptly. The earl does not like to wait for food. You have the place of honour at his side." He turned to John and Jack, "When I have taken your lord to the earl's side, I will take you to the kitchen."

In many ways, the two would have an easier time. They would have to work and carry platters to serve us but they would be kept busy. I would have to watch every word I said. As we approached the earl I saw that he was roughly my age but there the similarity ended. He was not an active man and I saw the development of a paunch on his jowls and belly. His hair was thinning but he had oiled it and he wore expensive garments.

He nodded as I was seated, "And now we can begin. Food."

I saw the shrug from Edward Gilling. He had to bow and scrape if he was to get on. I did not like my welcome. I suppose that I was used to being summoned, both the Duke of Gloucester and the Earl of Suffolk had done so many times but I had always been greeted with courtesy. This was rude. Jack or John should have placed the cloth on my shoulder but they had been whisked away and I placed it there. I saw that there was a spoon and a knife already placed before me. The earl had money, for both of them were made of metal and well-made. The platter was also made of metal and not wood. The food for the first course was a large sturgeon. The fish was well decorated and had been made to look as though it was alive and leaping. The earl took a large portion and most of the roe. His wife, Lady Alice, picked at her food. I saw that she was pregnant and the tiny sliver of fish she took was merely to show she had eaten this most expensive and royal of fish. I

The Knight's Tale

waited until the clergyman to my left had taken his portion before I took my own. I did not take a large piece. This might be a meal of many courses and I did not wish to offend the earl by refusing to eat one. Far better to nibble my way through it.

The earl ate and clearly relished his food. His goblet was already full and he drank well. When the game birds were brought in, my goblet was filled. It was John who did so while Jack placed the quail on my platter. They both gave me reassuring smiles. It was not until the beef was brought in, to great applause, that the earl spoke to me. He had exchanged words across me to the bishop and to his wife but I had been assiduously avoided.

I was so distracted that when he did speak to me I almost jumped, "I thought after the long ride you would wish to eat. Now that we have had two courses, I can tell you the reason for the invitation." Perhaps I had misjudged the earl for he had been thinking of me rather than simply ignoring me. "You fought alongside Sir William Strongstaff and Sir John Talbot."

I nodded, "I did, my lord. Both were great knights. Sir John still serves England and the king in France." My part in the taking of the Pays de Caux and Pontoise were still a secret and I would have to watch my words.

"And you were charged with the protection of the king." I nodded. "The Duke of Gloucester showed misjudgement, in my view, when you were dismissed." He leaned in and I could smell the drink on his breath, "My part in the council was also ended so we both suffered from the wrath of the king's uncle. I hope that when my cousin, the Duke of York, returns from France where he has been placed in command of the king's armies, we shall see a change in those who guide our young king."

This was politics and I wanted none of it. The earl wanted to control young King Henry.

The serving of the beef and the rich sauce that accompanied it allowed a halt in the conversation but, when the beef had been consumed and the earl had refreshed his mouth with wine, he turned to me again. "You now have a manor that is in Yorkshire."

I was wary. "Yes, my lord, it was one of the king's manors."

"As Warden of the West March, I can command your men to serve me."

"There are few men in Easingwold, my lord. I have spent the last months trying to make the hall habitable, and the land to produce enough food."

"I know. I have had you watched."

The Knight's Tale

To cover my shock, I drank some wine. I had not known that there were men watching me and, more importantly, I did not like that it had happened at all. I found it sinister.

"Your efforts confirm all that I have heard of you. That is why I sent for you. My brother has sent me word that the lands of Durham are being threatened by Hugh Douglas, the Earl of Ormonde. His father, James the Gross, was for many years, a thorn in the side of Durham and his son looks to be the same. I want you to take some of my men and go to the aid of my brother. I have good soldiers but none have commanded in battle. You were the one who captured the Maid and one of the few to emerge with any honour. I wish you to lead my men. I have some mustering here and the rest have been warned. You shall pick them up as you travel through the Neville lands of Yorkshire and Durham."

I was stunned and this time I could not cover my shock with a drink. My mouth simply dropped open. "But, my lord, I do not know your men."

"From what I have heard you led men in France that you did not know. You are a soldier. I can see that. From the moment you strode in I knew that I had made the right choice." I was going to argue although I knew that it would be a waste of time when he said, "I know the problems that you have in Easingwold and, as compensation for the time you are away from your new manor, I will give you a pair of oxen, a flock of sheep and some pigs. Your manor can begin to grow." He smiled as the desserts were brought in and added, "And there will be no service for the men of Easingwold."

He had me and I knew it. The animals would be the saving of the manor. "And when do I leave, my lord?"

"I began the muster yesterday. The men from Middleham and the land around here will be ready to leave the day after tomorrow."

I nodded, "Then I shall have to return to my home at dawn. I have much to do."

He laughed and banged the table, "I knew I had chosen the right man and your words confirm it. You are a man of action." He nodded to the desserts which were rich with marchpane, "I am not. I hope that my son might become as skilful as you. You may leave the table whenever you wish, Sir Michael, I will not be offended. My gentleman, Edward Gilling, will be your lieutenant. He has ambition and you might be his hope."

I picked at the dessert and then rose. Few people noticed my departure. Lady Alice had departed long before I did and the bishop who was next to me was happily swimming in Malmsey. John and Jack followed me. "Did you eat?" I knew the problems of being a squire. You ate at the end of the feast. You dined well but on leftovers.

John grinned, "Jack told me to eat when we cleared the platters. We are both well fed."

Jack had a cloth in his hand and he opened it to show a leg of ham with just a few slices taken from it. "And we can dine on this in our chamber, Sir Michael."

"Keep it for the morrow. We have to ride back to Easingwold and then return here. We go to war."

Neither of them was taken aback by my words. In John's case, it was all that he wanted. He wished to go to war. Had his mother been present then there might have been some argument from her, but he would don a sword, wear a helmet and carry my lance. He was happy.

The guards must have been told of my early departure for, after being the first to breakfast in a hall which stank of stale ale and wine, we found our horses ready and the guards preparing to open the gates for us. We left and headed southeast towards the faint glow in the sky that heralded dawn. While we galloped, I told them all that I knew.

"We do not have much time. When we reach Easingwold we will need to load mail and weapons on two sumpters and then return here. Our horses will be weary when we reach the borderlands."

"We fight the Scots?"

"We face the Scots but we may not have to fight them. I have learned that a show of strength can often defeat an enemy, John."

He looked disappointed, "Then we may not have to draw a sword?"

"That will depend upon the Earl of Ormonde. In any case, John, you are not even a squire. Your task will be to take messages and watch Jack's horse and mine if we are dismounted. Your sword will be used in your defence only."

Jack asked, "And will we take men too?"

I had thought of little else since the earl had told me of my commission, "I will need a couple but who I have yet to decide."

We clattered into my yard well before noon. Will and my four men all emerged from behind my hall where they were still working on the bread oven, "My lord, you are back early."

"We are. Gather around." The five of them closed with me. "Jack, John, see to the horses."

The two led off the animals. They would be watered and fed. We would ride other horses back to Middleham. If nothing else, this had shown me that I did not have enough horses. We would be riding sumpters. If we rode our war horses, we would risk ruining them and they were far too valuable for that.

"The Earl of Salisbury needs me to lead men against the Scots. I need two of you to come with me. I will not command you to come, for I do not know what we will face."

Will said, "I am the archer, my lord, and I have fought in France. I will come."

"You need not, Will. You are now married, you are my steward and this is your home."

"Mary will understand."

The other four all wished to come too. I chose Alan Red Hair because he was the closest I had to a man at arms. He had a leather jack, a good helmet and was more than a competent rider.

"We leave two hours after sext. Will, say your farewells."

We ate hurriedly and then packed the mail and weapons on sumpters. We would be taking every horse that we had. It was good that when Jack had returned from Houghton Regis he had brought eight horses. We would leave six at Middleham. There were no tears from Mary as we left. She was young but had a strong heart. The three men I left to continue the work would look after her. We headed back up the road to Middleham.

Chapter 12

The earl gave me fifteen men at arms and twelve archers from Middleham as well as five knights and their squires from the manors around Middleham. I could have taken more archers but there were not enough horses for them. Edward was ready there, too, and he had a spare horse. With no squire, Jack had to lead Edward's mount. We dined, not in the Great Hall but in the more modest warrior hall. I needed to get to know the men. They had all heard of me. The capture of the Maid was the stuff of legend and so the meeting was a warm one. They were happy to have me as their leader and that meant I did not have that battle to win. Edward was keen to be of use to me and he supplied all the information readily.

"This is a modest retinue that you will lead, but when all the muster is gathered, there will be five hundred men. Those lords, like those from Masham and Ripon, will lead their men here tomorrow. It is a short ride to Richmond and my home of Gilling where we shall collect even more men. The men of the Palatinate will gather at Durham. The bishop has promised us St Cuthbert's banner."

Even as he read off the names my hopes rose and then the name stuck in my head, Masham. Sir Walter Wolsey and his son Sir Marmaduke would know me as Sir Ralph. The necessary lie I had told was coming back to haunt me. I would have to speak to those knights and give them a version of the truth. I prayed that they would remember my deeds and not my lie or else any hope of my bonding with a disparate body of men was doomed to failure from the start.

A combination of worry about the campaign and the meeting with the knights from Masham ensured that I neither slept well nor long and I was awake before dawn. I roused a sleepy John and Jack. "John, I have a delicate task for you this day. There will be knights this day who come from Masham and I need the senior knights brought to me. I shall use Sir Richard's solar. They will have a livery with three red game birds. If one has a red bar across the top then that is Sir Marmaduke and if not, and the man is an older knight, then that will be Sir Walter. Bring them to me."

"But why?"

I sighed and Jack shook his head. My squire answered, "Master John, you do not question Sir Michael's orders. I understand the need for this order. Just obey it. You are the only one who can do this. I cannot."

He brightened, "Me?" We both nodded. "Then I will not let you down."

The Knight's Tale

The earl was not an early riser and with no other guests in the castle, we had the place to ourselves. I was anxious to leave as soon as I could. Richmond was just eight miles away. I had all the men woken and breakfasted as dawn was breaking. The riders from the south would be there soon after and I intended to make the crossing of the Tees by dark. It would be a twenty-mile ride and leave us with just twenty odd miles to Durham.

I left Will to organise our men and John waited at the gate. Jack would be at the door of the solar. I did not like the deception I had been forced to use and I now had to use another trick. I sat on the chair with my back to the door. I had to count on the fact that they would be anxious to meet me and Jack would escape scrutiny.

I heard the clatter of mounts in the ward and sat. Jack was behind the door and when there was a knock upon it I heard it open and Jack said, "Sir Michael, Sir Marmaduke Wolsey."

I waited for the door to close before I stood and turned. "Sir Ralph! What is this?" It was not anger on the face of Sir Marmaduke but confusion.

"I am Sir Michael of Weedon. When you met me in Normandy, I was playing a part. I can say no more about it except that the king and Sir John Talbot were privy to the deception which, for a variety of reasons, was a necessary one."

He looked from me to Jack and then John. He was a clever young knight and I saw him taking in all the information. Eventually, he nodded and gave a slight bow, "You are still the same knight who gained the Pays de Caux for us and I now know that the unknown knight we heard affected the entry into Pontoise was also you."

"And the men you brought? Would they recognise me?"

He looked at me, "The livery is different and your hair and beard are gone. What if I say that Sir Ralph was your older brother?"

I nodded for it was a good plan, "And died at Pontoise."

"Aye, that would work." The confusion left his face and was replaced by a grin, "I was looking forward already to a chance to bloody Scottish noses and now I have confidence that we shall do so."

I held out my arm and he grasped it, "And, for my part, I know that I have at least one knight and retinue upon whom I can rely."

"All the knights I bring are doughty fellows."

"Your father?"

"He is getting old. The campaign in the Pays de Caux will be remembered as his swan song."

I was relieved that the young knight had chosen to believe the best of me.

By the time we left Richmond, we had two hundred men. There were too few archers, just eighty, but that was because we rode. I had already decided to make Will Willow Tree their captain but that appointment would have to wait until we met the bishop. I wanted the Palatinate to pay my captain.

We camped at the old Roman fort by the river at Piercebridge. The men were in good spirits for the Scots were an old enemy and it had been many years since the men of Yorkshire had been asked to fight against them. As we sat around a fire, surrounded by the twenty knights, tales were told of past battles. They had all been passed down from father to son and, as with all such tales, changed a little in the telling. The story of the Battle of the Standards, when an ancient Archbishop Thurstan had led a hastily cobbled army to rout the Scots, capture the king and chase the Prince of Cumberland, was a particularly stirring one, as was the Battle of Neville's Cross when the Scots, keen to take advantage of the English army fighting at Crécy, had been trounced.

When we left, the next morning, the men sang songs of the battles and I knew that while I had a small number of men, they were made of the right sort of metal.

Durham was an armed camp and this time I saw that there were more archers. That was good in one way, we had the means to break Scottish hearts, but it also meant we would be travelling more slowly. I had asked Sir Marmaduke to be my lieutenant as he was a knight and Edward was not. Leaving him and Will to organise the sleeping arrangements, I went to speak to the bishop. He was a Neville and being born, as was his brother the earl, at Raby Castle, was a Durham man. He was more of a priestly bishop than many of his predecessors. It explained why the earl had needed a military mind to lead his men. I was taken to a quiet office where we could speak.

"The Earl of Ormonde is trying to make a name for himself. I believe he has aspirations for the crown itself. It has been some years since the Scots enjoyed success in the borders and I fear that the failures in France have encouraged their ambitions. In the days of the late king the Scots were fearful of reprisals across the border but King Henry, well, he seems preoccupied with Normandy and France."

I agreed with the bishop but I was still a loyal knight and I could say nothing.

"Where have they raided?"

He sighed and poured us some wine, "You know, I think, of the history of the Nevilles and the Percies?" I nodded. "As a man of God, I would end this divisive situation but…Northumberland controls the East March as we the West March. The Scots have raided the lands north and east of Carlisle. That castle is too mighty a nut to be easily cracked and the Scots are making their way east to raid the Tyne Valley and the Durham Dales. We are lucky that they are not a mobile army. I sent word to my brother as soon as I heard that they had raided. The Earl of Northumberland will not cross to protect the West March."

"And we cannot cross into the East March for the same reason. Then they will be coming along the Roman military road south of the old wall?"

"That is our belief. Hexham will be their target. Prudhoe has been warned and that castle is well defended. Once they reach Hexham then they can spread out and ravage the land where farmers are planting crops."

"And do we have their numbers?"

He gave a wry shake of the head, "You are a soldier, Sir Michael, and you know, as well as I do, that farmers exaggerate numbers. There could be ten thousand or there might be just a thousand. I fear that the true figure will only be discovered by you. I have mounted as many men as I can. Here is the muster."

He pushed over a parchment. I added the men I had brought with me. "So, I have five hundred mounted men. Fifty knights, one hundred and twenty mounted archers, two hundred and thirty men at arms and the rest are squires and pages. The two hundred men on foot, who leads them?"

"Sir Roger of Stockton. He is an older knight but he has fought the Scots before."

"And are there any border horsemen that I can use to discover where the Scots are?"

He nodded, "Sir Alan Grey is from Corbridge. He knows the lands."

"We have plenty of arrows?"

"Ten thousand, if you should need them."

"I have brought my own captain of archers, my lord, Will Willow Tree and I would have him paid as such; two shillings a day. For my part I need nothing."

"Of course, but when this is over there will be rewards for your service. It is the least that Durham can do."

Even as I was speaking, I was working out a strategy and battle plan. I explained to the bishop what I intended. If I failed, then his brother would need to know that I did all that I could. There was a map on the wall and I went to it. "Haltwhistle and Haydon Bridge are places that promise the Scots plunder. They will raid there. We have a twenty-mile ride to Hexham. I would leave now but I need to speak to the leaders. We will leave at dawn and my plan is to hold them at Hexham. If Sir

Roger marches his men hard then they can be the difference that brings us victory."

The bishop was not a military-minded man, but the simplicity of my plan appealed. "I have sent riders to Norham, Bamburgh and Newcastle to warn them of the danger. Even if you fail to destroy them, I hope that you may slow them down."

"Bishop, if we fail then it is we that will be destroyed. I seek no glory. I intend to win by any means possible."

"Good, and I will give you the Banner of St Cuthbert."

"I will give that to Sir Roger to bear."

He frowned and then grinned, "And that will encourage the men who march on foot to make all haste. I can see why you were chosen, Sir Michael. Why are you not in France fighting alongside Sir John Talbot and the Duke of York?"

"I have served my time there, my lord. If the king commands me to do so, then I shall return but, until England is safe, my place is here." I studied the map. "And supplies, my lord? I hope to defeat the enemy but if they are persistent, we may have a long campaign. As I discovered in France, men who are not fed neither fight nor stand."

"You will be fed. The people of Durham know the danger in which we stand."

I stood, "Then, with your permission, I shall address my knights. May I use the Great Hall?"

"Of course, and I shall stand at your side. I may not be raising my sword in defence of my land but you will enjoy my support and I shall send priests and healers with you."

"Thank you, my lord." The priests would be useful but they would also slow down my progress.

It took time for the knights to be gathered. It was as well I had decided to leave at dawn, the next day. I saw some faces I knew: the knights from Masham, Middleham and Richmond but the Durham knights were an unknown quantity, and I knew that they would need to be persuaded of my skill. I would have to use my reputation. It would seem like boasting but I knew of no other way. I was not used to this. I would be leading a large army. Sir Walter had led in the Pays de Caux and Sir John Talbot or Sir William had been my generals at the other battles I had fought. I was more used to skirmish, ambush and chevauchée.

The men were noisy and I wondered how to silence them without sounding like a bully when the Bishop made the sign of the cross and began to pray. "Almighty God, we beseech you to come to the aid of

The Knight's Tale

our warriors who, once again, are gathered to fight the might that is Scotland. Amen."

"Amen." The amen brought silence.

The bishop and I were on a raised dais and I stared at the sea of faces. The squires and pages were gathered at the rear and I took heart from the proud looks on the faces of Jack and John. "I am Sir Michael of Weedon and the Earl of Salisbury has given me this commission. We are to send these Scottish raiders back to Scotland." I smiled, "Depleted in number I hope." That brought some cheers and smiles. "Before I take you into my confidence with my plans, I think that I should tell you why I was chosen. I served both this king and his father in the wars in France. I was the knight who fetched the Maid of Orleans to justice and I have campaigned with Sir John Talbot in the Pays de Caux and at Pontoise. I have rarely fought Scotsmen but I assume that an arrow or a sword will work just as effectively on them as Frenchmen." This brought another cheer and I noticed that there were fewer frowns. My words were working. "Edward Gilling will command the men at arms and the man who will command the archers is Captain Will Willow Tree. Show them who you are." The two of them stepped forward and raised their arms. There was no mistaking which was which. "My plan is a simple one. I want that noble border knight, Sir Alan Grey, to take some of his redoubtable border horsemen and find the Scots." I knew who the knight was from the arms that patted his back. "The rest of us will leave Durham at Lauds. I intend to make a stand at Hexham. Sir Roger of Stockton will bring the men on foot as quickly as he can. To help speed him on his way the bishop and I are entrusting the Banner of St Cuthbert into his care. I doubt not that it will be defended well."

The portly knight was instantly recognisable with his red face, thinning hair and paunch, "My lord, I thank you for the honour and know this, the only way the Scottish bandits will get the standard is over my dead body."

Another knight, I did not see him shouted, "Aye, and they will need good swords to get through that belly."

I wondered if Sir Roger might be offended and I would have to chastise the knight, but Sir Roger laughed and said, "Aye, I eat well and for good reason, Sir Giles, to sustain me when I fight England's foes."

I knew then that all would be well.

"Until Lauds, I bid you goodnight but know this, I am happy to explain my reasons for each and every action but they are commands and not requests."

The Knight's Tale

I waited with the bishop while most of the men left. Notably, Sir Alan approached me, "My lord, thank you for the honour. When do I leave?"

"You know the land, when do you think you should leave?"

He grinned, "I will take my twenty best mounted horsemen and leave the other twenty to act as scouts for the main body. I can be at Hexham by nightfall, my lord, and scout out the enemy tomorrow."

"Then go with God."

He hurried out and I was confident that we would have intelligence when we reached Hexham.

The bishop said, "If you do not need more of me, I shall prepare for Nones. My priests and I will pray for you."

That left me with Edward, Will, Jack and John. All four looked happy. "My lord, thank you for this honour. Are you sure that it is within my compass?"

"Of course, it is, Will. You have a sharp mind and have campaigned in France. I need one who knows when to loose, when to fall back and when to attack. I trust you. The bishop will pay you two shillings a day and it began when we left Easingwold." He smiled. "Edward, none save Sir Alan asked questions of me. Go around them and discover if they have worries."

"I will, my lord, but your plans seemed simple and, to my mind, good. I look forward to the day."

"It will be a bloody battle, whenever it comes. The Scots are always brave soldiers. They are not always well led but they will fight and die, hard." When he left us I said, "And now, you two. All is prepared? Horses, weapons, mail? Once we leave here, we cannot get more."

"It is all ready my lord and we have oats for the horses."

"Then let us go to the cathedral and pray by Cuthbert's tomb. Any divine help is to be welcomed."

Chapter 13

We trooped out of the city well before the sun was up. The bishop stood by the bridge over the Wear to bless us all. We had twenty-seven miles to go and I intended to push the horses. I had no intention of fighting on horseback. I wanted the horses to be rested when we reached our destination so that if we won, we could chase them back to Scotland. With Sir Roger's men on foot and the archers, we had the chance to make the Scots bleed. I was not being reckless like Sir John Talbot but I was using his dash and speed to get to a place where we would have the upper hand and not our enemies.

We travelled on the Roman Road that led to the wall, that edifice which had been a barrier to keep Roman Britain safe. The bishop had told me that it was designed to guard the start of productive land in the south from the more barren wilderness of the north. Consequently, there were few settlements lying close to the wall. Hexham, thanks to its abbey, was the largest village. There was a wall but with few men to defend it, an army would be able to sweep through it. The abbey would be sacked and its riches taken. Crops and animals would be taken and the harm it would do to this part of England was unimaginable. The Earl of Ormonde was a clever man. He was attacking the soft underbelly of the border. With one savage slash, he could eviscerate the north of Durham. With no castle closer than Carlisle in the west and Prudhoe in the east, he could do as he wished.

Edward Gilling rode next to me. He was keen to learn. He knew how to use a sword and both his horse and weapons were as good as any I had seen. I did not doubt his ability to be a successful participant in a tourney. War was different. I had been brought up in war and seen its ugly face at close hand. Fine blows that brought applause in a tournament were wasted where men were hacking, slashing and butchering in a fight to the death.

"My lord, why do we not make a mounted charge against the Scots? Some of the knights from Middleham wonder at the wisdom of your decision. We will have many more horsemen that they do and ours will be better mounted and armoured."

"And their mounted men will not be the ones we would have to charge. The Scots like to use the schiltron. Even at Falkirk, where King Edward trounced them, the schiltron held out longer than one might have imagined. King Edward's knights failed to break them and he had to use archers to kill them and even then they died hard."

"Schiltron?"

The Knight's Tale

"A long pike, up to fifteen feet long held by men who can, if they need to, make an impenetrable circle. They wear a small shield or buckler in their left arm and with a helmet and leather jack, they are hard to beat. Horses cannot get close. We stand a better chance of defeating them with a combination of mailed men on foot and an assault of arrows descending from the sky. A victory will only come our way if the archers are successful."

I saw him taking in the information and I studied the land which had been steadily rising as we closed with Hexham. The Romans had chosen a natural feature upon which to build their wall, a long ridge of rock that ran east to west. I had never seen the wall but I knew that there were ditches along both sides of it. The road we would travel, to the south of the wall, was the fastest way to get from the east of the country to the west. The distance between the two seas was less than ninety miles.

"And will you fight in the line, Sir Michael?"

I turned to look at him, "That is a good question, Edward. When I fought in France I fought in the front line alongside my men at arms. At Pontoise and in the Pays de Caux I fought alongside knights such as Sir Marmaduke, but here I lead. I need to see the battle and so, my answer is no, but as I have never been in this position before, I do not know where or how that will be. We have few enough knights in any case. I will be close to the front line of knights but where I can see the whole battle. Until I view Hexham and the land around it, I cannot say."

We reached the village well before noon. I knew that Sir Roger would struggle to catch up and would not arrive until very late in the afternoon. Sir Ralph of Hexham met us as we entered the village which was clearly preparing for war.

"Sir Michael, Sir Alan told us of the danger and he rode west before dawn. I have four men at arms, six archers and we have twenty men from the village. We are at your command."

I nodded, "Sir Marmaduke, take command. Have the horses secured at the eastern end of the village and then have the men cook food. As Sir Alan has not yet returned, I am assuming that the enemy is not yet close. Have hovels built."

"Yes, Sir Michael."

"Edward, Sir Ralph, we will walk to the west and see the way that the land lies. Jack, see to my horse."

We walked to the bridge over the River Tyne. This was the crossing that the Scots sought. As we walked Sir Ralph pointed west and explained, "Less than a mile and a half away the two branches of the Tyne join. That is why there is this bridge here." We stopped in the middle of the bridge. The main part of the village lay to the southwest of the bridge. There were a few isolated farms to the northeast. He pointed north, "The wall lies just three and a half miles that way." He chuckled, "If you visit it, you will find that there are fewer stones on the wall than there are in Hexham village, but it is still an impediment to those who would steal animals. It is a barrier." He tapped the parapet of the bridge. "This is the barrier to the east of this land." He pointed south and west, "There used to be a castle there, just south of Haydon Bridge. Langley Castle was a powerful barrier but the king's grandfather took it and destroyed it two years after Shrewsbury. It is but a ruin now."

"And the Scots will come from the west."

"There is but one road and this is it."

I pointed north, "What about the Roman Road south of the wall? Could they not use that?"

He rubbed his chin, "Aye, they could and the bridge close to the old fort at Chesters crosses the North Tyne."

"Then why could they not cross there?"

"They could."

"We will examine the land on the approach from the west, but, if Sir Alan returns with no evidence of a Scottish army, then we will march north to Chesters."

Edward said, "That is a huge risk, my lord."

I sighed, "I know, but until we came here, I did not know that there were two places the Scots could come."

We passed the abbey and I saw that it had high walls, "We can use that for archers." There would be no fighting platform but something could be improvised. Our archers were the key to the encounter.

The houses became sparser as we moved along the road and the ground descended a little. Sir Ralph said, "Haydon Bridge lies four miles down the road."

"If the Scots come then I want the village of Haydon Bridge to be abandoned and the people brought here. Their men can defend with us."

"But their village might be destroyed."

"Houses can be rebuilt. It is harder to do so if all the men are dead."

Edward said, "Could we defend the bridge?"

Sir Ralph said, "That is a good idea."

I shook my head, "Until Sir Roger arrives with the men on foot, we do not have enough men. You say the Tyne is a more powerful river after Hexham?" The local knight nodded. "Then it can be forded upstream?"

I saw his face fall, "Aye, it could."

"Then this is where we fight." I pointed to a stand of trees that had grown close to the road. "We cut those down and make them into stakes to slow an enemy down, but we wait until Sir Alan brings us news. Until his men arrive we are in the dark." In my mind, I knew that the abbey with its attendant riches would be the lure for the Scottish earl. The village would give him a base and he would be able to raid at will.

Sir Ralph's men approached. They were all mounted, "My lord, do we camp with the others?"

He looked at me and I shook my head. "Have your men stay here. I may need to use you."

Even as we turned to walk back to the abbey, I heard the sound of hooves clattering on the cobbled road and riding hard. I turned and drew my sword. Both Edward and Sir Ralph did not draw a weapon, they just turned. I was the soldier who was alert to danger. I sheathed my weapon when I saw that it was Sir Alan and his twenty light horsemen.

He pointed behind him, "The Scots are just the other side of Haydon Bridge. They will reach it by dark."

Sometimes a leader has to make instant decisions and this was one such occasion, "Sir Ralph, the villagers know you, ride to Haydon Bridge and command them to leave their homes or face death."

He mounted the horse his men had brought, "Yes, Sir Michael." Sir Ralph's men had fresh horses and knew the area. There were only five of them but the knight and his men at arms were all mailed.

"Edward, fetch our men."

He turned and ran back to the village.

"How many men, Sir Alan?"

"More than a thousand. We found them at Haltwhistle. They were plundering but we were seen. I did not have the luxury of time and so my counting was, perforce, perfunctory. I estimate fifty border horse and another fifty who are mailed, heavy horsemen. The rest are men on foot."

"Then their approach will be slow."

He nodded, "It is eight miles from Haltwhistle to Haydon Bridge. Their men on foot cannot reach it before dark. Their horsemen, however…"

I rubbed my chin, "Thus far this Earl of Ormonde has shown himself to be both clever and careful. I cannot see him risking all. This is where we fight. You have done well. Take your men into the village. There are fires and there will be food."

"You will stay here, alone?"

I laughed, "I will be safe enough and I need to walk this land while it is still light to see how it can be made defensible."

The Knight's Tale

He showed he was a true horseman when he had his men dismount and walk their animals back to the centre of the village. I turned and squatted. It was easier to see the rise and fall of the land from such a position. I saw the natural rise. That would be where we would stand. The ground before would become littered with stakes to slow down the enemy. I headed across the rough ground towards the river. I saw that there was a stream, they called them burns in this part of the world, and it ran north to the river. It could be easily crossed but it was boggy and would disrupt a schiltron. I began to adapt my plan. When I reached the river, the plan had become clearer. We would put the stakes on the east side of the stream where they could be embedded easily and we would defend on the more solid ground a few paces from the stream on the slightly higher ground.

Edward returned with the first of our men and I ordered them to cut down the saplings to make stakes. "I want a line of stakes embedding from the river to the walls of the abbey." I saw Edward frown. "I have paced it out. It is five hundred paces from the walls of the abbey to the river. We have enough men now to cover that and we can use the walls of the abbey to give our archers a longer range." I did not like having to explain but Sir William had taught me that men needed to know a leader's mind. That was the difference with Sir John. He did not share his thoughts.

The abbey would only give forty or so archers the extra range but they would be able to loose over our heads and they would have protection from Scottish bows, although I knew that their archers were neither as strong nor as skilled as English bowmen.

Sir Ralph rode in, the horse he rode was lathered and weary. His men led another eight horses. He dismounted. "They were not happy but I gave commands and they will come. It will be close, but they should be here before dark. It gives us an extra twenty-five men."

"We will use that burn as our first line of defence."

"The Cockshaw Burn."

"If that is its name then, aye. We face well over a thousand men but most are on foot. If we can hold them then we can destroy them with our horsemen but, first, we must break their hearts and their spears." I saw Edward listening, "This will be bloody and the outcome will be decided by who wants this land more; those who come to take it or those who wish to defend England. Did you see their scouts?"

He laughed, "We saw them and we slew them. We took their heads. These are their horses. They will know that men defend the village."

By the time it was dark, we had the stakes embedded and the horses had been brought to the green area inside the abbey. They would be protected by the walls and we could reach them quickly if we had to pursue the Scots. The men were fed and the hovels were built close to the stakes. Best of all, Sir Roger and his men had arrived. Our numbers were swollen by the men on foot and we had the banner of St Cuthbert. As I had anticipated, the carrying of the banner had encouraged the portly knight to make all haste. He was weary but proud of his achievement. I ate with Sir Roger, Sir Alan, Sir Ralph, Sir Marmaduke, Will and Edward. The last two were honoured to be eating with what amounted to the five leaders of this army, but in the short time I had known them, I had come to realise that Sir Alan and Sir Roger had much in common with me. They believed that knights had a duty to lead and to set an example.

We ate, but it was as much about planning for the battle as anything. "Will, I know you do not know your archers yet but have you any idea of the range of the men you lead?"

He swallowed the stew-soaked bread and nodded, "There are fifty that I would call archers who could fight in France. With the height of the walls then those fifty can rain death on the Scots when they near the burn. The rest, the ones who are Sunday morning archers, will drop them on the stakes."

"Sir Roger, I am placing you on the left of the line. I would have you command those who do not have good armour. If you have to, then I am happy for them to fall back."

"You do not mind being outflanked?" There was curiosity in his voice.

"I plan on blocking the streets of the village with wagons and to have the slingers and boys be a nuisance. The Scots cannot flank us on the right as the river lies there and I am happy for them to be stretched. Will's archers can switch their arrows to those on the flank. All that I ask is a steady withdrawal. Sir Ralph, you and the men of Hexham will be on the right. There are fewer of you, but you know the land and the river."

"And what of me?"

I turned to Sir Alan, "You are the key part of my plan. Your border horsemen are lightly armoured but they are well mounted and fast. I would have you take your men and ride around the rear of the Scots. When you are in position, I wish you to blow your horn and attack their rear. They will not count your paltry numbers, merely fear an attack in the rear."

Edward could not contain himself, "And that is when you will attack in the centre which will already have been weakened by the men spreading around our flank."

I smiled and nodded, "Just so, and I hope that the horn and the fear that it is an army of horsemen attacking at their rear will eat their resolve and they will break."

The others took that in. I saw the frown on John's face. He was a clever boy and knew the danger in which I would be placing myself.

"And who will be in our centre?"

"I will be in the centre with you, Sir Marmaduke, the men of Masham and the knights of Middleham. The Earl of Salisbury's men shall be the rock on which the Scottish are broken."

The plan was a good one. I was not arrogant but I believed I had measured all the possibilities. This one played to our strengths. Will and his archers were the most potent weapon we possessed, especially against men wearing no armour. He could use the walls of the abbey to move easily and attack any target that, from his lofty perch, he deemed the best. I was trusting my archer. I knew his worth and only a fool would not use his archer's brain. For the rest, it relied on our mail and plate being stronger than the long spears of the Scots.

After we had eaten, I walked around the camp to speak to the men. I remembered at Agincourt where King Henry had done so in secret. Sir William always did it openly. I emulated my mentor. I wanted to afford men the chance to speak to the man who might order them to their deaths. It took a long time, as there were many men who had heard of me but did not know me, and they all had questions. Most were about the Maid. Some called her a witch but I quickly put that lie to bed. "She was anything but a witch. Many of those who had been defeated by her circulated that lie, for they could not believe that such a simple girl could have beaten them. The French believed that God had spoken to her and it was ordinary men who fought like Achilles to protect her." I nodded towards the banner of St Cuthbert, "I hope that tomorrow the banner inspires Englishmen in the same way the Maid inspired the French."

The priests also wandered the camp to hear confessions. It gave men comfort knowing that if they died they would be granted a place in heaven. To die unshriven was a frightening thought.

When I eventually went to my bed, John was weary beyond words. It was not just the work that had tired him but the excitement of a prospective battle. I remembered it well. Despite the rough ground on which he lay, he was asleep even as his head touched it. Jack covered him with a blanket, and I said, "Watch over him tomorrow, Jack. Do not let him be foolish."

He nodded, "I am your squire, should I not be watching you?"

The Knight's Tale

"Watch John and I pray that God and the spirit of Sir William will watch over me." I shrugged, "Surely the knight chosen to watch over the king should not need a minder?"

"The Scots will come for you, my lord."

"I know. In fact, I am counting on that. I want them to push hard, for in their eagerness they will open themselves up for Sir Alan's attack from the rear. This time he will not be attacking with those who scouted but all his border horsemen. This is their land and they hate the Scots more than any. They might be few in numbers but they will surprise the enemy."

By the time the sun was fully up, we had breakfasted and were standing ready for an enemy we could not see. I was at the centre of twenty knights and we stood close to the bridge that led over the burn. It was the only place where we could not place stakes and the weakest section. If the Scots chose the road, we would be vulnerable to an attack from their flank. It was a risk but every battle had risks.

Sir Ralph had local men watching the road and it was two hours after dawn when they ran in, "Sir Ralph, they come."

It was one thing to expect an attack but the news that they were close had an effect. Those who had yet to fight in a battle found the need to make water and empty bowels while those who knew what to expect checked the edges of swords, tightened straps and made the sign of the cross. I turned to John, "Now is the time for my helmet."

The abbot himself came from the abbey to bless us. The whole army knelt as he invoked God's help. The priests and healers from the abbey stood close to the wall that surrounded the abbey. They would tend to any wounded. We waited.

The lone voice that started the song was soon joined by all the locals. It was Cuthbert's song, a paean to the saint and to the men of Durham. I did not know the song but most of the Hexham and Durham men did and their voices were swollen by others as parts were recognised. The singing seemed to bond the men and the fluttering banner of St Cuthbert added to the effect.

The Scottish banners appeared through the trees in the distance. I had not seen their scouts but I knew that they must have had them. That was confirmed when the Scots began to form ranks. They knew what to expect. I saw that their front rank had men in mail and plate. They carried the long spears of the schiltron but they were men at arms and knights. As the sun, shining from behind us, glinted from the metal, I was able to see that their strongest part was in the centre. Their leader, the earl, sat with his household knights, all fifteen of them, on horses. He would be able to see how the battle went and his small reserve could

The Knight's Tale

exploit any weakness. The enemy had five ranks and that suited me for had they used three ranks then Sir Roger would have been in danger of being outflanked before the battle began. The five ranks concentrated the Scottish in the centre. They would be going for the bridge over the burn. The twelve hundred men with the spears were in a block two hundred and fifty men wide. Such a mighty army could have swept over us but for the burn and the stakes.

"Lock shields and brace spears." The noise of shields touching rippled down the line, and I shouted, "Captain Will, the battle begins upon your command."

I could not see him, he was eighty paces from me standing behind the walls of the abbey on the improvised fighting platform the archers had constructed, but I heard his reply, "Fear not Sir Michael, England's archers will not let you down."

The Scots would have seen the line of spears and shields but the archers were hidden behind the walls of the abbey. The Scots knew to fear English archers and seeing none would advance more confidently. The shout from the Scottish line heralded their steady march towards us. They sang a song just as Cuthbert's had aided us. It helped them to keep time and to put heart into them. We were just two ranks deep, the squires and pages were behind us with spare weapons. I braced my spear next to my foot. When it was shattered Jack would hand me the war axe. It would be the best weapon to shatter spears.

Will would be watching the approach and choosing his moment. The Scots were just twenty paces from the burn and sixty paces from the stakes behind which we waited when I heard the cry, "Loose!"

Not every archer had the range needed and Will had chosen his best archers. The fifty arrows were followed in rapid succession by another four flights so that two hundred and fifty arrows fell quickly. The Scots were not expecting them and Will had used some bodkins. Men fell and in their falling brought down others. The Scots were brave and came on, but they were now looking up. Their bucklers were small but they raised their arms to afford some protection. In that rising they made their spears a wooden wall and they did not see the burn. Even as Will commanded the rest of the archers to ready their bows, men fell in the burn. Some were drowned and crushed by the press of men behind. The exception was the body of men who hurried across the wooden bridge. They came for me. I was flanked by Sir Marmaduke and Edward Gilling. The three of us would be the first that the enemy would reach.

The stakes were not in regular lines but unevenly spread and that, along with the fact that the twenty men who ran at us were no longer in a line meant that we would be attacked piecemeal. We would have the chance to choose our targets. My shield was held not only by my left arm but also by a guige strap that ran around my body. If I had to drop my shield, I would still have protection.

When the arrows from the rest of our archers struck, it was as though the whole Scottish army had been slapped. These were not bodkins but war arrows, but even a war arrow could penetrate a leather jack. Men fell and the twenty who ran at us became twelve. One brave knight, an arrow sticking from his shoulder, came directly for me. His spear was almost twice as long as mine and he rammed it at my chest. I lifted my spear and shield at the same time. The shield blocked the long spear and deflected it up. I thrust my spear at the eyehole of his full-face helmet. The narrow aperture afforded protection but restricted the view and I pushed so hard that the spear not only entered the hole but drove into his eyes and stuck. He screamed behind the mask and sank to his knees. I released my now useless spear and shouted, "Axe!"

I held up my right hand and grasped the haft proffered by Jack. I brought it down to split the helmet and skull of the Scottish knight. The arrows had thinned out the mailed and plated men. Now they slammed into men who had little protection from the missiles raining like hail. The bridge over the burn was now filled by the Scots who had seen the problems created by a piecemeal attack. They came purposefully towards us but they still had the stakes to contend with. Instead of a solid wall of spears, we had the odd spear and my axe was able to hack through them before the heads could scrape and scratch my armour. I could not see it, but the Scots must have crossed the burn along the line and were engaging our men, for I heard the rattle of spears on shields and the cries and shouts of men engaged in combat to the death. I raised and hacked with my axe. I relied on the strength of my shield and my armour. The ground near the stakes was slippery with blood and water from the burn. It made it harder for spearmen to thrust. We were on the more solid ground, and I chopped through spear shafts and bodies as though they were parchment.

When I heard the horn in the distance, it seemed a long way away but I knew that was an illusion. The noise of battle made it appear that way. I shouted, "For King Henry, St Cuthbert and England, charge!"

The combination of the losses they had endured, allied to the disconcerting horn from their rear, made men stop and we took advantage. I led the charge through the stakes. I was mindful of my footing as I swung my axe at the heads of men, many of whom had not even a helmet. When they began to drop their spears and to run I knew that victory was close. However, being close was not good enough, we had to keep on. When I reached the other side of the bridge I had many bodies to negotiate. As I took the arm of a man at arms who was too slow to bring up his spear, I saw that, ahead of me, I could no longer see the Earl of Ormonde and his retinue. Either they were engaged with Sir Alan, or they had fled.

A sea of northerners surrounded me as we hurried towards the trees towards which the Scots were fleeing. The men of the north were in a vengeful mood and no prisoners were taken. Men were struck in the back as they ran and then butchered where they lay. When we reached the trees, I stopped. I turned and saw a joyful Edward Gilling with a bloody and notched sword and an equally ebullient Sir Marmaduke wielding a poleaxe. John and Jack were so close to me that I knew they had watched my back. I took off my helmet and said, "Well, Edward Gilling, I think this victory today is cause enough for me to ask the Earl to give you your spurs."

He knelt, "My lord, it was an honour to follow you. This victory will be sung of."

I shook my head, "Edward, this was a small battle. Outside of those who fought here, none will know of it. This saved part of England from deprivation but do you honestly think that those in London would care? No, we have done our duty, and we are alive."

Sir Marmaduke said, "You are right, my lord, but it feels good to win again."

The men around us all cheered and I smiled.

Chapter 14

We stayed for a week in Hexham. Sir Ralph and Sir Roger had managed to take prisoners for ransom and we waited for it to be collected. The dead were stripped and their weapons and mail were reused. Their bodies were burned. We had lost men, but not enough to cause distress and we had made the land safe. The abbot blessed my sword before we left and Sir Ralph and Sir Alan swore that they would follow my banner anywhere. I headed back to Durham with Sir Roger and Sir Marmaduke. It was a leisurely ride back to Durham for we went at the pace of marching men. I had sent word to the bishop and there was a celebratory feast for us. My name was spoken of in the same terms as Sir John Talbot and Sir William Strongstaff. I felt a fraud for it had been little more than a skirmish. The bishop rewarded me with a purse and a cross made of silver and jet.

We did not go south to Piercebridge but went via Stockton where Sir Roger also feted us. By the time we neared Middlcham, it was almost three weeks since the battle. The earl was at home and, when Sir Marmaduke and the other knights told him of the battle, he happily concurred with my request for Edward to be knighted. When I left two days later he promised me animals for my manor. "You are a man I would have fighting for me again, Sir Michael."

I nodded, "Of course, Sir Richard, but I am still the king's knight and he has first call upon my services. All my manors are royal ones."

He shook his head, "A true knight. I hope the king appreciates what he has."

As we rode back to Easingwold, I doubted that he did.

I was keen to get back to my family but I still had a manor to leave in a sound state. It took a fortnight to do so but, when the animals from the earl arrived and were distributed and Will was confident in his duties, I left with Jack, John and the two men who had sweethearts in Houghton Regis. I almost wept when we reached my home for it seemed a long time since I had seen it. Maud had grown and while we had been away, Queen Catherine's daughter had become a young woman. I had missed the change.

That night, as Isabelle lay in my arms, we told each other of the events we had seen. I learned that Margaret had become a woman just two months before my return. Isabelle said, "And now there will be suitors. She is of royal blood, although just we know this, therefore we must be careful."

In the dark I sighed, "And the king is still to wed. So long as he is single and without issue there will be plots."

"Even with issue there will be plots. Visitors have told me that the Duke of Gloucester is raising his head again. The Earl of Suffolk is not as popular as he once was."

"I just pray for some peace and the chance to see my children and land grow."

She was silent for a while and then asked, "Jean did well?"

I smiled for she always pronounced our son's name in the French manner. "He did but he has learned that war is not as glorious as he thought." I had not described the butchery that had followed the victory but Jack had confided in me that it had made John physically sick. That was no bad thing. I did not want my son to be a warmonger.

I waited until the next day to tell her all about the new manor, "I do not expect an income any time soon but the treasure we found and the gift from the earl means that the land will grow and Will Willow Tree will be a good steward."

"And he is married. That is a good thing, too."

"I do not think that he will have to use his bow in war but he can train the young men of Easingwold to follow in his footsteps." I smiled, "And now, this manor."

She then went into great detail about all the improvements that had occurred in my absence. Houghton Regis was a rich manor as one would expect having been owned by the queen and, more importantly, used. The bad news I had was that I had many cases to hear. None were major crimes but theft, boundary encroachment, and disagreements over the ownership of animals all needed an arbitrator and that was me.

During my first months at home, I had little time for anything other than just being the lord of the manor, as my long absences meant people were keen to see me. When I did have time, I went hunting with Jack and John. I rarely used my falcon, Ajax, but I was aware that John would need to know how to hunt with a bird of prey and it was my duty to teach him. Jack could teach him many things but falconry was not one. I had neither a cadge nor a cadger. My horse master, Peter, liked all animals and it was he who looked after Ajax. As luck would have it, he had not been flown to hunt for a month or more and he was keen to do so. We went to the woods where my gamekeeper told me that the pigeons were becoming a nuisance. With the season for seeding almost upon us, we needed the numbers kept down and the best way to do that was with a bird of prey. Ajax was a powerful bird and we took five pigeons quickly. I gave John the chance to fly him. It proved to be successful and the look on my son's face was a reward for me. He showed his increasing maturity not to mention his kindness, when he offered to let Jack fly the bird. Jack enjoyed it, too, and by the time we headed home, we had twelve pigeons that would make stews and pies for the next days. The bounty was only part of the happiness I felt when we returned home.

It was in February that the messenger arrived from the Earl of Suffolk. I recognised the man at arms, it was Henry of Oxford. I greeted him warmly although his arrival did not bode well for me. The last time had seen my departure for Easingwold for months. I looked for the parchment but there was none, "You are from the earl?"

"I am, my lord, but there is no letter this time. The earl wishes you to visit with him at his manor of Great Bradley."

"And where is that?"

"Fifty miles or so east of here, my lord, in Suffolk." He paused, "I am requested to return with you."

It was clear that I was commanded rather than requested. "Jack, have quarters made ready for our guest and see the horse master. We have a fifty-mile ride tomorrow."

"Yes, my lord. If you would follow me, sir."

I went to tell Isabelle first for she would need to organise the food. "How long will you be away?"

"I know not but I doubt that I will be away more than one night. I think that this is a delicate matter which the earl does not wish to commit to parchment."

She shook her head, "You do not wear it, but the crown ties itself to you and your life almost as much as it does the king."

She was right and Sir William's wife had been of the same mind. When I told John he was delighted. He saw intrigue in the matter. He would change.

Henry was an older warrior but he had obviously been chosen for his ability to be discreet. Despite my son and wife's attempts to extract information, he said nothing to reveal the purpose of my summons. I did not even try. I would find out soon enough, instead I spoke of those soldiers we had both known. He, like me, had been at the failed siege of Orléans. What I learned was that the love of his life had died of the plague while he had been in France, along with the rest of the family in the village where he had been brought up. Returning to England with the earl after the war, he had committed his life to serving the man he respected.

"Had I served someone like Sir William I would have done the same. I have a good life and it is a soldier's life. I am no courtier. The times he sent me to you were because he knew we were acquainted. For the rest, I command his bodyguard. He has enemies, my lord. I am not speaking out of turn when I say that the Duke of Gloucester seeks to undermine the earl in parliament." He shook his head, "There is support for the duke as many people think that his wife was wrongly accused of witchcraft."

"Witchcraft?"

"Yes, my lady, she was accused and convicted of the crime. She was made to walk barefoot to three markets, divorced from the duke, stripped of her titles and imprisoned in Chester Castle." He leaned over to me, "When we travel through Kent we are especially wary for that is where the duke has his support."

With a fifty-mile ride ahead of us we left early. I loaned Henry a better horse than he had brought with him and we used his horse as a sumpter to carry our clothes.

The manor was small and far from grand. It felt to me like a home. I had learned, from Henry, that the wife of the earl, Lady Alice, had given birth to a son, John, He was a sickly child and Great Bradley was a cosier home for the two-year-old and his mother. When I met Lady Alice I was surprised. She was over forty years of age and I knew that she had been married three times. She was beautiful but I could see that the birth of a son at such a mature age had taken something from her. The retreat to rural Suffolk made sense. She took John and Jack to our chamber while the earl and I spoke in his solar. Henry guarded the door.

"I am sorry to have fetched you again, Sir Michael, but you are one of the few men I trust and your connection with the king is also useful. I will tell you why you are summoned now, while we are alone. Your son and squire need not know the meat of the matter until… well when it is too late for the news to be of interest to another." I was both intrigued and fearful. "I believe that we cannot win the war in France by force of arms. Sir John Talbot and the Duke of York have done their best but now that the Burgundians have abandoned us we have little hope of victory. I seek peace through other means." He looked over to the door even though it was guarded. "I will travel to France to negotiate a marriage between the king and Margaret of Anjou, the niece of King Charles of France and the second eldest daughter of René, King of Naples, and Isabella, Duchess of Lorraine."

I was taken aback because it mirrored the marriage of King Henry to Catherine of France and that had almost brought France to the English crown.

"Now you see the need for secrecy. I have enemies, not least the Duke of Gloucester, and if it was discovered what I planned then they might consider murder. You have met Henry who is the best of bodyguards. You would be his equal and I would feel safer with the two of you. Even the Maid came to no harm while she was in your care and there were many who sought her death."

I nodded, "And we leave when, my lord?"

"By the middle of April. We must take ship before Lady's Day. You have time to make plans and to prepare others for your absence. You are clever and will devise some subterfuge that will allow you to meet me at Ipswich, where we will take ship. You will return here and we shall depart from this manor." I took it all in. "Once we reach Tours then all need for deception will be over. There will be a reward for you. The king would make you Baron Michael of Weedon. He heard of what you did at Hexham and approves."

I could not help a wry smile, I had said that none would know of it and yet the king had heard. "Thank you, my lord, I am honoured."

He beamed, obviously pleased that I had raised no objections. "And now you can wash before we dine."

Henry took me to my room where Jack and John awaited me. They looked at me expectantly. "We eat tonight and return home on the morrow."

John asked, "And?"

"And that is all."

"But why were you summoned?"

"If the earl wished you to know that, John, then he would have invited you to hear his words. As he did not then you should assume that it is none of your business."

Jack laughed out loud, "I told you, Master John, that your father is a man of much importance. Know that whatever it is, it will be an adventure."

We dressed and descended. Of course, I would tell Isabelle. I had no secrets from her but she knew how to keep a secret, too.

Lady Alice was a delight. She was a granddaughter of the poet and diplomat, some said spy, Geoffrey Chaucer and she told tales she had heard of his life and travels. "Have you read his most famous work, Sir Michael?"

"The Canterbury Tales?" She nodded, "Parts only."

"I think, from what my husband tells me, that you and the knight in his Knight's Tale have much in common. You should read it again. Perhaps he knew a knight like you. My grandfather was a great observer of people." She told us of the origins of the characters like the wife of Bath and the miller. I could see why the earl had married her. She was beautiful and clever.

I enjoyed her company but my mind was distracted by this latest task. It would not be as hard as recovering the cross but it would be both more momentous and dangerous. This time I would have my son with me. I knew that I could not leave him at home. He would see that as some sort of punishment.

It was towards the end of the meal that the earl spoke of Sir John Talbot. "You have heard of the tragedy that has struck Sir John?"

I shook my head. Since I had returned from France the battle for Normandy was a distant memory. "No, he is not hurt, is he?"

"No, but his son, Sir Christopher, has been killed in a tournament. Sir Gruffudd Vychan pierced his heart with a lance and is now banished from England and declared an outlaw."

"I knew Sir Gruffudd, he was a valorous knight at Pontoise. Surely it was an accident."

"It is thought not and Baron Dudley has now been given his estates. I mention this as it is rumoured that the Welshman fled to France." I could see that there was more to his words and I waited. "You know that Sir Gruffudd was knighted at Agincourt for saving the life of the Duke of Gloucester? They are friends."

I understood why he had mentioned the incident. It was not gossip but he was warning me of, perhaps, some of the dangers we might face.

When we left, John was full of the excitement of meeting the earl but Jack was more pensive and, when John had finished babbling on, said, "Are we going with the earl when he travels to France, my lord?"

So much for secrecy and discretion, "What did you hear?"

"Just that the earl and his bodyguards will be travelling in a ship and the gossip is that the voyage will be to France."

That was not as bad as it might have been but it was still worrying. Even without the purpose of the visit being known, the earl could be in danger from his enemies. To kill the earl in England would bring forth great repercussions but in France...

"We may be travelling with the earl but keep all speculation to yourself." Even as he was opening his mouth to speak I said, "And that goes double for you, John. If one word leaks out, then you will stay at Houghton Regis." My tone left him in no doubt that I meant what I said. He nodded. "And now no more debate. I have plans to make."

By the time we reached home, it was dark and food was already cooking for our meal. Sarah and Elizabeth got on well as cooks and Isabelle had few duties in that area. Now that Maud was growing, my wife was able to give her whole attention to me. While John and Jack saw to the horses I sat before the fire and, having ensured that we were alone, I told her of my task.

She was pleased and smiled, "That is the most sensible thing I have heard for some time, husband. It worked with the king's father and if it saves those in Normandy from being slaughtered then that is all to the good." She sipped the wine. "Margaret of Anjou…if I recall she is the same age as our Margaret."

I don't know why, but I had assumed that she was older. "That seems young to be married."

"The king is not much older. How old is he?"

"He is twenty-two."

She looked surprised, "I thought him younger." She shrugged, "She is young enough to bear him heirs and that may silence the king's enemies."

I was silent and sipped my wine.

"What is wrong, husband?"

"I am not sure that the king is well-advised. When I was in the north the nobles there were unhappy at his policies. They see a king who is wholly focused on London and the acquisition of France. The Scottish raids are ignored. I know that is not completely true, I am to be made a baron for my service in the north, but…"

"A baron? You did not tell me. That is a great honour."

"I am sorry, my love, the thought went from me as all that I could think of were the problems awaiting us in France."

She put her hand on mine, "You will cope and this will give Jean the chance to use his French."

When he was little, my wife had spoken to him in French. It had made her feel a connection with her home in Normandy but it also ensured that our son was bilingual. I could speak French and speak it well, but I sounded like an Englishman. John sounded French.

"I will have my ladies make you all new clothes for the journey. If you are meeting the Duke of Anjou, it would not do to appear as beggars." She was an eminently practical woman. She suddenly stopped speaking and a frown appeared, "I am assuming that the earl has written permission to travel through Anjou and Touraine?"

I shrugged, "As would I but I do not know for certain. The first part of the journey should be safe enough. We still hold Normandy and Maine but you are right, Anjou and Touraine could be a problem. For all that René is King of Naples as well as Duke of Anjou, he is still French."

Just then we heard voices as Jack and John entered the hall and we stopped talking. That evening, the two girls were desperate to know more about the mysterious visit to Suffolk. I approved of the way that my son and Jack managed to answer the questions but in such a vague way as to leave our destination hidden still. My wife's words about Margaret made me look at her more closely. We were her guardians and we had a responsibility. None save the two of us and Sarah knew her parentage. I doubted that Sarah had even told her husband, Thomas of Chester. Certainly, he had never given me any indication that he thought that there was anything exceptional about her. If anyone discovered that the blood of the Tudors and Queen Catherine coursed through her veins she could be used by the enemies of the king, and there were many of those. She was now becoming a woman and men would court her. Isabelle and I would have to ensure that, when she married, it was for the right reasons.

We had just three weeks to prepare. That sounds like a long time but the reality was that it was not. My wife had her women sewing clothes that incorporated my livery and my colours. We would need at least three sets: one for the journey and two for the times we might be presented to court. I was not certain that we would be. So far as I could tell, our presence was necessary as protectors for the earl.

It was when Jack and John wore their new clothes for the first time that I saw Margaret take an interest in the two of them. I suppose I had forgotten that we lived an isolated life for that suited me. We did not invite other lords to dine and Margaret rarely left the house. The young men that she saw all the time were John and Jack. Jack had grown into a fine young man. The urchin who had come to us from the bandit's forest had grown into a young man who could have been taken as a noble's son. The clothes helped but he had learned, as a squire, manners and phrases which marked him as different from the other young men who came into contact with Margaret. Whatever the reason she began, from that moment, to take an interest in how she dressed. That pleased all three women in the house. Sarah and Isabelle felt maternal towards the child they had raised and Elizabeth came into contact with her every day. Margaret was a likeable soul. It comforted me for they would have something to occupy their minds whilst we were in France. I had no idea how long the negotiations would take.

It would be a hard two-day ride to Ipswich or a leisurely three-day one. I chose the latter as we had no idea what might be needed once we were in France. John, as usual, was full of questions as we rode to the sea.

"Where will we land, when we reach France?"

"The earl will have his own plans, John. I cannot think that this is a purely speculative mission. He has to have spoken to someone in France and they will have suggested where we will meet." His questions mirrored my own although my enquiries were to myself. Margaret of Anjou's situation was not the same as Catherine of Valois had been. She was not the daughter of the King of France, A marriage would not bring King Henry the crown of France. At least, not unless something catastrophic happened to King Charles and Prince Louis. The best that could come of it was peace. Humphrey, Duke of Gloucester, wanted the war to continue. The Earl of Suffolk wanted peace. War was expensive. There were more questions from John than I had asked myself. He wanted to know the name of the port, and the number of men. Jack's smile told me that my squire was enjoying my interrogation. I suppose he was normally the recipient of such attention.

I had never sailed from Ipswich. It was a small port and, from the tiny number of vessels I saw tied up, few other ships did. There were more fishing boats than anything and they must have returned recently as there was an impromptu market. The crews were selling their fish from the quay. In fact, there was only one vessel of any size in the harbour, the *'Maid of Suffolk'*. She was a cog with both a bow and stern castle. I saw that she flew the earl's flag and that she was guarded by two liveried men. We dismounted and walked our horses through the milling people trying to buy the best fish at the lowest price.

When we reached the ship I asked, "Is this the vessel belonging to the Earl of Suffolk?"

"It is, Sir Michael." My livery had been recognised. He turned and said, "Passengers, Captain."

A disembodied voice came from the stern, "I will come."

The sentry continued, "The earl is here already but he is in the town where he talks with the mayor. He said for you to board when you arrived."

A tubby seafarer with the bow-legged gait of sailors came down the gangplank. "You must be Sir Michael of Weedon."

"I am."

He rubbed his white flecked beard, "You know your horses better than any I suppose. Can they be walked aboard or should we rig slings?"

"We will try the former. I will go first for my horse is the leader." I had chosen Gilles for he was a French horse and younger than both Storm and Shadow.

The captain shouted, "Horses."

His men quickly took away another part of the tumblehome and placed another plank next to it. They deftly and quickly fastened the two together with ropes and then stood back. I guessed that they had suffered kicks from horses that resented the treatment.

I spoke in French and stroked Gilles' head as I walked up the gangplank. Gilles walked confidently up the planks and once aboard, a seaman handed me an old apple, "A reward for your horse, my lord."

The Knight's Tale

I gave Gilles the apple and said, "John, you are next. Jack, watch him." I handed Gilles' reins to the seaman who led my warhorse to the bolt on the deck where he would be secured. There were eight horses already fastened there. I was pleased that they would not be below deck. Horses became fretful if they could not see the sky. John was keen to impress and he spoke to his horse as he led her up. She did it as though it was the most natural thing in the world and John beamed when the sailors complimented him. Jack's horse was a courser and having seen the other two successfully walk aboard, he did so too. The captain and his crew breathed a collective sigh of relief.

The captain came aboard and the crew began to disassemble the horse gangplank. He took us to the bow castle and opened a door. Inside were three hammocks and he said, "This is your cabin, my lord. You can stow your bags here." Jack and John deposited the bags and I saw the fearful look on John's face. The room was tiny and there was no aperture for light. The captain said, "We will not be sailing now, my lord, until the late tide."

"And which inn would you recommend, Captain?"

He pointed, "***'The White Cockerel'*** has good food." He shrugged, "And my brother is the innkeeper. Tell him you sail with me."

I understood the arrangement. The cog's captain would keep his brother supplied with smuggled goods and in return, the innkeeper would not rook the captain's passengers. We would eat well. The inn was crowded but the use of the captain's name gave us a table and good service. The food was good. The innkeeper had bought fresh fish and the stew was both hearty and tasty. Washed down with local ale, I knew that this would be the last hot meal until the voyage ended. It was Henry of Oxford who fetched us.

"His lordship is aboard. We do not sail for an hour or so but he would have all aboard."

We paid the bill and left. Darkness had fallen while we ate. The quay was deserted and ours was the only vessel tied up. The others had sailed on the afternoon tide. "Henry, why did we not sail on the afternoon tide?"

He grinned, "The earl is careful, my lord. We leave in the dark and no eyes can see the direction we take. The earl spent the day with the mayor, ostensibly on business but really to give a reason for our visit to the port. The mayor thinks that we are sailing north for the earl has land on the Humber."

It all made sense now and confirmed that this was a mission that was both secret and, inevitably, dangerous. John asked, as the gangplank was pulled aboard behind us, "Will we have to go to our cabin?"

The Knight's Tale

I shook my head, "Go to the horses and comfort them. They came aboard easily enough but once we leave the harbour and reach the open sea they may become fretful."

Grateful for something to do, John walked towards the horses and Jack approached, "Do you need me, my lord?"

"No, Jack, go with John." Left alone with Henry, I said, "How many men does the earl have with him?"

"He has his squire, Edward, a household knight, Sir Rufus and his squire. Then there is me and three men at arms. In addition, there is a priest and a clerk. They are the ones recording the negotiations."

"I only counted eight horses."

"The earl will hire animals when we reach St Gilles Croix de Vie."

"Where is that?"

"In the Vendée. It is a small fishing port a hundred and fifty miles from Tours. That is where we are headed. The port is south of Nantes at the mouth of the Loire." A smile creased the man at arms' face, "The earl is clever, my lord. We will be seen sailing along the French coast. It cannot be avoided. When we pass the mouth of the Loire any watchers will assume that we are headed for Bordeaux. The earl has a manor there, too. We have four days to cross through Poitou to reach Tours." I cocked an eyebrow. He shrugged, "I know, my lord, it is a long way and we will be vulnerable but that is another reason for your inclusion. You showed, when you fetched the cross, that you are resourceful and I am not without skills."

"The earl has great confidence in two men who are not noble born."

"Perhaps that is why, my lord. Eh?"

The earl remained below decks until we sailed. We slipped away from the quay, silently, secretly and with not a sound except for the billowing of the sails. We were well offshore before he came from the stern castle. "And now it begins, Sir Michael. This is Sir Rufus." We nodded to each other. "Like you he fought in France and, like you, he can be trusted. I know that we are a small band but that, I think, will mean we have less chance of having our mission spoiled by those who wish the war to continue."

"And how long to get to St Gilles Croix de Vie, my lord?"

"The captain tells me that it is eight hundred miles. I hope that it will take just a week but it may take longer. We are well supplied with food, water and ale."

I nodded towards the horses, "I was not thinking of us, my lord, but the animals." His frown told me that he had not thought of that. "If it takes too long or we endure storms then we will have to rest them before we can leave for Tours. Will we be safe in St Gilles Croix de Vie?"

"I hope so. I have a manor there but…" he nodded, "you are right to bring that up. I will tell the captain to make all haste while we enjoy clement weather."

He disappeared and I was left with Sir Rufus and Henry for company. Henry smiled, "The earl has been a courtier for so long he has forgotten what it is like to be a knight in hostile lands."

Sir Rufus shook his head, "He knows all about hostile lands for he treads a path each day between snakes and daggers but you are right, Henry. It is we three who will have to keep him safe until it is time for him to work his magic and find the peace that England and Normandy need."

The sea kept the squires busy all the way to the small port. The winds were brisk and the sea was lively. The horses had to be calmed more frequently than any had expected. My horses seemed, somehow, to deal with the voyage easier than the others but when, at the end of April, we saw the small port, we all breathed a sigh of relief. The earl had planned well and we stayed off shore until just before dark and then sneaked in. We were unloaded and the captain continued south to Bordeaux. Any who had been following our progress along the French coast might have expected us to still be aboard the ship. The horses, however, even our three, were in no condition to make the one-hundred-and-fifty-mile journey east. The earl saw that and we walked our horses through the Poitevin countryside to his manor three miles south of the port at Givrand. Some of the horses staggered as they walked, showing the effects of the voyage.

Henry was philosophical about the inevitable delay, "My lord, it means we can acquire the extra horses we need from your manor. We can hide there for the day or so we need and then head northeast."

"I do not like the delay, Henry."

The man at arms shrugged, "Until we can fly here like a bird, my lord, then such inconveniences are to be expected."

I agreed with both men for I knew that while we could do nothing about such things as the sea and the weather, any delay helped the enemies who might seek us.

The Knight's Tale

Poitou 1444

Chapter 15

The manor was a small one. There were just four houses and a tiny church. The manor house itself was also smaller than any I had seen in England. There was a wall surrounding it, but it was a wall for privacy and not for defence. Henry knew the layout and he took command as the earl, Sir Rufus, the priest and the clerk entered the hall. "Squires, I will show you the stables. That will be your home while we stay here."

He gave me a quizzical look for I had not gone into the hall with the others. I smiled and said, "Call it the old soldier in me, Henry, but I will reconnoitre the land. I would have my bearings."

Jack said, "We will sort out your clothes, my lord."

I left through the gate. One of the men at arms, Mark, stood watch at them. "I will identify myself when I return. Close and bar them."

"Yes, Sir Michael."

I did not draw my sword but I was wary as I walked back the way we had come. I passed the houses but there was no chink of light indicating that the people within were curious. It gave me the chance to observe the dwellings. They were small and single-storied. I could see that they were, in effect, smallholdings with the Poitevin equivalent of a hog bog, but I heard no pigs, just the clucking of hens. Each of them had a row of what looked to be vines. That made sense, they would make their own wine. The trellises of beans told me about the other crops that were tended. The church was very small and the door was open. I peered in. I saw a small altar and the church looked as though it would hold less than twenty people. I doubted that there would be a priest. It was as I walked down the road that led northeast when I almost took a tumble. What I had taken as ditches were, in fact, bodies of water. Once I saw one I was able to identify others. I saw eel traps in the water and that let me know how they fed themselves. There had been few stands of trees on the way south. Most of the woodland appeared to be pine. This was as unlike England as I had seen. I guessed that it was similar to parts of East Anglia and the earl's home in Suffolk. Perhaps he felt comfortable here. I headed back to the manor house satisfied that there was no immediate danger. We had passed no one on our way south and Henry had used another of the men at arms, Robert, to ensure that we were not followed.

I knocked on the gate and said, "It is I, Sir Michael."

The gate opened and I saw that Mark had been joined by Henry. "Anything, my lord?"

"As quiet as the grave. There is no priest?"

Henry shook his head as he led me to the door of the manor house, "The priest comes from St Gilles if there is a death or a marriage. If the villagers need confession then they walk back to St Gilles."

"There is much water around here."

"It is low lying and the water began life as drainage. Now they are used by the villagers for food. The earl likes it here. It is peaceful and no one bothers him. Since he took charge of the affairs of the king we have not visited."

The steward was an Englishman, Harry, and he welcomed me. "I am afraid your room, my lord, is a small one."

"It does not matter, Harry, a bed is a bed and we will only be here for a few days."

"His Lordship and the others are in the dining hall. I think he awaits your presence."

He was right. Food had been hurriedly prepared, and the rest were around the small table, "What kept you, Sir Michael?"

"You brought me, my lord, so that I could keep you safe. You might know this manor but I do not. I have the layout in my head now."

"We will be safe here for the two days Henry tells me that we need to rest the horses. We will keep within the hall and Harry and his wife, Sophie, will buy food in the market. Perhaps this might not be a bad thing. Here we are hidden."

I felt a little excluded from the talk around the table. Henry and the men at arms ate in the kitchen as did the squires. Harry and his wife served us. I was happy when we were able to retire to our beds.

The only servants were Harry and Sophie. That meant they could not leave for the market until the earl had been fed. It was not until noon that they returned. We had stayed within the walls and all that I had done was to exercise our horses in the small yard. When Harry returned it was with the disquieting news that a foreign ship was in the port. Harry had discovered that men had been landed but that was all. The ship had left not long before Harry and Sophie returned to the manor.

The earl dismissed Harry's fears, "It has nothing to do with us, Harry."

"My lord, few ships land at St Gilles Croix de Vie. Les Sables d'Olonne is a much bigger port. It is just fishing ships that land here."

The earl waved a dismissive hand. I said, "So when we landed, last night, even though we think that no one saw us, the ship would have been seen?"

Harry nodded, "Yes, my lord."

"Then we can assume that as your steward here has bought a larger amount of food than normal, that there will be speculation?"

The Knight's Tale

Harry was a clever man, "There was, my lord. We were asked if there was a feast at the manor."

I said, "We should leave tomorrow, my lord."

"Pah!" He waved a hand, "You worry about nothing."

"My lord, you brought me here as a watchdog. When a dog's hackles are raised then it is as well to heed them. You have enemies as does the king."

The earl stared at me.

Harry said, "There is something else, my lord."

"Yes?"

"When we were passing the inn on our way back here, I am sure I heard Welsh voices."

We all stared at him and the earl said, "Welsh voices? You are sure? Could they not have been Breton? I know that sometimes the languages of the two Celts share common words."

"They were Welsh, my lord. I heard the name Glendower spoken."

The steward used the English pronunciation. The Welshman had been dead for more than twenty-five years yet his name was still revered amongst the Welsh. He had almost done what no Welsh king had done since Llewellyn the Great, he had almost defeated the English.

"Could it be a coincidence?"

Sir Rufus said, "Owen Tudor is Welsh, my lord."

The earl shook his head, "I cannot think that he would be so ungrateful as to bite the hand that feeds him. He has a pension from the king as do his sons."

"And I cannot believe it either, my lord." The earl looked at me, "And it matters not if this is Owen Tudor. Harry here says he heard Welsh voices and that is rare in these parts, is it not, Harry?"

"I have not heard Welshmen here, well, not since I have been steward."

"And a ship docks the day after we arrive…my lord, no matter what the condition of the horses, we need to leave tomorrow and do so mailed and armed."

My words and those of Harry had alarmed the earl and he nodded, "Ask your wife to rouse us early and the food you brought prepared so that we can eat it on the road." He shook his head. "That a Welsh voice should upset my plans…"

Sir Rufus said, "It might have nothing to do with Wales, my lord. These could be Welshmen hired to thwart the king's plans."

"And that makes it worse, Sir Rufus, for mercenaries are not men to listen to reason and we are parlous few."

The Knight's Tale

I shook my head, "More would simply have attracted greater attention. I will go to speak to Henry."

When I told the man at arms he concurred with my plans. "The horses are not in perfect condition but we would have to wait for four or five days to ensure that they were. Do you know the land through which we travel, my lord?"

I shook my head, "I campaigned with Sir William and Sir John north of the Loire. This will be new to us all. The men at arms, you know them better than any, who has the best eyes and ears?"

"Walter is the best hunter and while he is no longer a young man, he has forgotten more about scouting than most men have learned."

"Then we need him one hundred paces before us on the road. We need another man at arms fifty paces behind us to listen for pursuit. The squires can guard his lordship and the other two. If there is danger then it will be up to you, Sir Rufus, Will and me to do something about it."

He looked glum, "It is many years since I fought in a war, my lord, but, as I recall, the advantage always lies with the ambusher, does it not?"

"That it does and what we lack here are archers. In my experience, they have not just five senses but sixth and seventh ones." I shrugged, "There is little point in bemoaning what we do not have. I leave you to speak to the men at arms. I will go to speak to Jack and John."

I found them with the horses. Both knew the value of our animals and were making sure that we, at least, would be well-mounted. I waved them over and gave them my news. John looked excited while Jack had a worried look.

"We will be able to deal with a handful of Welshmen."

Jack said, "Master John, when your father and I were ambushed on the road from Pontoise, we were lucky. A man cannot count on luck all the time."

"Jack is right. When we ride tomorrow, wear your leather jack and your helmet. You two will be needed to protect the priest and the clerk."

"But is it not our job to protect you, Father?"

"I am mailed, plated and well protected. The priest and the clerk are not. If we are attacked then put yourself between the attackers and the two men. You have your bucklers and, whilst they do not afford the protection of a shield, they can be used to stop a bolt or an arrow. If these are Welshmen then they may have bows."

Jack knew as well as I did that if they had bows then there was a good chance that some of us would die. My archers could penetrate good plate with a bodkin and Welsh archers were at least as good as they were.

The Knight's Tale

The news that we might have hunters seeking us made our isolation threatening rather than reassuring. Harry and I arranged the watches. We included Sir Rufus and his squire. We all lost sleep but, so far as we could tell, there were no watchers. As we breakfasted, before dawn, I said to the earl, "One good piece of news…"

"There is good news?"

I smiled, "I am just making a deduction, my lord, but Harry did not mention horses being landed."

Harry had just entered with fresh bread from the bread oven and he shook his head, "No, Sir Michael, and the landing of horses would have attracted attention. All that we heard was that a ship had docked and men had come ashore. They were cloaked and cowled."

"Then if they wish to either come here or to follow us they need horses. To my mind that is good news. In my experience, the acquisition of horses is never as easy as one expects. If we ride hard then we may outrun any who wish harm to come to us. It also means that they will be unfamiliar with their mounts."

I looked at the priest and the clerk, both of whom had been listening to my words and looked decidedly unhappy.

I smiled, "I have asked the squires to be your bodyguards. If there is trouble heed their words and keep your heads down." In my heart, I knew that they would be safe, in the initial attack, at least. Any mercenary would come for mailed men first.

We walked the horses towards the small road that headed east towards L'Aiguillon-sur-Vie. The ditch-filled land would be treacherous in the dark and we dared not risk the priest and the clerk falling from their horses. We did not mount until we reached the hamlet. They would hear us as we clattered through the houses and our passage would be marked but it could not be helped. From there we had a short ride until we reached the main road. Dawn broke as we joined the main road leading to Tours at La Joubretière. This was a larger village but as it was daylight we would be just seen, I hoped, as cloaked riders heading east. Henry and I rode at the fore with Alan and Sir Rufus flanking the earl. The squires and our human baggage followed. With Walter at the fore and Mark at the rear, we trotted along the road.

We rode as hard as we dared although the priest and the clerk both looked like untidy sacks of grain and I feared that they might fall. In the end, we had to slow down to a walk to avoid a disaster. It did make the journey longer. We stopped to water the horses in the small town of Aizenay. I saw men's gaze on us and knew that if there was pursuit then we would be marked and identified. Our liveries were hidden by cloaks but war horses could not be disguised, nor could the mail and helmets.

The Knight's Tale

Had we not feared an ambush then we might have ridden without those clear markers of warriors. If we had ridden without the clerk and priest then we might have been another eight miles along the road, but anything more than a walk was too hard for the men who were more used to ink-stained fingers than a saddle sore rump.

The earl was impatient and he ordered a faster pace once we left the village. The squires were forced to flank the two men and keep them in the saddle but we made better time. The land through which we were travelling was more like Normandy than anything through which we had passed. It was like the bocage country. Stands of trees stood next to the ditches and provided both shade and shelter. It was a more comfortable ride for the sun was making the metal of our helmets hot. The road twisted and turned. Often, we lost sight of Walter, our scout, and then he would reappear.

The cry from ahead made both me and Henry draw our swords. I knew that John and Jack would copy me. Walter's cry was a warning of danger and Henry shouted, "Mark!" We would not need our rear to be protected but there was danger ahead. Walter appeared around the bend in the road. He was shouting something when I heard the distinctive sound of an arrow followed by a crack as it hit his back. Walter wore a breastplate, but his back was only protected by mail. He slumped forward in the saddle.

Henry and I reined in. I shouted, "Beware, my lord, this is an ambush."

Just then two arrows soared in the sky. Henry shouted, "Arrows." If we had held shields then we would have raised them. We did not. We would have to watch their flight and avoid them. It was a clever move by our ambushers as we could not watch the sky and the road. When I saw that they were going to miss me I urged Gilles on. I heard a crack behind and risked a glance. Jack had managed to deflect with his buckler, the arrow that would have skewered the priest. It was then that the six horsemen rode at us. They were mailed but only one was plated and I recognised his livery. It was Sir Gruffudd Vychan. There had to be at least two archers with them. We had a chance, but it was a slim one for even as I watched them I saw Walter slip from his horse. We were at a disadvantage.

Sir William had taught me well and I took the initiative, spurring Gilles to ride at the men. Henry gamely followed. I held my sword slightly below and behind me. The men who rode at me had their swords pointed at my head. My helmet was open-faced and while that meant I was in danger of suffering a wound it also ensured that I had better vision than the first three men who rode at Henry and me. Any

The Knight's Tale

sudden movement by me would render them temporarily blind. It takes courage to trust in your own ability but I had been chosen as King Henry's protector because of my skill. I jinked Gilles to my right at the last moment. It meant that the sword aimed at where my chest had been struck fresh air. I hacked my sword at the man's side. His left hand was holding the reins and my sword swept into his side. Like Walter, the man wore a breastplate but my sword hacked into the mail. His gambeson diminished the effect of the sword, but I had a strong right hand and I drew blood. He veered towards the man next to him and seeing Sir Gruffudd Vychan, whose livery I recognised, and another mailed man ahead, I rode at those two. Sir Rufus and Mark had to have joined Henry for I heard the clash of swords behind. It was as I neared the Welsh knight and his companion that I saw the three archers. They had no sight of the men on the road but were loosing in the sky. All it took was one lucky arrow and the earl would be dead. I had to get to the archers but that meant facing a champion of tournaments and another.

Sir Christopher Talbot had been the champion of England with a lance and for Sir Gruffudd to have slain him showed that he had skill. My skills were not in tournaments but in war. The more dangerous of the two was Sir Gruffudd. He had a full-face helmet but I heard him shout, "Owen, kill the earl!"

I could do nothing about that and this time I rode at the Welsh knight so that we were sword to sword. He tried a thrust at my face. It was an inviting target but I had quick reactions and, even as I moved my head to the side, I was slashing at his waist. Sometimes luck plays a part and while his mail and armour protected his body my sword sliced through his reins. His horse moved, naturally, away from the danger and as the Welshman passed me, I backhanded my sword into his back. I broke no plate nor sliced through mail but I hurt him. Glancing back, I saw Mark riding at the Welshman. I spurred Gilles towards the three Welsh archers. They were not alone. There were two men with spears. Five against one were not good odds but when I saw the archers draw back, I had no choice. I rode at them. The spearmen were slow to react and the sight of my huge war horse, teeth bared, put the archers off. One lowered his bow to aim at me while the other two loosed hastily. Gilles savage bite crunched through the bow and the arrow of one man as my sword cleaved the head of one of the others in two. A spear was rammed at me but my plate held and I slashed at the neck of the third archer. Blood spurted. The archer whose bow had been chomped, turned and ran and I pulled back on Gilles' reins and stood in the stirrups. As he had been trained, he raised his hooves and I let him smash down on one of the spearmen.

The Knight's Tale

I heard Jack shout, "Sir Michael!"

I turned and saw that Mark was down and Will was clearly wounded. The tournament champion was winning. Sir Rufus and Henry were fighting three men and I saw that Sir Gruffudd was heading for the earl. It was a race but Gilles had the bit between his teeth and we galloped after the Welshman who had grabbed at the slashed reins. He had a little control but not enough. I brought my sword down to smash across his back. He was a tough man for I knew the blow had hurt him. He kept his saddle but veered away from the earl. He rode at John and the priest. My son did the only thing he could, he held the buckler before him and deflected the blow that was aimed at him. Both he and the priest were knocked from their saddles as the Welshman rode back down the road.

I turned and saw that Sir Rufus was also wounded. I rode at one of the men he was fighting. I shouted, "Turn and face me!" The man did so but I was standing in my stirrups and bringing my sword down even as he turned. His helmet was a fatal choice. He did not see the sword come down and when I hit the helmet it dented and he fell from the saddle. The last two men at arms, seeing the knight's flight followed him. I cursed our lack of numbers. We had three wounded men at arms as well as a knight and I knew not what injuries to John and the priest. We had won but some of our enemies had survived. I saw that the earl, who had his sword drawn, lived and I dismounted to join Jack, kneeling next to John.

His eyes were closed but as I raised his head he opened his eyes and said, "Do not tell Peter the Horse Master that I fell from the horse."

It made Jack and I smile. My son was unharmed. As I stood, Henry said, "Thank you, my lord. I fear that but for your intervention, the earl might be a dead man."

"What of your men?"

The earl's squire, Alan, was with Mark and he said, "Mark will live."

Sir Rufus' squire said, "As will, Will, but I fear that Walter is dead."

The priest stood a little shakily and said, "I will tend to their hurts. I thank you, Sir Michael. I am no warrior but I know how to heal."

Jack pointed to one of the men at arms who had attacked us, "One lives still, Sir Michael."

Henry was angry. Walter had been his friend and I saw the man at arms draw his rondel dagger, "Hold, Henry. Let us question the man first."

I took off the man's helmet. His eyes were closed but when I put my fingers to his neck I felt a heartbeat. I held out my hand and Jack gave

The Knight's Tale

me a water skin. I poured it into his mouth, and he coughed. His eyes opened. "I cannot feel my legs…nor my hands."

I saw no other wounds on him and said, "Then your back is broken."

"Give me a warrior's death, I pray you, my lord."

I nodded to Henry, "That you may have and, when the priest is finished, absolution, but I need information." The earl had joined us but he did not kneel. His face showed the shock of the attack. He could have died. "Sir Gruffudd Vychan was your leader."

"Aye."

"Who was the paymaster?" Even as I asked the question, I prayed that it was not Owen Tudor or his sons. If it was then I would have to break my oath to the queen and kill them. The man looked from me to the earl. "Come man, you are dying. This was murder. Do you wish to die without being shriven?"

"The Duke of Gloucester."

I looked up at the earl who nodded, "Just so."

"And are there others like you?"

"Aye, but further south. We landed here for we knew there was a manor and Sir Gruffudd thought you would head here. The rest went to Bordeaux."

I turned to the earl, "Then we have time but we must get to safety soon. We are few in number."

"Yes, Sir Michael and getting fewer by the mile."

I stood, "He is yours, Father, and then, Henry of Oxford, you can send him to the next world."

The priest heard the words of the wounded man, whispered in his ear and made the sign of the cross. He stood and Henry knelt to slit the dying man's throat.

The three wounded men were bandaged and we helped them to mount. The squires slung the bodies of the dead on their horses. The spearman and archer had taken two and of them, there was no sign. This time I led and Henry brought up the rear. If we were attacked again then it would be the squires who would have to do the fighting.

Chapter 16

By riding as hard as we could with three wounded men, we reached the small walled town of Mauléon before dark. The earl had been given a passport by the representatives of the Duke of Anjou and we were forced to use it. We were given shelter and the dead promised burial. Henry and the other two men arms, even though they were wounded, insisted upon burying their friend themselves. That was the bond of brothers in arms.

That night the wounded slept for as the priest, Father Richard, said, "Sleep is the best medicine."

The earl was in low spirits. Henry and I kept him company and we nursed some wine as we examined our shattered plans. "The snake of a Welshman escaped us and we know that there are men further south seeking us. If Sir Gruffudd is able to find more killers, then we could do little to stop them."

I shook my head, "In this land, there are many men whose lords died and they now have to make a living hiring their swords to any paymaster. I do not think that this is a case of 'if' but 'when'. The road we took marks, quite clearly, our destination. It is either Chinon or Tours."

The earl nodded, "You are right and Chinon no longer enjoys the importance it did when Queen Eleanor lived there. They can get ahead of us for the priest and clerk slow us down."

Henry held his fingers up as he illustrated the problems, "We cannot leave our wounded men here for, wounded or not, they are some defence against an attack. We were slow enough with the priest and the clerk but the wounded men will slow us more. Our enemies could be anywhere."

The earl was irritable and he waved an angry hand and snapped an irritated retort, "Do not give me problems, Henry of Oxford, give me solutions. Find me some spark of hope in this dark land."

"Sorry, my lord." He looked at me in case I had an answer. "Sir Michael, you never give up, what hope can you spy?"

"Little, I fear. If we were in Normandy, we could make for my manor and pick up men I know to be loyal. Here in Anjou, I know no one."

Henry's eyes widened as though he had just been poked by a sharp point, "I am a fool, my lord, there is hope."

"What are you rambling about, hope? You have said there is none and you are right."

The Knight's Tale

Henry of Oxford shook his head and the words poured out like water over a waterfall, "My lord, you know when we fought in the wars there was a French lord who fought for us. His name was Sir Robert of La Flèche."

I saw the earl struggling to remember, "The name La Flèche sounds familiar, but I cannot remember why."

Henry turned to me, "The knight was loyal to England and Aquitaine. He was called Sir Robert, as I recall. His manor lies to the east of the city of Angers. He was descended from a squire whose lord served Empress Matilda in the time of the first civil war. He was rewarded with the gift of this manor. At that time, it was part of King Henry the Second's lands. Over the years the family lost touch with England, but thanks to the first knight who held the land they kept their loyalty to England. If Anjou fights England, then the knight's hands are tied. Let us use the passport from the Duke of Anjou."

The earl still seemed in low spirits but I saw light, "And how far away is this place, La Flèche?"

"It is not far out of our way and would mean that we might lose our pursuers, for we would approach Tours from the northwest and not the southwest. It is sixty miles from here."

I saw the glimmer of light on a dark night, "My lord, Henry has given us hope. At the very least we put off our pursuers and even if this knight cannot aid us, he can offer shelter. We have three spare horses now. Riding as fast as our wounded men will allow might enable us to reach there in one day." He looked up at me and I smiled at him, "Rouse yourself, my lord. We cannot allow the Duke of Gloucester to win. He offers no hope for England and this is a petty attempt to stop England having peace."

It was that argument that won the day and he nodded, "You are right, Sir Michael, and I owe it to the king to succeed. When this is over, I will have my vengeance on this man. He might be of royal blood but he has no nobility."

We left at dawn and headed along the road towards Tours. We turned north after Loudon when we found a crossroads masked by trees so that none saw us change direction. The squires each rode next to a wounded man and John accompanied the priest. The poor clerk had to manage his mount as best he could. Henry and I were now the only real defence and we rode at the fore. We kept up a steady pace and changed any horse that showed signs of weakening. As we rode Henry and I spoke. We were both hopeful that Henry and the earl had rightly remembered the allegiance of the knight we sought but we spoke of the other dangers.

"The Welshman might well seek others as well as Frenchmen to follow us. There are Italian, Burgundian and even Spanish mercenaries in Aquitaine and Anjou. We have to be prepared to fight a second time."

Henry nodded, "But this route buys us a day. Why do you think the Welshman became an assassin? I heard from Jack that Sir Gruffudd fought well at Pontoise."

"He did but he was declared outlaw when he killed Sir Christopher Talbot."

"I am no knight, Sir Michael, but that was not murder, it was in a tourney. Surely it was an accident."

"He pierced the heart of the knight with a lance. When knights fight in tournaments, it is not with weapons that can penetrate plate. I heard rumours that he was seduced by a dream of an independent Wales. Perhaps he saw himself as another Glendower."

As we rode north we found that the people in the villages through which we passed were less hostile than I expected. Perhaps it was the ancient associations of Anjou and Aquitaine. Both had been English longer than they had been French. Whatever the reason, we were welcomed but I also know that our passing was marked. Once our pursuers discovered that we were not on the southwest road to Tours, they would seek us out and a wounded knight and two wounded men at arms identified us clearly. We had to use a ferry across the Loire and that too identified us but, once that was crossed, we made good time to the walled town of La Flèche.

Henry's predictions proved correct for, when we were identified as English, we were allowed through the gates and led to the castle on the north bank of the river. I was impressed for it was a strong castle and, unusually, had a triangular wall. It reminded me of Caerlaverock but without the moat. We spoke French but the steward's English was good. He fetched the knight and his lady.

"I am Sir Leofric of La Flèche, welcome to my manor." He saw the wounded men being helped from their saddles and snapped to his steward, "Henri, these men have wounds. Have my men take them to the warrior hall and send for the doctor."

"Yes, my lord, I am sorry, I did not see their hurts."

Sir Leofric said, "And I am sorry for snapping, Henri. Perhaps it is the surprise at seeing such an eminent lord as the Earl of Suffolk at my door."

"And now, my husband, can we bring them in and not keep them waiting like beggars at the gate?" She was English and her smile took away the sting from her words. "I am Lady Anne, Sir Leofric's wife.

The Knight's Tale

We will have chambers prepared for you. Come within. I know this is not as cold as England, but a warm fire always welcomes."

No more was said until we entered the Great Hall. It was cosier than I expected for this was a large castle. Sir Rufus had insisted upon accompanying us and Henry had gone with Will and Mark. Our squires were taken away and we sat with Sir Leofric and Lady Anne. When the wine was served, the servants were dismissed and Sir Leofric said, "And now the tale, my lord. I can tell that this is not some happenstance. You have suffered violence and seek shelter."

The earl smiled, "I am sorry, Sir Leofric. I would not have brought this danger to you but Henry here remembered Sir Robert, was he your father?"

"He was and he died last year. I remember you, Sir William, from the wars although I was just a squire then."

The earl smiled, "Your father was a good man and loyal to England."

"Our roots go back far and our forebears came from the north of England. Although we have lived here for almost three hundred years, we still feel half English."

Lady Anne smiled and put her hand on her husband's, "And I, Earl, am all English. My father, Sir Richard of Arden, was given lands by King Henry Vth in Maine and it was there that I met my husband, so you see that this is an English enclave."

Sir Leofric kissed the back of his wife's hand, "Yet we have a perilous path to tread. Now that the Duke of Anjou is so closely tied to France then we cannot fight France. If that is why you came here, Earl William, then I fear I cannot help."

I saw the earl vacillating and I spoke, "I am Sir Michael of Weedon, and I have to tell you that the earl is on a mission from King Henry."

Sir Leofric said, "Sir Michael? The knight who took the Maid?" I nodded. "Then you are most welcome and your presence here tells me that this is not a petty diversion. You make speak freely, Earl. We are loyal here and whatever you tell us will not leave this hall."

The earl nodded and, after drinking some wine, he began to tell the tale from the very start through to the attack on the road.

Sir Leofric nodded at the end and said, "Then I can, with all honour, help you and be a loyal servant to both England and Anjou. I would suggest that you leave Sir Rufus and your wounded men here. I have a good doctor."

Sir Rufus looked as though he was going to object and I said, "Sir Rufus, if you and the wounded men come with us then you will slow us

The Knight's Tale

down. You know that. With Sir Leofric's help, we can make quicker time and should not need your sword."

He was the earl's knight and when the earl said, "Sir Michael is right, Rufus." The wounded knight nodded his acceptance.

Lady Anne said, "I will have food heated for you and supplies laid in for the morrow."

I asked, "How far to Tours?"

"Forty miles. We can make it in one day. I know the road and, unlike you, we have archers who can scout."

I was surprised and that showed in my voice, "Angevin archers?"

He laughed, "Aye, Sir Michael. When the first Sir Leofric came to this land he brought with him archers. Griff, James' son, was the first and he trained others. Hamlin Jameson now leads eight archers. I think you will find them the equal of any that were raised in England. Griff laid down the rules and strictures for the training of archers and we have adhered to them. The archers may speak French, but they have English blood in their veins. We also took in some archers who were lordless after the siege of Orléans. They will be happy to serve King Henry's son."

While we ate, we shared stories of the wars in which Sir Leofric had fought. He was particularly interested in the exploits of Sir William Strongstaff. That night, as I lay in a soft bed and was warmed by good food and wine, I felt more confident about our task. We had, it seemed, a chance. One day of hard riding would bring us to Tours and then my work would be done and it would be down to the earl to negotiate.

The horses had been well cared for and our squires had also enjoyed good food. We were ready to ride at dawn. Sir Leofric chose eight men at arms and six archers as our escort. As he said, any more might well attract attention and we were enough to defend against an attack. We bade farewell to the lovely Lady Anne. It felt like leaving a safe haven and the parting saddened me.

The archers rode ahead of us and were a reassuring presence. With four men at arms at the rear as well as two protecting the priest and the clerk, I felt safer. Sir Leofric's squire, Charles, was the same age as John and the two of them chattered like magpies as we headed south and west to Tours.

Sir Leofric chose to ride next to me. Henry, as the last of the bodyguards, rode next to the earl. Sir Leofric pointed south. "I hope that we will have a journey that is free from incident but I have to warn you, Sir Michael, that the land north of the Loire, through which we pass, is heavily forested and perfect country for an ambush."

"I am hoping that our deviation may put off our enemies."

"From what you say this Welsh assassin was not hurt and he sounds resourceful." He looked over his shoulder at the earl, "I believe that your mission was kept secret and your preparations sound yet they were waiting for you. It seems to me that your mission was known before you left England. If there are two bands seeking you, why not a third, or a fourth? The Duke of Gloucester, I believe, is a rich and powerful man still."

"What are you saying?"

"If your enemy knows that you are heading for Tours then would it not make sense to have killers waiting closer to the city? It is not just some of the English who do not want this peace, there are Frenchmen, too who wish the war to continue. They see the war as almost won. It would be in their interest to stop the earl from getting to Tours. Once the marriage is arranged then they can do nothing, but if they stop you…"

"You expect an attack?"

"I will be surprised if we reach Tours unscathed." He shrugged, "You are mailed and plated and, from what you told me, you handled yourselves well against a determined foe. Enemies may plan for your demise but they cannot know that you have enlisted our help." He pointed ahead, "It is our archers that will sniff them out."

His words worried me. I had thought that we were safe and we had been clever. I saw now that Sir Leofric was right. The Duke of Gloucester was a rich and powerful man. Since being ousted from the king's side he had become an isolated figure. This made perfect sense to me. He would not just rely on one rogue Welshman. It may have been that he had used the Welshman to throw suspicion on the Tudor family. The earl was right, the duke needed to be stopped.

The road passed through many patches of woodland and each one had me more nervous than the last. When we reached villages and watered our horses I found myself looking for danger in every face. The archers and men at arms Sir Leofric had brought inspired confidence but we still seemed few in number. The first attack had halved our fighting force. If there were more men waiting for us then it might be the end of the road to peace.

We were just ten miles from Tours when the attack finally materialised. This time it was Hamlin Jameson and his archers who gave us the warning. They stopped and when I saw them stringing their bows, I drew my sword.

"My archers have stopped. There is danger."

Henry and the earl drew their swords, "John, Jack keep your eyes open."

"Aye, my lord."

Sir Leofric was just as vigilant and he gave orders for his men at arms to close up. His men at arms had shields and the earl, as well as the clerk and priest, had a wall of wood and metal around them.

I turned to Sir Leofric, "This is your land and your men, what do we do?"

He smiled, like me he had an open-faced helmet, "We wait. See, Hamlin has tethered his horses and he and his men are filtering through the trees. He has sensed danger and they will flush the enemy out." He shouted, "Keep a good watch on the trees."

Suddenly we heard the crack of a crossbow from ahead followed by the whoosh of arrows. There was a cry and then the clicks and cracks of crossbows were punctuated with the twang of bowstrings. Jack shouted, "Ware right!"

I turned Gilles as the horsemen, each carrying a spear, burst from the trees to our right. Numbers were hard to ascertain and all that I could do was to put Gilles between the earl and his attackers. The earl had a couple of men at arms with shields but a spear could easily unhorse a man. The horsemen had moved up silently. I saw now the plan. The crossbows would have drawn our attention allowing the horsemen to attack unseen. The spear that came at my chest bore a metal head. I swashed it away and urged Gilles at the would-be killer. I pushed at the man's shield with my sword and strong right arm. It made him veer his horse and that allowed one of the men at arms to hack at him with his sword. It was a confused mêlée. Horsemen appeared in our faces and it took quick reactions to use my sword and my horse to both avoid being punctured and stop them getting close to the earl. I found myself facing two men and both had spears. I thought my time had come until I heard the bodkin arrow slam into the back of one of them. Wearing only mail allowed the arrow to penetrate through to the front. I was able to slash at the shoulder of the other. He dropped his spear, turned and fled. The archers' appearance won the day. Leaving four horsemen dead, the rest raced west.

I turned and saw that not only the earl but also Jack and John were unharmed.

"Collect the armour and weapons. Secure the horses. Are any left alive?"

"No, Sir Leofric." Hamlin pointed ahead. There are four dead crossbowmen. Another six fled. We would have had them but saw that you needed our help more."

"And right glad I am that you did so." The Angevin knight turned to me, "Hopefully, that will be the last attack. It almost succeeded."

The Knight's Tale

"But thanks to your archers it did not."

"We keep the old traditions alive and they have saved us. All is well."

We took the horses but left the dead, stripped of all that was valuable, in the forest. They all had gold crowns in their purses. They had been paid well for their treachery.

When we saw the bridge over the river ahead, I breathed a sigh of relief. The city of Tours was the end of our journey. We would be safe.

The passport afforded us entry to the city and the men at arms, archers and squires were all taken to the warrior hall while we were greeted, not by the duke but by the Bishop of Tours. It was he who would initiate the negotiations. My work was done and now I would be a mere observer.

I was glad that I was not a diplomat. It took days for the protocols for the negotiations to begin. I was lucky in that Sir Leofric was known and respected. I was able to wander the castle and the town and be occupied. The prospective bride was presented to the earl on the 4th of May when the negotiations proper began. I was told she was fourteen years old but she looked younger. Each day I presented myself to the earl but was told my services would not be needed. I spent the rest of each day with Sir Leofric. We planned our journey home, whenever that would be. He told me that it would be easier if we left Anjou from Angers. We would take a riverboat to Nantes and pick up a ship there. Each night I met with the earl and the priest. In that way, I was kept up to date with the negotiations.

There were good parts. King Henry would gain the islands of Mallorca and Menorca. There would be a dowry, although at 20,000 francs it was not a large one. The most important part was the two-year truce. That would give England and the king some respite. I knew when the negotiations were coming to an end for King Charles himself appeared. He was closeted with the duke and the earl for some time. That was the day, the 24th of May, when Margaret of Anjou was married, by proxy, to King Henry. The actual wedding would be in April a year later.

I had expected the earl to be jubilant, having achieved what had seemed impossible, but he was a little unhappy. It took until we had almost reached Sir Leofric's home before he told me the reason. "There will be angry men in England, Sir Michael."

"Why, Earl? We have peace and a bride for the king."

He nodded, "Aye, but the cost is that King Charles wishes us to give up our claim to Maine. I may have to give away another jewel."

The Knight's Tale

As we entered the castle, I knew the reason for his mood. There were many English nobles with land in Maine. If Maine was given away then they would be subjects of the King of France. I saw the reason for the late arrival of the French monarch. He was waiting until the earl had almost everything signed and sealed. I wondered how this would affect England. Only time would tell.

We reached England on Midsummer's Eve. I had hoped for a swifter return to England but we were fêted in Tours and again at Sir Leofric's home. It took time to find a ship and when we did the journey was longer than we might have hoped. However, I learned much on the journey back. Thanks to my efforts, the mission had been a success and the earl confided in me. I had missed much of what went on in France and when the earl told me it filled me with disquiet. The two sides of the family descended from Edward the Third had two branches. One was descended from John of Gaunt and was Lancastrian. The other was descended from the Duke of York. Richard the Second's death without children caused many problems. King Henry had tried to placate both sides of the family and both the Duke of Somerset and the Duke of York were given senior positions in Normandy and France. When the Duke of Somerset made himself Lieutenant Governor of Aquitaine and all the income from that land, he used his position to deny the Duke of York men. When Somerset was defeated and then died it had left the English position in France untenable. I now understood the haste for the marriage arrangements and the possible shedding of Maine. The earl had shaken his head when he spoke to me of the problem, "The Duke of Gloucester was behind all of this. He allowed the Duke of Somerset to undermine the Duke of York. Between you and I, Sir Michael, I would not have let the Duke of Somerset command the fyrd. Richard, Duke of York, is a far better leader. Still, I have done my part and I hope that England appreciates our efforts, although I doubt it."

I went with the earl to the king who was also pleased with our efforts. In a small ceremony at Windsor Castle, I was made Baron Michael of Houghton Regis. Along with the title came responsibilities. I could be called to Parliament. I knew that while the king was happy to reward me, he was also gaining an ally in a Parliament that consistently opposed him. The earl was also rewarded and made the Marquess of Suffolk. It was a lower rank than Duke but showed that he was gaining power. With gifts of weapons and armour from the Marquess of Suffolk, I rode home with my squire and my page. They had also grown during the mission and both had a confidence that boded well for the future.

Chapter 17

We did not tell Isabelle all that had happened for there was no need. I had been the only one of the three of us to have been close to death and I had returned without a scratch. The less she knew of how close we had all come to death the better. She was flattered by the new title, Baroness, but wondered why there was no financial reward attached to it.

I shrugged when she asked, "We have more than enough money, my love, and extra payment normally means that there is an obligation associated with it." She nodded and I added, "You will, of course, be invited to the wedding of the king. As one of his envoys, I am invited."

She brightened, "A royal wedding followed by a coronation? They are something to which I can look forward." Putting her hand on mine she said, "You are at home now, though? There will be no other calls upon your time?"

"A Parliament, but that will be just one day. I will have to stay in London for one night only."

Before I had left the marquess he had told me that there would need to be a Parliament to ask for funds to bring the new queen to London. I had asked if the terms of the marriage would be disclosed. His silence told me that they would not, and I feared the outcome of such a decision. It would have to come to light that Maine might yet be given away and the delay would anger many nobles. The truce meant that our leaders would return from France and Richard of York, for one, would be unhappy.

John and Jack had returned richer. The ambushes had been dangerous but to the victor went the spoils and both had benefitted. The new weapons and armour that they had received also made them both look nobler. In Jack's case, this made his mother weep when she saw the transformation. Each time we returned from an adventure, it seemed as though he had grown and changed. I did not see it for I was too close but my wife and Jack's mother, not to mention Sarah, did.

A few days after my return I happened to be passing through the kitchen on my way to examine the new bread oven when I heard a snippet of conversation. I paused to listen. It was Elizabeth and Sarah.

"Your Jack is a changed man, Bet." Sarah used Elizabeth's diminutive and it was a measure of their closeness. "He will turn many a young woman's head."

"He is a handsome young thing is he not? I thank God for the salvation that Sir Michael brought. Had he not scoured the woods of the bandits then who knows what might have happened. There were evil men there and I feared for both Jack and myself."

"Now you are safe and he has money. With Sir Michael's permission, he could marry."

I heard a tinge of sadness in her voice as she said, "There is but one for our Jack and I fear that she is beyond his reach."

"Who is that?"

"Have you not eyes? Have you not seen the way he looks at her? Why, it is Margaret. The bairn you brought to be raised by Sir Michael."

I chose that moment to enter the kitchen. I was right to do so for I saw the look on Sarah's face. Margaret knew nothing of her parents and believed that she was the daughter of Sarah and an unknown man. Sarah knew that Margaret was the daughter of a queen.

Both women curtsied and Elizabeth said, "Good morning, my lord, can we help you?"

It was a veiled criticism for the kitchen was the domain of women and not the lord of the manor. I pointed to the back door, "I was going to examine the new bread oven. This saves a trek around the hall."

Elizabeth beamed while Sarah remained silent, "It is well made, my lord, and we can now bake more loaves. We can use the old one to bake raveled and Carter's bread."

"Good." I paused, "Your son did well in France and acquitted himself well. The Marquess of Suffolk was well pleased with him. He shall accompany me to London next year when the king is wed."

Her face erupted in a smile as wide as a summer morning, "The king will be there." I nodded. "Oh, Sir Michael, to think a child of mine should rub shoulders with nobility."

I smiled but my eyes were on Sarah. I saw the questions on her face. I would need to speak to Isabelle and then we would speak to Sarah. We had known that the day would come when someone would seek the hand of Margaret but we had all put it to the back of our minds. People did that with hard questions. They simply got on with their lives and hoped that such decisions would not be needed. Isabelle and I had been appointed Margaret's guardians and an oath to a dying queen was as binding as a blood oath.

Later that morning I was practising with John and Jack in the yard. This was a time of peace and my men at arms could get on with their lives and families. They did not practise with us. Indeed, I wondered if they would ever go to war again. My squire and page, although John felt himself a squire rather than a page, both had new weapons. They were keen to hone their skills. I allowed them to spar and only intervened when I could improve their strikes. They were not using their fine new swords but the old, blunted, heavier ones. It was how I had learned. The heavier old blades strengthened the arms and when one used a good sword it felt like a feather rather than a club. The other advantage was that a blunted old sword gave bruises and not cuts. Both wore padded gambesons and their arming caps. It was more like a game to both of them. They had similar skills. That was inevitable as they had both been taught by me and brought up in the same environment. It meant they looked for tricks to defeat their opponent and that was no bad thing. When I had fought Sir Gruffudd I had not used the predictable blows of a tournament knight, I had improvised and that had brought me a victory. Men attributed my victories to skill. I had ability but I also used my mind to outwit an opponent. John and Jack did the same. Both wore gauntlets and Jack won the first bout by using his left hand to push away John's sword.

"A hit!"

"Well done. John, you need to be lighter on your feet and be ready to dance away from your opponent."

"Dance, Father?"

I laughed, "Aye, a squire needs to learn how to dance to impress the young ladies that he courts but it has a benefit when you fight on foot. Those who lumber forward like oxen can easily be defeated by a deft turn of foot."

Jack asked, "When do I continue my training as a squire, my lord?"

We had not kept up all of Jack's studies and that was largely because we had been called away so often. "As soon as you like. Your French is now almost perfect and you have shown you know how to behave at court. That leaves the learning of the crowd."

I saw his face fall. He had been dreading learning to play the instrument. I had never had to for I had been knighted in war. There was no war for Jack.

"It cannot be hard." John had yet to master the stringed instrument and I knew that Jack feared it. He had a good voice but the fingering of the strings was hard for him.

"It is the composition of the song for a lady I fear."

I was mindful of the overheard conversation, and I said, "Is there no young lady you have in your head you could use as your muse?"

John laughed as Jack blushed, "You know there is, Jack. If this were me, I would do so as quickly as I could for then you will be knighted."

Jack shook his head, "That is some time off, Master John."

John was a clever youth and he shook his head, "No, Jack, now that my father is a baron he can make you a knight. It is true, is it not, Father?"

I nodded, "I can but the question is, are you ready?" I saw him debating. "Your namesake, Jack, who was your predecessor, chose not to be knighted. He is now a steward and married to John's aunt. He is happy that he is not a knight. He chose a life of peace and yet he could have won his spurs. The choice is yours, Jack."

John gave me a quizzical look, "If he was knighted would he be Sir Jack?"

I shook my head, "Jack is a diminutive. What was your christened name, Jack?"

"James."

John asked, "Then why, Jack?"

"Jack was my grandfather's name. My mother called me Jack after him but I was christened James."

"Then if you are knighted you would be Sir James but that is some way off, is it not, Jack? You are not yet twenty one and there is no maiden who is the object of your desire?"

I saw John about to say something but Jack shook his head and said, "No, my lord, there is time."

Isabelle and I could not speak in the hall for John, Margaret, Maud and Jack were all around. I waited until we retired to our bedchamber and while Isabelle undressed in the flickering candlelight, I told her what I knew.

She was not as surprised as I was. "I thought as much. You do not notice such things but a woman does. He has doe eyes when Margaret enters the room and, for her part, I think she is attracted to him. It is Jack she asks after while you are away rather than John."

"What do we do about it?"

"Do?"

"The queen charged us with the care of her daughter."

Isabelle patted the bed and I sat next to her, "The queen had four children did she not?"

"She did."

"Three of them were given into the care of the church. Owen, I believe, is still there." I nodded. "If she did not wish Margaret to have a normal life then she would have been placed into a nunnery. Instead, she gave her to the Queen's knight whom she trusted to give her a life, a real life. Is Jack such a bad choice? Is he not kind, brave, hard-working and loyal? Does he not have all the attributes needed to be both a knight and a husband?" She took my hand.

"Of course he does, but she is the daughter of a queen."

She shook her head, "Queen Catherine was no longer a queen when she gave herself to Owen Tudor, she was a woman and a mother. If she was alive now and in this room, what would she want for her daughter?"

Isabelle was right and I kissed her hand, "You are the wisest of women. What do we do now?"

"You? Nothing. From what you say there is a conversation I need to have with Sarah. I know that, as the wet nurse for Margaret, she has bonds, but Margaret was given into our care."

I was relieved for such matters were uncomfortable for me and I was able to throw myself into the running of my manors. My stewards were all diligent men and Edgar, Jack and Will constantly sent accounts to me. Charles, in Normandy, was different. My three English stewards sent riders each September and April. In Jack's case, it was easier for Weedon lay closest to Houghton Regis but Will's rider had a long journey. It was always Hob who rode from Easingwold. His mother still lived close by Houghton Regis and it was a chance for her to see her son.

The September reports were all good ones. The crops had been harvested and having had little rain to spoil them ensured that those manors, like Houghton Regis, would have food for the winter. The animals had birthed and that boded well. With peace, even in the north, then men could father children and the reports all spoke of babies born to the men at arms, archers and yeomen of my manors. The future of my lands was a little more secure. The only cloud came when I spoke to Hob. He had stayed longer than the other riders to allow him to see his mother and that meant I could talk to him about life in the north.

"Life is good there, my lord, but…"

"Go on, you know me, Hob son of Dickon. Speak openly."

"Will is worried for there is disquiet in the north. The earl has been visited by the Duke of York when he returned from France to his lands in Yorkshire. They passed along the road and we saw their passage. We heard rumours that the duke is unhappy with both the Duke of Gloucester and the peace that was made by the Earl of Suffolk."

"They talk rebellion?"

"No, my lord, but they question the king's advisors." He shrugged, "It may be gossip, my lord, we hear it from those who pass along the road from York."

"No, you are right to warn me."

His words caused me disquiet. The Duke of Gloucester, since his wife's imprisonment, had ostensibly retired from public life but I knew

The Knight's Tale

he was still actively plotting. Was the Duke of York right to fear the uncle of the king? I knew that when I went to London for the Parliament I would be embroiled in the politics of the land and that I might learn more.

In preparation for the trip, I took Jack and John to one side. Both were excited about the Parliament but I did not want them to think that this was a holiday. "I now have great responsibility and that means you have more to do. Men will seek to use you to get at me. You must be guarded and not make promises that you cannot keep. You will need to keep your eyes and ears open."

"Will this be a regular occurrence, Father?"

I shook my head, "The king only calls a Parliament when he needs something. In this case, the Marquess of Suffolk needs money to bring Margaret of Anjou to England. You cannot reveal the terms of the marriage settlement."

Even Jack was surprised, "Why not, Sir Michael? Surely it is common knowledge."

"The marriage? Aye. The possibility of giving away Maine and the paltry dowry? No. When you have your spurs, Jack, then you will feel a weight upon your shoulders. It is why John's uncle chose not to wear the spurs. When we return from London, then you and I shall sit down and decide your future. Your skills with the crowd have improved and John here is ready to become my squire. Let us use this ride to London and back to clarify your thoughts, eh?" He looked at me and I added, "About everything."

I had never attended a Parliament, but Baron Strongstaff had and I knew what to expect. Parliaments were not always held in the same place. Oxford had hosted some in the time of Simon de Montfort and even York had hosted one, but this time we would be using the old palace of Westminster. It meant that the king could travel down the river from Windsor. The Marquess of Suffolk had invited me to stay with him at his house just north of London. It lay beyond the walls of the city and we could be at Westminster within an hour of leaving his home. It suited me as it meant a shorter ride from Houghton Regis and more privacy than if we stayed at the old palace.

We left Houghton Regis on a day filled with black clouds and autumn showers. We pulled the cowls of our cloaks up, grateful that we had thought to wear the woollen hats that stopped the wicked wind from freezing our ears. I rode Shadow. He was getting old and while I would not ride him to war, he was a comfortable horse to make the relatively short journey to London. Both Jack and John had better horses and we made a steady pace. It was just thirty miles to the manor of the

The Knight's Tale

marquess and even though it was small, he had guards there. Henry of Oxford strode from the hall to greet us. He shouted over an ostler, "Nob, take these horses and care for them well."

"It is good to see you, Henry. How are Will and Mark?"

"Thank you for asking, my lord, they are both recovered well although both now have an abiding hatred of Welshmen. You are all given your own chambers in the manor. There will be just you and the marquess."

"Sir Rufus?"

"Back in his manor. His recovery was slower." He shrugged, "He is a noble. Those who are lesser born seem to have more resilient bodies."

Even though I was a knight, a baron even, Henry knew that we were closer because of our backgrounds. The manor was, as one might expect from such a rich man, well-furnished. More importantly, after the rigours of the road, it was both warm and cosy. Even the first floor, where our rooms were to be found, was not as draughty and cold as I expected. The marquess was busy with a visitor and so Henry took us to the dining hall, it was too small for the title grand, and the steward fetched us wine, bread, ham and cheese. The chairs were padded and cushioned. John and Jack each had one and they both looked like the cat that had got the cream.

When the marquess entered, with his squire, Alan, they both leapt to their feet. The marquess smiled, "After what you did in Aquitaine, I think that you can keep your seats. They sat on two chairs further away from the fire. He nodded to me, "We have a hard task in Parliament, Sir Michael. The wolves are gathering. The joy at the peace was short-lived and there are rumours being spread about Maine."

I held up my hands, "Not from me, nor these two, I swear."

"I know. I have my suspicions. The king can be a little loose with his confidences and has a tendency to trust the wrong people. The Yorkist faction is also making demands for remuneration. The Duke of Somerset benefitted from the war yet the Duke of York became poorer. The Duke of York is still in Normandy and I have persuaded the king to let the Duke be the one to escort his bride-to-be from France. I fear that the king intends to appoint Edmund Beaufort, the new Duke of Somerset, as commander in France. That will not sit well with the Duke of York. We will need to find something for him." He smiled at me as his squire poured some wine, "Those matters are above your station, Baron," he exaggerated my title, "let me toast you. I am finding, as did the king's parents, that you are a rock upon which a man can depend."

"My lord, I feel like a fish out of water. When I am in Parliament, what do I do? I am a warrior and more comfortable with a sword in my hand rather than a plot in my head."

"It is simple, Sir Michael, you support the king but do so more vocally than you are used to. I will be frank with you, you have a reputation for chivalry and honour. You showed courage and, along with Sir John Talbot, one of the few men to emerge from the wars with any dignity. Your capture of the Maid appeals to both the opponents of the war and those who wish to see it carry on. Men will listen to you and your vote may well sway those who are undecided. The enemies of the king, and there are many, will not heed you and his friends will vote the way they always do. You may be the one who sways the mass."

I sighed, "I am flattered and I will do all that is asked of me but I confess that I cannot wait to get back to my manor."

He laughed, "Aye, you are a warrior and I know that I am not. The road to Tours showed me that. Even these two youngsters were more comfortable than was I." He nodded towards Jack, "And are you ready to be a knight? I can happily dub you."

"I am honoured, my lord." I saw the squire of the marquess, who was older than Jack, looking enviously at my squire. "The baron spoke to me on the same matter before we came. I give the same answer to both of you. Shortly after Christmas, I shall be twenty-one. I will make my decision on the shortest day of the year. I am still wrestling with the dilemma."

The marquess laughed, "You are rare, Master Jack, most squires, mine included, would jump at the chance to be knighted. You have shown that you have courage and skill. To my mind, you would be, like the baron, a perfect knight."

I knew the dilemma was in female form and I jumped in to help Jack, "That is a good answer, Jack, and it means I do not need to think about training John here until the new grass. By then he will be almost fifteen and that is a good age to start to learn to be a knight."

The steward came in, "My lord, we need to make this hall ready to dine."

The marquess stood, "Then we shall retire to our rooms and freshen our clothes and faces."

"I will ring the bell, my lord, when all is ready."

We went to our chambers. John and Jack had the luxury of a bed each and a shared room. They were more used to a paillasse on the floor. It also meant that I was alone and that suited me, too. Jack said, "Would you like me to help you to dress, Sir Michael? Shave you?"

The Knight's Tale

I shook my head, "Prepare yourselves, for tonight you dine and do not serve. That should be a pleasure, eh?"

We had brought fine clothes with us and as there was a chimney in the wall of my room I put the chair there with the clothes upon its back. This was a luxury for the warmth would drive away the dampness and cold of the journey south. The room had a mirror and that, too, was rare and showed that the marquess was rich. I filled the bowl with water and realised that the stewards must have had a servant use boiling water. It had cooled somewhat but it meant I would be able to shave. I had a beard but it was not the wild one I had adopted as Sir Ralph of Stoney Stratford. It was trimmed and my cheeks were bare. Isabelle liked the look and it was a relatively easy one for me to manage. By the time I had shaved, I felt cleaner and my fresh clothes felt warmer to the touch. I dressed and took my eating cloth, spoon and knife from my bag. I did not doubt that the marquess would provide some but it was a habit. The bell sounded and when I saw Jack and John waiting outside my chamber, I knew that they were eager to partake of the potentially fine table.

We were not disappointed. There were dishes of finely cooked fish to start and then the pie was one of beef and oysters. That surprised me a little as oysters were considered poor man's food although beef was definitely the food of the rich. I could not remember the last time we had eaten beef. My son and squire enjoyed the pie so much that the servants would not have their normal treat for they devoured every last crumb. I enjoyed the cheeses because they were my favourite course. The desserts were also to the liking of my two companions. One was a hot fruit pudding that was heavily spiced and served with cream while the marchpane was also their favourite. We finished the meal with a fine Malmsey.

Jack had been careful about his drinking but not so John and when he adopted a silly grin, Jack said, "My lords, it has been a long day. Do you mind if I put Master John to bed?"

"That would be a good idea, Jack."

When they had gone the Marquess asked, "What stops him from becoming a knight, Sir Michael? I am more than a little intrigued."

"His predecessor shunned knighthood and chose, instead, a bride."

"Surely a man can have both."

I was uncomfortable, "My lord I am not sure how to say this." I shifted in my seat, "You are nobly born. Like Sir William Strongstaff and me, Jack is not. We have different expectations of life. I believe he will take the spurs but if he does not then I will find a place for him in my household."

The Knight's Tale

He laughed, "It is a most interesting experience seeing life with you, Sir Michael. I have high hopes for you on the morrow."

We left early and poor John suffered. He had drunk too much and it showed. I gave him no sympathy for he had brought it upon himself. We reached the old hall just outside the city walls less than an hour after we had left our lodgings. Even so, there were many knights already waiting at Westminster. Our arrival, with the marquess, identified us as supporters of the king but I was gratified when I was warmly greeted by many of the nobles already gathered. Jack and John would stay with the horses and the marquess hurried off to the river to await the arrival of the king by boat.

It was the welcome from the Earl of Salisbury that surprised me. I had thought that, being a clear supporter of the king, I might be shunned by Sir Richard Neville who, as one of the leading Yorkists, had his own ideas about the family that should rule England.

"It is good to see you again, Sir Michael, and elevated too. My brother, the bishop, will be pleased for he liked you and the last time we met he spoke highly of you and your actions." He waved an arm around the nobles. "You have now entered a den of snakes. See how they all gather in little groups. Each one has its own plans and thoughts. I fear that you might be unique in this body."

"Unique, my lord? Why do you say that?"

"Because all men say the same thing about you. You are honourable and do the right thing. Even when the Duke of Gloucester dismissed you from the care of the king you stood by the royal family and the queen. Those actions garnered you much support. Even those who do not like the marquess speak well of you and that is a rare thing." He leaned in and said, "Do not change, my friend." He waved at another knight and left.

I am not sure if any other wished to speak to me for there was a fanfare of trumpets and the king, flanked by the archbishop and the marquess, entered. We all bowed and parted. The king saw me and gave me a smile.

The proceedings were very formal and much of it was in Latin. The important parts, however, were in English and spoken, not by the king but by the marquess. He laid out the terms of the marriage settlement but managed to avoid the mention of Maine and the amount of the dowry. Instead, he concentrated on the length of the peace and the benefits to the economy. When the request for the money to pay for the queen to be brought to England was made, the marquess cleverly pointed out that the Duke of York would bring her. That ensured the support of the Yorkists and when we were asked to vote, I saw that my

The Knight's Tale

raised hand encouraged the neutrals to vote. The king and the marquess had succeeded. The money was promised, and I saw the look of relief on the face of the marquess. He had been right; I was the deciding factor for some men and, as we left the hall, I was able to reflect on that. I had more importance than either my title or my lands gave me. It was my reputation that was important. I would have to tread very carefully in the making of friends. Some might choose me for the wrong reason and there lay the path to betrayal.

Inevitably we were not able to leave quickly. The marquess had a short meeting with the king and that allowed me to observe the knots of men who gathered outside the palace. Their cowled cloaks and their heads close together made them all look conspiratorial. I stood with Jack and John. They had learned now to keep silent but Jack told me that other squires had enquired after us. They wished to know when we would be travelling. Jack shrugged, "It may have been innocent chatter, my lord, but I have learned to be suspicious of such things."

"You said nothing?"

"No, my lord, but Alan said we would all be glad to get back to the manor and out of the cold."

I debated what to do. In the end, it was the marquess who decided for us. The king boarded his boat and the marquess strode over, first to his squire who waited with their horses close to the river, and after a few words, to us. I watched him approach us. "The king and I have matters to discuss. I will be returning with him to Windsor. My squire, Alan, will head for my manor and I offer you a bed for the night there."

"Thank you, my lord." I waited until he had boarded the ship and Alan had led the horse of the marquess towards us before I mounted.

"I have been told to offer you the hospitality of the marquess' home."

John and Jack mounted. They both turned the heads of their horses to follow the squire. I shook my head, "I have remembered some business that I need to conduct. You will make a faster time riding alone, Alan. Thank the marquess for his offer but I will make other arrangements."

I saw the dilemma on Alan's face but I was his superior and, nodding, he headed off.

I waited until he was out of sight and then wheeled Shadow towards the gate leading to the city. Jack knew to keep silent but John asked, "Where do we go, Father?"

I smiled, "A little excursion." I urged my horse on and we followed a group of knights and squires towards the gates. I had a plan.

Chapter 18

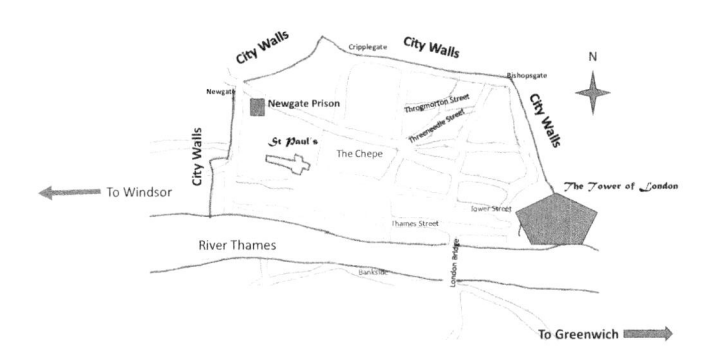

I did not like that there had been questions about our plans. I was suspicious of almost everyone. Sir Gruffudd was still at large and, as an outlaw, he had little to lose. There were others who would see me as an enemy. Many Frenchmen hated me as they saw me as the captor of the Maid. Finally, there were men who would see me as more than a pawn in this game of chess. My elevation meant I was now at the top table. I was a supporter of the king. With an escort of what amounted to two squires, I was in a vulnerable position. I intended to lose any pursuers in the melting pot that was London. With crowded streets and other knights passing through, I hoped to disappear. As we entered the city through the Newgate and the prison where Owen Tudor and Father Bertrand had been held, I said, "Do not look behind you but keep your eyes fixed on me." I knew exactly where I was going. We had to dismount as we passed the Chepe and the thronged market that was London's maelstrom and that suited me. As I dismounted, I examined the faces of those behind us. We walked our horses through the crowded streets and crossed London Bridge. It was as we reached the south bank that we mounted, and again I studied the faces behind. I saw no signs of any followers.

The land to the south of the river was a rougher and wilder place than the city. There were cockpits and low inns. I knew that brigands and bandits lived here. The road east led to the Les Plaisance, the home of the Duke of Gloucester. I would avoid that route and instead, we took the road south. The traffic soon thinned out and I was able to confide in my son and squire. I waved for them to flank me.

I gave them my reasoning for the departure from our expected route home. "I did not like that men wanted to know our plans. I cared not what the other barons intended so why should any take an interest in me? It is some years since I saw Edgar White Streak and I will visit with him for a few days. We then have a choice of routes home."

"Will Mother not worry?"

"Perhaps, but she will understand, John; your mother is wise and, most importantly, sensible. I chose my bride well."

I glanced at Jack who flushed a little and then smiled at me, "You must know of my interest in your foster daughter, Margaret."

"I do."

"It is another reason that I have not decided upon my acceptance of spurs. If I am denied the opportunity to wed Margaret then I would leave your service, Sir Michael. I am a soldier and have skills. I would join the mercenary companies in France, Germany and Italy."

"You have already decided that I will reject your request?"

He shrugged. Jack had been brought up with low expectations and saw opposition from me. "I am poor and have little to offer you. Margaret is the foster daughter of a baron. I cannot see why you would allow me to ask for her hand in marriage."

I was not angry but I was disappointed. I thought I had been open and honest in my dealings with Jack, his mother and the others who served me. I believed I had treated Jack like a son but he clearly had not seen it that way. "In all of this, there is no mention of Margaret and her views on the matter."

John piped up, "Oh, she is all in favour, Father." I turned and withered him with a glare. "Sorry. It is none of my business."

"Well, Jack?"

"She is as enamoured of me as I am of her. We both know that she is young but when we came back from Tours, we realised that Margaret of Anjou is younger. It gave us hope."

"Yet still you do not do me the honour of voicing your desires."

He said, in a small, fearful voice, "I was afraid."

"Afraid? The young man who happily charged with me against arrows and spears is afraid to ask a question?"

"You might have said no."

"So, instead, you do not ask the question and, in doing so risk losing her."

"How so, my lord?"

"There may be other lords whose sons wish to marry Margaret. As you say her foster father now has more importance. There may soon be a queue of young men wishing to win the hand of a baron's daughter."

His voice was filled with fear when he said, "You would not do that, would you, my lord?"

The Knight's Tale

I was toying with him and I gave a wry smile and shrugging, said, "In the absence of a request from you, why should I not consider offers of marriage from others?"

"Because I wish to marry Margaret and be a knight!"

I said, quietly, "Then ask."

Even though I had given him enough clues as to my potential answer he hesitated. John said, "Go on, Jack, you have naught to lose."

Jack sighed, "Sir Michael, I would like to ask for the hand of your foster daughter, Margaret."

I waited for a heartbeat and then said, "I would be honoured to have you in the family, Jack." The relief on the faces of the two of them made me wonder about how they viewed me. Was I such a terrible ogre that my son and squire were afraid of me? The two chattered like magpies all the way to Sevenoaks where there were two hospitals that provided accommodation for pilgrims. I knew that I would have to convince Sarah that it was a good idea and Owen Tudor and Father Bertrand would need to be told, too. The latter was easy for he knew about the existence of Margaret. I was not sure if Owen Tudor knew he had a daughter. Once I had visited with Edgar White Streak, I would find Margaret's father and tell him. I knew that he was the Keeper of the King's Parks in Denbigh. I believed Father Bertrand was still with him.

The hospital we used was more used to serving the poor than a baron and his squires. I rewarded the monks well for their hospitality. The next day we rode the thirty odd miles to Iden close to Rye and the coast. I had only visited it once. Edgar was the most trustworthy man I had ever known, and he had been my right hand for many years. As we rode into the manor, I reflected that it was as different from my others as was possible. It was close to the sea. It was not far from the South Downs and the site of the Conqueror's victory over the English. It was a land of rolling hills and sheep. Iden lay just three miles from Rye. Rye had been the most important of the Cinque Ports, but the harbour needed constant work to prevent its silting up. The masts of cogs as well as fishing ships could be seen below us as we rode into the manor.

A young man I did not know approached me but as he had the same white streak as Edgar, I took it to be his son. I did not know he had a son. I dismounted. He saw my spurs and bowed, "Can I help you, my lord, do you need directions?"

I smiled, "I think not for this is my manor. I am Sir Michael of Weedon."

He bowed even lower, "Forgive me, my lord, I did not see your livery. Come within, my father will be pleased to see you."

The Knight's Tale

"And you are?"

"Ralph the Wanderer, although now I am Ralph Edgarson. My father will tell all for it is his tale." He paused at the door, "I have to tell you that he is not a well man."

I turned to Jack, "Take the horses to the stables and then bring our clothes inside."

The manor was built on one level although, as we headed down the corridor, I saw that a door led down to what I assumed was a cellar. We passed a dining hall that was cosy and Ralph stopped outside a door. He paused with his hand on the handle, "I need to tell you that the priest calls each day and I have been told that my father is dying."

"Why was I not told of this?" I could not keep the anger from my voice.

"My father forbade it." He shook his head, "I am sorry, my lord. He is my father. I will see to your squires." He opened the door and said, "Father, there is a visitor for you."

I do not know what I was expecting but it was not the skeleton beneath the sheets that greeted me. Edgar White Streak had been an archer with a broad chest and an arm that could have felled a man with one blow. I was not expecting the desiccated shell of a man who looked to be more bones than flesh. His eyes widened when he saw me, "Sir Michael!" His face became angrier, "Were you summoned?"

I sat on the bed and taking his hand in mine, shook my head, "The Three Sisters we spoke of all those years ago are at work. I came here… well, the reason is immaterial but I knew nothing of your illness. Had I known I would have been at your side long ago. The reports you sent did not speak of this."

He gave a wan smile, "I am pleased that Ralph obeyed me. He is the one who wrote the reports, my lord, and as for this…it is a worm and it eats at me every day. None can do anything about it and I wanted you to remember me as I was and not as I am. I am dying, my lord, and when I wake each day, I am surprised. When the priest comes for the final absolution there will be nothing left to confess."

I nodded, "Your son?"

He chuckled and in his eyes, I saw the old sparkle of Edgar White Streak. "I did not know I had a son. I sired him when I was a young man and his mother raised him. I was in France with Sir William and knew nothing of his birth. She told him my name and when she died, he left home and came to France to seek me. He became a man at arms. He was at Verneuil with the Duke of Bedford. He was one of those who guarded the baggage train. He came here two years after I was given the manor. He had met Will Green Hose who told him where I lived. He has been here ever since."

"Yet you told me nothing."

He sighed, "Do not reproach me, my lord. I gave my life to England, Sir William and to you. Ralph was the one piece of me that I had and he has given me comfort. I now have a grandson, Edgar, and he brings me joy for the toddler will live after I am dead and there will be another Edgar White Streak." He winced.

"Are you in pain?"

He opened his eyes, "Aye, my lord, and so long as I have left I will be in pain but I cling to life every day for I do not wish to die. I want to see another day of my son, grandson and daughter-in-law. When I close my eyes at night, even though it brings some relief from pain, I know that it may be for the last time. Your visit has made me happy."

Just then there was a knock at the door. I stood and opened it. Jack and John stood there. Jack said, "We have placed our gear in our room, my lord."

I opened the door wide and said, "Come in and see a great old warrior, Edgar White Streak." Both had heard his name but never met him. I saw their shock as they tried to marry up the description I had given and the shell of a man who lay on the bed. "This is Jack, my squire, and John, my son."

Edgar smiled, "And I am pleased to meet you." He winced again.

"Go find Ralph and see if there is a medicine to ease the pain."

They left and I sat by him once more, "Can we give you wine? Will that help?"

"Aye, it does but it dulls the mind too, my lord, I endure the pain."

Ralph arrived carrying a leather flagon. "Here, Father, have a draught of this. You are due one."

"It will make me sleep."

"We will bring Edgar to you before he sleeps and you can tell him another story, but a little rest after this excitement is needed. Father John will be here later so a sleep now will make life easier for all."

"Then give me the draught and I will sleep, but swear that you will wake me for my grandson."

Ralph nodded, "You know that I shall for Edgar dotes on his grandfather." He held the skin to the dying man's lips and Edgar took a single swallow. He smiled and I saw it take effect almost immediately. "Now sleep and I will take Sir Michael and he can meet Edgar and Mary."

I squeezed Edgar's hand, "I will return, I swear. I still have tales to tell."

The Knight's Tale

"Good." He closed his eyes.

We shut the door and Ralph said, "The doctor put a draught in the wine to dull the pain and to help him sleep. If the pain is too much we can give him a larger draught and end his pain forever."

"Would you do that?"

"If he was an animal we would have done so long ago for it is painful to watch him die by degrees. The doctor has been treating him for a year and does not know how he manages to survive. He is a tough old man. He adores Edgar and he clings to life for him."

"He is happy that you came into his life."

"Aye, I sought him for years. It is strange that the three of us were on the same battlefield in France and yet we did not meet. Had we done so, then I would have had even more time with him."

"Do not bemoan what you did not have but be grateful for what you have." I took his arm, "I came here seeking refuge but now I see that I was guided here."

"Refuge? You are in danger?"

I shook my head, "I do not think that I will be bringing danger here but I have enemies. I will tell all but first I would meet the young Edgar, for he has brought joy to my friend."

The boy was about three years old. He had a streak of hair that was slightly different in shade to the rest and that marked him as Edgar's grandson, but he would not be white streak. He was a delight and bombarded both me and my squires with questions. His mother was appalled at his apparent lack of respect. He spoke to me as though I was an ordinary man.

"Edgar, this is a baron, show respect."

I shook my head, "Mistress Mary, titles are not important here. I am his grandfather's friend and I am honoured to be so. Edgar can talk to me any way he wishes and I will tell him tales of his grandfather that will make him proud."

The little boy said, "I am proud already for my grandfather was a hero!"

I laughed and ruffled his hair, "That he was!"

The manor had just one servant, a young woman called Anne. While we ate and talked she watched over a sleeping Edgar. I learned that the manor was, as I expected, well run. The profits were less than Weedon and Houghton Regis but that was as a result of its small size. It had been a small gift, given while Sir William was still alive.

"My father will die, my lord." I nodded but made the sign of the cross. I did not wish it any time soon. "What of my position?"

I smiled, "You do not know me, Ralph, what you should know is that I am loyal to those who serve me. Sir William taught me that I serve them as much as they serve me. I am happy for you to continue as steward. I know from talking to your father that you have shouldered the burden during his illness. I see no reason to change the arrangements."

They both looked relieved. "You spoke of a refuge, my lord, what did you mean?"

I sighed, "We serve the king as we did his father. King Henry has enemies as does the Marquess of Suffolk. I am seen as a supporter of the king and men seek to undermine me. Sometimes they try more than that. I was at parliament and rather than doing what my enemies expected, I did the unexpected. I now find that it was meant to be."

When Anne told us that Edgar was awake his son, grandson and I returned to the bedroom so that he could tell a story. Edgar seemed to come alive as he regaled little Edgar with tales of our adventures in France. For his part, I saw the adoration in the toddler's eyes. He would miss his grandfather more than any. When the priest came it was time for young Edgar to sleep and Ralph and I left the priest with Edgar White Streak.

When the priest came out of the chamber, he was smiling, "Sir Michael, it is good to meet you and I have got to tell you that it has revived Edgar. I feared for him when I called last night. You have given him more days of what passes for life. I fear that there will be few of them and they will be painful ones. When he goes to heaven then God will make up for all the pain that he has endured. I will visit on the morrow when my other duties are done."

We gave Edgar his last draught before we were due to retire. Ralph said, to me, "I will see you in the morning."

"You sleep in your father's room?" He nodded. "Then tonight the lord of the manor will sit by his old friend." I held up my hand, "I will brook no arguments. If you are needed then I will wake you."

He left and I settled into the chair. I put my cloak about my shoulders for it would be cold in the night and I watched the old man as he slept, albeit fitfully. He had watched over me when I was young. He and the other archers had stood the night watches and kept us safe. I was repaying him. Edgar had often mentioned The Three Sisters. He had called them the witches who determine our lives. He had been a friend of Ulf the Swede, a huge warrior who came from the Baltic. He had filled Edgar's head with the story. I had always been a little sceptical but I could not explain our arrival at Iden in what seemed like the nick of time any other way. We were meant to come.

The Knight's Tale

I was not asleep when Edgar woke. If truth be told I needed to make water but I did not want to leave. I saw his eyes open and he started, "I thought it would be Ralph."

"And I thought to allow him to spend a night with his wife. How else will you have more grandchildren?"

He smiled, "I will not see them."

"One day at a time, eh Edgar? Do you need anything?"

"Aye, I need to make water." He nodded to the pot in the corner. I had not seen it. "You had better call Ralph."

"Why, am I incapable?"

"You are a lord."

"Edgar, you were there when I was pulled from that cell. Come let me help you."

It was like picking up an empty sack. There was no weight to him and once out of the bed, he looked even thinner. When he made water he winced and I saw, in the dribbling stream, the specks of blood. He saw my gaze and nodded, "Aye, my lord and each day is worse."

The noise we had made and our conversation woke the house and Mary came in, "Come, my lord, I will clean up Edgar. Anne and my husband are preparing food. Little Edgar is desperate to hear more of your tales. Your son and squire are doing their best but he wants to hear of the Maid you caught."

Little Edgar made me smile and I realised, after an hour in his company, that he had given Edgar White Streak a lease of life. His smile and his laughter made me feel better and for my old archer, it must have been doubly joyous for he was his grandson. Over the next days, we all spent as much time with Edgar as we could. John and Jack were with me as often as they were allowed. Edgar liked them both and I saw, in his eye, the sparkle he had once had around the campfires of France. He saw their hopes and their dreams. When Little Edgar joined them then they were Edgar White Streak's happiest moments.

When he slipped into a deeper sleep than normal we knew something was amiss and we sent for the doctor and the priest. To our relief the doctor, through the use of strong-smelling salts, roused him but, while Mary and Ralph cleaned him up, the doctor told me that the old man had hours left. "The next time he slips away will be the last. I will not be able to rouse him." He shook his head, "I do not want to rouse him for he has endured more pain than a man should. He is now in God's hands."

Father John nodded, "And Edgar is well prepared." He waved a hand at the hall, "You will need, Sir Michael, to prepare the others. In the short time I have known you I have seen a strong man and a fair man."

"Thank you, I will do my best."

I spoke to Edgar once more. Ralph and I took turns to watch over him and on my shift, Edgar suddenly opened his eyes and writhed in pain. I heard him say, "I come, Sir Willliam." He looked over to me and held out his hand. I grasped it, "I am tired and ready to go, Sir Michael."

"Ralph!"

"Farewell, it was an honour to serve you. I was blessed."

Ralph entered, "Father." He dropped to Edgar's side and grabbed Edgar's other hand.

"All is well and now I shall sleep." He might have wanted to say more but as the door opened and Mary stood there, Edgar White Streak joined his dead comrades. Ralph and I unmanned ourselves and wept. Mary put her arm around her husband and John and Jack came in to comfort me. We had no words as Edgar's soul hovered above our heads.

Edgar White Streak was buried in the churchyard at Iden. I commissioned a stone mason to carve the stone. It had a simple inscription: **Here lies Edgar White Streak, Father, Grandfather and archer**. We stayed for one day after the funeral. "I will return if only to tell Little Edgar more tales."

"And I would thank you, my lord. I can think of few other nobles who would have done what you did."

I shook my head, "I am not a noble. At best I am a knight. I was not nobly born and I feel more like Edgar than a noble. Sir Michael is just a title. It is not the man."

Chapter 19

We did not return through London. There were too many prying eyes. We had disappeared to Iden and I hoped to reappear, magically, at Houghton Regis. I knew that Isabelle would now be worried and we rode hard on horses that were well-rested and refreshed. Jack was also keen to get back for I had given him permission to be wed and that meant he could accept, after Christmas, my offer of spurs. John was also eager to get back for he would no longer be a page but a squire.

Word of our prospective return must have reached my wife for she, along with Maud, Margaret, Sarah and Elizabeth were waiting for us as we clattered through the gate. I saw the relief on all their faces when they saw that we were whole. It was as we dismounted that I saw the look of love on Margaret's face as she beamed at Jack. She and Jack were meant to be together. I had much to tell Isabelle and then Sarah and Elizabeth. First, there were the welcomes and the hugs. Peter the horse master took away the horses. He tut-tutted at their lathered coats. While Sarah and Elizabeth went to the kitchen to fetch food and drink, we went to the dining hall. We sat and looked at each other.

"Well? I thought it was a journey of two nights. You did not return and there was not a word."

I sighed and took her hand. "I went to Iden."

"That does not explain..."

"Edgar White Streak is dead."

She had not known Edgar but she had heard his story for my archers and men at arms often spoke of him. Thomas of Chester would be as upset as any when he heard the news.

"I am sorry, but why did you go to Iden? Did you know he was ill?"

"No, I went because men were too curious about my plans." I glanced at Maud and Margaret, "I have more to tell you when we are alone."

She nodded, "Then I shall be patient." She looked at Jack and John, "And you two look as though you are the cats who found the cream."

I said, "And that too, will have to wait. What say, my love, that when we have refreshed ourselves, you and I take a walk to church?"

She nodded.

It suited the rest that we left. Elizabeth, Margaret and Jack had time to speak and Maud, who had grown into a curious nine-year-old, questioned John who had a fine line to walk between lying to his sister and revealing a secret.

The Knight's Tale

I started the story when we left the hall to walk down the lane to the church. I started with Jack and Margaret. She nodded, "They are well-suited, if not by birth, then by disposition. Sarah may not be happy."

"Sarah has nothing to do with this. I will have to travel to Denbigh to speak to Margaret's father. I had planned on doing so before the wedding but time and the death of Edgar have changed my plans. It was the queen who put Margaret in my care and I shall tell Owen Tudor after the marriage. Who knows, I may be able to tell him at the wedding of the king if he is invited."

"Sarah said that Owen Tudor thought Margaret was dead. Why tell him?"

"Because she is still his child, and he has a right to know. Father Bertrand also needs to be informed. He was the one who arranged this. He will be happiest of all, I think."

I then went on to tell her of the fears I had. I concluded, "Becoming a baron is a double-edged sword. I am no longer a simple knight." I patted my chest, "In here I am but to the world, I am now a man of importance and one who can be an ally or a threat."

We had reached the church, "To me, you are always the same, an honourable and chivalrous man. I am honoured to be your wife and now let us pray that God may guide and protect us. These are parlous times and while I do not doubt that we will prevail, God's help is needed." We knelt in the empty church and prayed.

When we returned to my hall, Isabelle and I summoned Elizabeth, Jack and Margaret. I first asked Margaret if she was happy to be Jack's wife and her affirmative answer filled the room with joy. "Then we will have a wedding in March. The king is to be married in April and it would not do to steal his thunder with another April wedding. Jack, I shall give you a dowry of a thousand crowns."

"That is too much, my lord."

"Jack, that is for me to say. You just say, thank you, my lord." I said it with a smile, and he nodded. "You shall be knighted in January. It is a cold and harsh month. Let us give the manor a cause for celebration and you can begin to train John for me. You shall need a squire yourself."

"I have time, my lord, and besides, I need to get used to my new position."

The meeting with Sarah was harder. Her eyes welled with tears, "My lord, she is like my own daughter!"

"Yet she is not, but if she was your daughter would you be happy with a marriage to Jack, Sir James, as he shall be titled?"

"Of course, but her mother was a queen."

"Who charged me with making the decisions about Margaret's life."

The Knight's Tale

I saw her taking that in. She nodded, "Thank you for speaking to me, my lord, and forgive my impertinence."

I shook my head, "You were concerned for Margaret and that speaks well of you."

Houghton Regis was a large dwelling but, while there would be enough rooms for Margaret and Jack to live in the hall, Isabelle felt that they should be given their own quarters. He would be a married knight. It was Thomas of Chester who came up with an innovative solution. As a man at arms, he had been both brave and clever. He had taught me how to fight an opponent and use my mind to do so. He now put his mind to the problem.

"My lord, there is a spare piece of land at the rear of the kitchens. It is large enough for a single-storey building. If we attached it as a wing we could build a bed chamber, a room to dine and a room to receive. It would be both separate and attached. Elizabeth's quarters are close to the kitchen. If Jack and Margaret wished for privacy then they have it."

Isabelle nodded, "A clever idea but what of children?"

Thomas smiled, "Let us get them married first, eh my lady?" Thomas suffered a dig in the ribs from Sarah for his impertinence, but my wife smiled and nodded.

The men of my manor, archers, men at arms and farmers alike all liked Jack, Margaret and Elizabeth. We all set to with a will and dug the foundations, hewed the wood and carried the stones. With huge trees felled and embedded as the four corner pieces of the house, it began to take shape quickly. Stones were mortared into both the foundation and the lower course of the house. I knew that some nobles were now having bricks made for their houses but we had enough masoned stones to make the walls we built attractive. We made wind holes with shutters in the wattle and daub walls. Isabelle liked glass but it was expensive and Jack was happy to have the simpler shutters. We were able to give the rooms more height and while that made them harder to heat, it made the small dwelling seem larger. As it was attached to the kitchen it was simplicity itself to add a fireplace and use the existing chimney in the kitchen. By All Saints Day, the house was finished. There was no furniture but Elizabeth knew a carpenter in the village who was happy to make what they needed. In the first instance, it was a bed and the carpenter worked in situ to build the bed in the bed chamber.

All the while I was working with Jack to finish his training as a knight. He threw himself into the training and John, seeing his future, helped him. It was a harmonious time. The time flew for not only were we building a house and training a knight, but we also had the normal demands of a manor to contend with. Crops were harvested, animals culled and their flesh preserved, and trees were copsed for kindling and firewood. No one complained for the land was at peace and we were working for each other.

That Christmas celebration was a special one. It marked the end of one part of our lives. Edgar White Streak was dead and his death still hung heavily over both me and the men who had served with him. When they had heard the news they had held a wake to remember not only him but the others who had fallen. It was a time of change. Jack would be a knight and within a few months, he would be wed. This one marriage would send ripples through the manor. Maud and John would see their own future in the young couple. The marriage would be a foretaste of what they could expect. Young men would seek Maud's hand in marriage and when John became a knight, he would need a bride. We ate well and celebrated even better. It seemed an appropriate way to remember Queen Catherine, Edgar White Streak and the others who were no longer with us. We were the caretakers of the future and I hoped, as we snuffed out the last candle, that the dead approved.

I had written to the king and the earl to tell them of the ceremony. I invited both of them to witness the knighthood but I was not surprised when they did not take me up on the offer. The king did not bother to answer my letter but the earl did and he approved. We held the ceremony in my Great Hall. It was crowded and the table had to be put against one wall whilst the chairs were removed to make room for all who wished to attend. Jack was popular. His mother spent the whole time dabbing her eyes and shaking her head. She and Jack had lived in the woods with bandits and for him to be knighted was a dream beyond words. Margaret's eyes were wide with wonder. She thought of herself as Sarah's daughter as well as ours. We never dispelled the rumour and she was between Sarah and Isabelle through the whole process. As I put my sword on Jack's shoulders and said, "Rise, Sir James of Houghton Regis," I wondered what she would say if she knew that her mother had been the wife of the King of England.

When Jack rose, there was a collective cheer. He looked almost embarrassed but the first thing he did was not part of the protocol and had the great and the good been there would have been frowned upon. He put his arms out to hug me and as I responded said, in my ear, "Thank you, Sir Michael, I know just how much I owe you and I swear that I will never let you down."

"And know that I am as proud of you as if you were my own son. Just be yourself, Sir James, and all will be well."

He shook his head, "The title and the name will take some getting used to, my lord."

John made the moment easier by bowing and saying, "Congratulations...my lord...Jack!"

Jack laughed and flicked his hand at John's head, "Cheeky young...was I ever this bad as a squire, my lord?"

We all laughed, and the three matriarchs ushered us out of the hall so that food could be laid on the table and we could celebrate properly. Margaret took Jack's arm and they led the party from the hall.

I knew it was hard for the couple to wait for the wedding but Elizabeth, Sarah and Isabelle all joined forces to ensure that everything was as it should be. The house into which Jack moved had a bed, a table and a chair only, but the carpenter had done the hard part and by the time of the wedding the furniture would be complete. The house was fine for Jack but as the plaster was still drying was unsuitable for a bride. She, along with the other women had a task to do. A large tapestry was being sewn to cover the wall without wind holes. It portrayed Sir William at the Battle of Agincourt. I was in it, too. My wife had designed it. Originally, she wanted to make one showing my capture of the Maid but I wanted Sir William honouring; I did not think he had enough honour in his lifetime and his children did not seem to celebrate his life. I hoped that when I died my children would. The frenetic work all came together a week before the wedding. The church had been prepared and Isabelle had invited every villager. We prayed for clement weather as the feast would, perforce, have to be outside.

God smiled on us and the wedding day had clear skies. Margaret looked regal and I could see her mother in her. She had her father's red hair but I also saw her mother's eyes. Sir James and John waited in the church and I escorted my foster daughter down the lane to the flower-bedecked church. The lane was lined with cheering villagers and the families of my archers, farmers and men at arms. Spring flowers were strewn at us as we walked.

Margaret held my arm tightly and said, as we walked, "I know what you and Lady Isabelle have done for me. My mother is as grateful as I am. I want to thank you for making me your ward."

I put my hand on hers and squeezed, "Margaret, it has been a delight and it is I who am honoured. Know that I could not be happier for Jack is like a son. This is perfect. As of today, you shall be Lady Margaret."

She looked up at me, her eyes wide, "Fancy that, the daughter of a cook a lady. It is like a fairy tale."

I smiled and said nothing. Her real mother, the Queen, had been prescient. Edmund and Jasper would not be able to make such choices. They now lived at court where every eye was upon them. When they married every eye would be upon them. As we walked into a church filled with simple spring flowers and the faces of those who had seen both Jack and Margaret grow, I knew that Margaret was the lucky one.

Isabelle had been invited to the king's wedding but on the day before we were due to travel, she became unwell. I suspected she had eaten fish that had gone off. My wife loved perch whilst I was not as keen. She had partaken and I had not. Whatever the cause she could not travel. In some ways, it was a relief. Had she travelled with us then the journey would have taken a couple of days as we would have needed Anne to wait upon her. This way John and I could ride hard and just use the warrior hall.

Since our return from Iden, John had filled out. It was not just his body that had grown but his mind and his maturity. Seeing Jack become Sir James had given him a target and he was determined to become a knight on his own twenty-first birthday. As we rode there were no questions and we chatted about the future. When we joined the queue of horsemen entering the city a local told us how the rooves of the houses lining the route to the city had been strengthened such was the interest in the marriage. When the King and Queen came to London for the actual coronation the following month, the city would be thronged. When the king's father and Catherine of Valois had been married the ceremony had been in Troyes. The coronation had been in Westminster Abbey. This time the king had chosen Titchfield Abbey in Hampshire as the place where he would be wed. The Marquess of Suffolk had done well. There was support for the king and the master stroke of asking Richard Duke of York to bring the French bride had also paid off in defusing the tension.

We stabled our horses, and I entered the Tower. Pursuivants checked the names of those entering and only those invited were allowed within. It was that day when I saw how my star had risen. Edmund and Jasper Tudor were there. Both were almost unrecognisable from the boys I had rescued all those years ago. King Henry had embraced the arrival of his half-brothers in a better fashion than one might have expected. They were nobly attired and presented at the fore of the guests. I was behind them. As we waited for the arrival of the other guests they turned, "Sir Michael, we never got to thank you properly for what you did for us. The king himself told us of your courage and how you kept your promise to our dear, dead mother. Many other men would not have risked the ire of a new king and the Duke of Gloucester."

I smiled, "Edmund, a true knight knows that his word is his best protection. If a man keeps his oaths then all is well." I saw them both nod, "Is your father invited?"

Jasper said, "Invited but he sent a letter to the king to say that he did not wish to cause any division in the kingdom. He knows that the Beaufort family still view him as an enemy. We might be accepted but that is because of our mother. He is happy in Denbigh."

I nodded. I had hoped to avoid a long ride north, but it was inevitable. I owed it to the dead queen.

We left the next morning to ride to the abbey. The king and the Marquess of Suffolk led the column that headed south. The king would be married and then we would have to return north to London. I was pleased that poor Isabelle did not have to endure the ride. It was seventy miles from London to the abbey and would be a hard ride.

Riding with the king's half-brothers was an interesting experience. I learned that they had not just good lives but rich lives. The king treated them both as brothers. They hunted and dined as though they were dukes rather than poor relations. The king rose in my estimation. When we stopped, Henry of Oxford rode back to speak to me. He was more than happy that I had knighted Jack. "If ever a squire was meant to be a knight it was Jack. He would have made a good man at arms." He beamed, "I can give no greater compliment than that."

It made me laugh. "And the other men at arms, they are well?"

"Aye, they are both fully healed. We shall soon see the conclusion of the work we did for England, eh Sir Michael? Let us hope that the people appreciate it."

I lowered my voice as I asked, "The Duke of Gloucester, will he attend?"

Henry shook his head, "As the king's uncle, one would have expected it, but I think not. Now the coronation is a different matter. He will be there for that one. Between us two, Sir Michael, I think that this abbey was chosen for the wedding as it is close to Southampton and small. The king was able to choose his guests well. The Duke of York will be a guest and I have heard a rumour that this is intended to build bridges." He tapped his nose, "Say nothing but I know the marquess trusts you and I owe you much. I thought you should know."

We were hosted in the vast grounds of the abbey. As was right and proper the king and his bride were kept apart until the service the next day. There was, of course, a feast but the king and his future queen were separated by the Archbishop of Canterbury, the abbot, the Marquess of Suffolk and the Duke of York. Even so, from my lowly position down the table, I saw that both Margaret and Henry liked what they saw in the other. It boded well. I had hoped to remain anonymous but the king doomed that thought to failure. He made a speech and in that speech spoke of my part in the arrangements.

The Knight's Tale

"My bride and I are particularly indebted to two men who made this possible: the Marquess of Suffolk and the Baron of Houghton Regis. Despite the treacherous attempts of some of our enemies, they managed to secure the hand of my bride and peace. Raise your goblets and toast, Sir Michael and Sir William."

Every eye turned to me for they all knew the part played by the marquess. The marquess, for his part, adored the adulation. I saw then the stare of the Beauforts who were there. Edmund Beaufort who was the new Duke of Somerset, Henry Beaufort, the Bishop of Lincoln, and Ralph Neville. Whilst not a Beaufort, Sir Ralph was the husband of Joan Beaufort. There were genuine smiles from many but not those three. Their thin smiles did not bode well. Sir Ralph Neville, in particular, had a grudge for I had helped his cousin who had taken the title he felt was his.

After the feast, I scurried to my chamber for I was anxious to become anonymous. John awaited me and he was full of pride at my notoriety. It had garnered him extra food from the royal cooks as well as the envy of his fellow squires. I just wanted to attend the wedding and get back to my home and my sick wife.

The wedding was, as one would expect, very formal. Margaret of Anjou had a large retinue with her but none of her family. I felt a little sorry for her but she had a steely look about her and the two looked a good match. I hoped that the king's fortune would change with the marriage.

As soon as the wedding was over, I sought permission to leave. It was the marquess who came to see me as I waited for an audience with the king. "Will you not stay, Michael? There are many men who wish to speak to you and I have much to tell you. Alice has borne me a son, John, and I have been granted many manors by the king. My life is rich and full."

"Congratulations, my lord, but my wife is unwell and I would be at her side."

"And that speaks well of you and confirms both my view and that of my wife that you are a truly noble and chivalrous knight. Would that others were as dedicated. You have our permission to leave but know that we may have need to call on you again. You are the first knight I have met whom Henry of Oxford respects. As a real warrior that is a compliment."

"Thank you, my lord, and for my part, I think that you have good men at your side and that is also testament to you."

We mounted our horses. I saw that we were observed although I did not recognise the men who stared at us. Their liveries were unknown but they were knights. As we headed north, I reflected that it was likely they were members of the Beaufort or Neville families. I would need to keep watch for them in the future.

We rode hard and reached Houghton Regis after a journey of two days. I was relieved to find that Isabelle had fully recovered. She wanted to know all that I had seen. The politics did not interest her but the dresses of the bride and the ladies did. I was relieved. I would worry and she would not.

The Knight's Tale

North Wales 15th Century

Chapter 20

I knew I had to go to Wales and to go soon. It was unfinished business. I doubted that Owen even remembered he had a daughter for he had not been living with Dowager Queen Catherine when the child was born, but I owed it to her to tell Owen that his daughter had married. Jack, of course, now Sir James, wanted to come with me, even though he did not know the reason for my journey, but I refused. "Your place is here, with your wife and to guard my home."

John was also curious, "Why do you ride to Denbigh, Father? What lies there for you?"

"For me? Nothing but we met with Edmund and Jasper and their father needs to know that they are well. Indeed, they are better than well. They enjoy the patronage of the king."

I could not tell my son the real reason for my visit. He accepted my answer and was a little excited to be travelling into Wales. I did need an escort. Wales was still a little too wild for my liking and I chose four archers to travel with me as well as two men at arms. Absalon and James were the men at arms and they chose themselves. They had been doughty warriors on our trip to Easingwold. The four archers were also easy to choose. They were young men whose fathers had served Sir William before me. William was the son of Alf the Grim. Seth was the son of Stephen the Tracker and I hoped he had been taught those skills by his father. Christopher was the son of Christopher White Arrow and Edgar was the son of Egbert Longbow. They all knew each other for they had trained at the mark on Sunday morning. They were all young men and in their prime. They were all keen to accompany me. We would ride mailed and armed for the Welsh rebellion had been less than thirty years earlier and there were fears that the charges against Sir Gruffudd might have stirred up nationalistic feelings again.

We left in the middle of May for the one hundred and seventy miles trip along the road travelled by the Roman legions when they had destroyed the Druidic religion more than a thousand years ago. As our hooves struck the cobbles, I thought about the Roman legionaries travelling the same road although in their case it was thousands of miles from their homes.

There were religious houses all along this road and we had a choice of accommodation. My name was known. Time had been it was because of my association with Sir William but since the Maid and the king's use of my name, I had a reputation of my own. I did not enjoy the notoriety but the ease with which we found beds, food and shelter made up somewhat. One thing I did not like was that our progress into

The Knight's Tale

Wales would be marked. I had enemies in Wales, not least Sir Gruffudd and, perhaps, the families of the Welshmen I had slain in Poitou. I had not known their names but, thanks to the king, men knew I was involved in the incident. I studied every face and developed a crick in my neck from turning around so much.

It was with much relief that we saw the royal castle of Denbigh or Castell Dinbych as it was called by the Welsh, loom on the horizon. The castle was held by Richard Duke of York, but he was absent. The rumour I had heard at the wedding was that he was set to become Lord Lieutenant of Ireland. A rich and lucrative post that would, so the Marquess of Suffolk told me, ease his financial losses incurred in France. It made sense that Owen Tudor would live in the castle. He was Welsh and his post was the keeper of the Royal Parks.

The castle was one of a ring of fortifications around the Welsh heartland. Harlech, Caernarfon, Conwy, Beaumaris and Chester had been strategically planned by King Edward, Longshanks. They penned in the Welsh. Each one had a good garrison. The men knew that if the Welsh rose, and rebellion was always simmering, then they would have to hold on until relief could be brought from England. We were scrutinised at the gate but, eventually, allowed in.

My men and John were taken to the inner ward and I was led into the castle. I was greeted warmly by Owen Tudor. The last time I had seen him had been at Newgate prison. That I was partly responsible for his release had not gone unnoticed.

He grasped my arm, "Sir Michael, forgive me, Baron Michael, this is an unexpected pleasure." I saw in the corner of the room, a woman rocking a young child to sleep. "That is…Myfanwy and my son David. Come, we will walk about the walls. The boy needs his sleep and the air on the fighting platform is invigorating, coming, as it often does, from the sea." He nodded to my cloak hanging over the back of the chair.

I donned the cloak and as we ascended the steps I asked, "And Father Bertrand, where is he?"

"He is with God now. He passed away a day after Christmas. It was as though his heart simply gave out and he died. He is at peace now but I miss his sage advice. I know that the queen found him to be a rock on which she could rely." The priest had died before Margaret was wed. The thought saddened me. I had delayed too long.

We reached the fighting platform and the sentries moved apart to give us some privacy. It was, indeed, invigorating. The view was equally spectacular. The sea could be seen down the valley and it was less than ten miles away. To the south and west lay the mighty

The Knight's Tale

mountain of Snowdon. I could see why this castle was so important. We both took in the view.

Eventually, Owen said, "Now what brings an important baron all the way here to speak to me? Has one of the dukes decided that I am an embarrassment? Are you here as an assassin?" He said the words without any rancour and I felt sorry for the man whose only crime had been to love a queen.

I shook my head, "I come on the queen's business."

I had shocked him. I saw it in his eyes as his head whipped around, "The Queen? She spoke to you from the grave?"

"Before she died, she entrusted me with the raising of a child, your child."

I saw him struggling with the news, "Jasper? Edmund? Owen? I do not understand."

"Your daughter, Margaret."

Had I slapped him he could not have been more shocked, "Margaret...but she died as a baby. Everyone told me so." Even before I could add more, he shook his head. "I was not at home and never saw the child so...Father Bertrand would have told me."

"Your wife's confessor knew of this, and he, along with the child's nurse, my wife and I were the only ones who knew of the child's ancestry. We still are."

"And now I do." He looked intently at me, "So why tell me now?"

"Your daughter has married, my lord. She married Sir James. You met him at Newgate, he was my squire, Jack, and they are a contented couple."

"And her life is a normal one? She is not scrutinised and every move and word examined for treachery?"

I knew then that Jasper and Edmund, for all their pampered lives at court, walked a perilous path. "She was raised like John and Maud, my children. She played in the yard and was brought up to be a kind and happy young woman. The marriage was not arranged, the couple chose each other. Jack, Sir James, is a good man and he will make her a good husband."

He suddenly launched himself at me and it took me aback. He grabbed me and hugged me. I saw the sentries further down the walkway start. He said, hoarsely, "Then I thank God for sending you to the queen. I know now that I have at least one child that will have a normal life. It was all that the queen and I wanted but we were denied it. Love drew us together, but politics drove us apart." He stepped back. "I am in your debt. Is there anything I can do to thank you?"

The Knight's Tale

I shook my head, "This was a promise made before God to a dying queen. I am not even sure if I have broken that oath by telling you for it cannot be mentioned again, you know that."

"Better than any and I swear that none shall hear of it from me. Your son does not know?"

"He was a toddler when she came to live with us and he, and she, believed that she was the child of the nurse, Sarah. They grew up together. He sees her as his sister."

"Then we will keep it that way. When I look at you, Sir Michael, I will know that I have a daughter and that she has a life. That will make me happy. I have another son, Owen, being nursed now by his mother and I know that he will not have a normal life." He stared across the land to the sea and we were silent. I respected the silence and I stood watching, too. Eventually, he said, "Although we will not speak of her again I would have you stay. I am the keeper of the king's parks and the land around here teems with game. I would be honoured if you would stay for a few days, at least, and allow me to take you and your son hunting. I was denied that pleasure with my own sons and I would like to do so with the youth brought up with my daughter."

I could not deny him that and I nodded, "A couple of days will do no harm."

We never did speak of Margaret again but I found the Welshman often staring at me and occasionally John. I worked out that he was imagining Margaret's life with us. He insisted on John joining us at the table, "We have servants enough to serve us and I would like to get to know this youth."

John liked to chatter and he happily rambled on about our adventures as well as speaking of Houghton Regis, his mother, sister and, of course, Margaret. I could see those stories pleased Owen Tudor. Now that the king had mentioned our adventures, it was safe for him to do so. When he spoke of Sir Gruffudd, Owen's face darkened, "That incident caused more trouble than enow, Sir Michael. It was an accident, or so they say and it was a tournament but Sir Gruffudd and others lost lands. It is said it was because he was a Welshman and the English Marcher lords feared any man who might raise the standard of rebellion. There is a rumour that he is back in England and he might now do as his enemies say and cause trouble along the border."

"Surely our castles are strong enough to keep the land safe."

"It is the land between the castles that would be ravaged. The Duke of York keeps men here but they are not the warriors you would want to take to France to fight in a war there. If there was an uprising they would stop the castle from falling but that is all. You will see, when we hunt on the morrow, that this is a land for ambush." He pointed his eating knife to the west, "The island of Anglesey is the lifeline to Ireland. If the Welsh rose in rebellion then Ireland would come under threat too."

"It is rumoured that the Duke of York may command in Ireland."

"Then he might regret not leaving stronger men here to defend the road."

We moved the conversation to more pleasant topics but the undercurrent was always his position here in this dangerous part of the kingdom. He was loyal but he knew that his loyalty to the crown won him no friends amongst the Welsh. To them, he was a traitor.

When we retired to our chamber, John asked me the question I had been dreading since I had first mentioned the trip. "Father, why did you come all the way here from Houghton Regis? Were you asked to do so by the king or the marquess? You told me before we left home that it was to tell Owen Tudor of his sons."

I could not lie to my son nor could I tell him the truth. If Margaret was to have a normal life then no one else could know of her existence. I was now convinced that her father wanted her anonymity to remain. "We came, John, because of a promise I made to his wife, Queen Catherine. I swore an oath and even though you are my son, I cannot tell you what it was. One day you will be a knight and you will understand."

"I understand now, Father. Since I began to serve at table, I have heard other squires give me their opinion of you and other masters. The one constant is that Sir Michael is a true knight. They say his word is his bond. Even those knights who do not like you respect you. I find it sad that you cannot confide in me, but it makes me respect you even more. It is enough that you tell me it was a promise."

We had not brought hunting clothes but garments were procured and with my archers and men at arms as beaters, we joined Owen Tudor and his men in the Royal Park of Denbigh. This was the land hunted by the king or those he chose to allow that privilege. It meant that it teemed with game. The punishment for poaching was blinding and that law was upheld rigorously.

"We will hunt on foot. There are deer that need culling and as you have brought archers to augment my own hunters, we will be safe enough."

I saw the looks exchanged between my archers and the Welsh ones. Archers were very competitive and my four would be determined to show their Welsh counterparts that they had more skill. It was good to hunt along the upper reaches of the Clwyd Valley. John and I managed to bring down a stag. That it was an old one did not matter for it had learned skill and it took two of us to throw the spears that ended its life. Our archers were ready with nocked arrows but they were not needed. The keeper of the parks also took two deer and then we allowed the archers to cull the old and the sick. The herd would be healthier.

As we headed back to the castle, Owen said, "There is more meat here than we can consume. We will share half of it with those who live in the surrounding farms and villages." He shrugged, "They cannot hunt there but they can benefit."

"You allow no hunting?"

He smiled, "Let us say that my gamekeepers turn a blind eye to the taking of rabbits and squirrels but birds, deer and wild boar are only hunted by those I allow."

"And the taking of kindling?"

He smiled, "I can see that you are as practical a lord as I am. Aye, I allow them into the woods. They are not allowed to use a blade to cut down trees but we have enough storms here that nature provides. It keeps the forests tidy."

I had promised we would stay for a couple of days and I kept my word. The next day we rode as far as St Asaph and Rhuddlan. We prayed in the cathedral which was being restored. It was little more than a ruin and Bishop Pecock was scathing in his condemnation of the rebels who had destroyed it. "That man, Owain Glyndŵr, was not a Christian man. No Christian could do this to a house of God. I hope he burns in hell."

I saw the looks some of the Welshmen with Owen Tudor gave to the bishop. The dead rebel still had supporters.

When we left the valley, after a longer stay than I had planned, Owen gave us food for our journey and his hope and desire to visit Houghton Regis. He smiled sadly as he said, "I passed there briefly when I was a fugitive. It would be good to see the manor restored and prosperous."

"You are welcome any time."

When we left, my son and I, along with our men at arms, wore arming caps and coifs. Our helmets hung from our cantles. My archers had their bows, unstrung, hanging from their cantles. We would be ready for any danger. The road from Denbigh Castle led south and was not a well-maintained one until we reached the Roman Road that led to Holyhead. The two men at arms led the pack animals with our clothes and the four archers were our eyes and ears. I had not worried too much on the way north for we had not told anyone outside of the manor our plans and the journey would not be marked. The conversations with

Owen Tudor, not to mention the gossip my men had heard in the warrior hall, meant that we rode south more warily than we had when we had come north. We had thought that the land was at peace, but the burnt-out St Asaph Cathedral showed me that I was wrong. Sir Gruffudd Vychan was still at large and I had hurt him. His pride would not allow that insult to pass unchallenged. Until we reached England we would ride as though to war. We had been advised not to travel through Corwen as that was the heartland of Owain Glyndŵr whose manor, Glyndyfrdwy, lay to the east of it. King Henry had destroyed it but it was said to be haunted by the ghosts of the rebels. The ghosts did not worry me but the thought of disgruntled Welsh enemies did. I planned on seeking shelter at Valle Crucis Abbey in Llangollen.

The ambush, when it came, was just a couple of miles from the abbey. Horseshoe Pass was well named for the road wound up the side of the valley in a large horseshoe. The horses were weary, as were our men, but we were within touching distance of the abbey. We rested at the top after the hard climb and then prepared to descend. There were trees to our left, on the north side of the road. Seth led the archers and but for his nose then the day might have ended in disaster. I did not know what alerted him, but his shout warned us. The ambush was in the trees on the north side of the road. The ambushers had the ridge behind them. The shout did not save poor William, son of Alf the Grim who was plucked from his saddle by a Welsh arrow. The other three archers dropped from their saddles and were already stringing their bows as my two men at arms dropped the reins of the sumpters and raced to our side.

I drew my sword and peered at the trees as arrows flew from the dark within. "Charge them!" It was the only choice we had. We had to get close to them. These were Welsh archers and until my three archers had strung their bows, we were easy targets. A charging man on a war horse could put even the most determined man off his aim. The arrow that struck my head could have killed me. I was saved by my charge and the fact that my head was down. The arrow struck the side of my coif and my ears rang but I was not hurt. It was a warning. Once I reached the trees where the ground began to rise, I saw the Welsh archer as he nocked another arrow to end my life. It was a race, and the result would be life for one and death for the other. Gilles' snorting teeth put the archer off and he released hurriedly. My sword struck his unprotected head while the arrow soared over my shoulder.

Now that I was in the trees, I had the advantage. I peered in the gloom and saw more shapes. I urged Gilles through the trees, twisting and turning to make me a harder target. Arrows flew at me but I led a charmed life although one hit my breastplate, it was not a bodkin and just dented my armour. I was like a man possessed. I had lost an archer and I wanted vengeance. I slashed to my left and right with my sword as I went after every man. The terrain and the fact that I was on a horse meant I had an advantage for the archers were above me, trying to get to the top of the ridge. When I reached the top I stopped for there were no more men before me. I turned my horse. I was alone. My wild charge had taken me to the crest around which the road wound. I made my way back down the slope. In the distance, I could hear the cries and shouts as men fought. John was not with me, and I urged Gilles towards the conflict.

The rider who emerged from the trees to my left was also mailed and armed but it was neither one of my men at arms nor John. The man, holding a sword, was a knight and wore a full-face helmet. He had a Welsh accent that was muffled by the visor as he spoke, "You bear a charmed life, Sir Michael. Sir Gruffudd said that you had more luck than a decent man deserved."

"You have the advantage of me. All that I know is that you are a Welsh murderer who ambushes men."

I heard the anger in his voice. I had deliberately insulted him for I wanted him angry. "I am Maredudd ap Llewellyn and you slew my brother Iago in France. I seek vengeance and to ignite the fires of rebellion once more. Perhaps the death of his knight might spur King Henry to lead an army north. He is a callow king and we shall defeat him and win back my homeland. Your death might bring the freedom of my land a little closer."

I smiled, "So treachery and murder do not run in your family, they gallop. Your brother died unshriven and so shall you."

I was watching his hands all the time I spoke and I knew when he would urge his horse at me. We were both on the slope leading down to the road and I knew that it would be treacherous underfoot for both of our horses. I knew Gilles but I did not know the quality of his horse. He came at me with a sword swinging at my head. My helmet still hung from my cantle and any blow to my skull would be fatal. I swung my sword from left to right and our blades rang together, sparks flying in the gloom. We both wheeled our horses as we passed. Gilles was the more sure-footed of the two and my opponent's horse slipped a little. It was a small error but in combat, such accidents can have a great bearing on the outcome. The slip meant he was below me and, in the gloom and with a full-face helmet he was unsighted. In a tournament, a knight would give his enemy grace. This was ambush and murder. I swung my sword at his helmet. He might have sensed the strike for his sword was

The Knight's Tale

already rising but was a heartbeat too late. My sword rang against his helmet and I urged Gilles on as the knight was unsighted. My next blow hit hard against his back, just above the cantle. I heard the muffled cry from within and I shouted, "Yield or die!" His answer was a sweeping backhand blow behind him. I had given him a chance of life but he had spurned it. I lunged at his underarm where there was no plate and the tip of my sword went through the mail links of his hauberk and into his body. As I twisted and pulled the sword out, I said, "Go to God." His lifeless body slipped from the back of the horse.

Below me, all sounds of combat had ceased but I heard Absalon shout, "Sir Michael, where are you?"

"I come." I dismounted and, after sheathing my sword, manhandled the corpse onto the back of his horse. I led both horses down the slope. When I reached the road, a horrific sight met my eyes. James was being tended to by Absalon while Edgar lay dead. I had lost two archers. Worst of all was the sight of Seth kneeling over John. The son of Stephen the Tracker looked up, "He is a game 'un, my lord. He slew two before an arrow struck his left shoulder. The arrowhead still lies within. He struck his head when he fell but he breathes."

"Put him on his horse. Are the other archers dead?"

Seth nodded, "We heard three horses heading north but none live here."

"Absalon, bring James. We shall head for Valle Crucis Abbey. Seth, gather weapons and horses. Bring the body of the knight and our dead to the Abbey."

"Yes, my lord. I am sorry that we were ambushed."

"It was not of your making and but for your shout, more of us would lie dead."

Thanks to the blow to the head, John was mercifully asleep. He would not have been happy about the manner of his transportation for he was slung like a bag of grain across the saddle. The abbey was Cistercian and, as I later discovered, had sixty monks. The abbot was no friend of Welsh rebels as his abbey had been damaged in the rebellion. We were welcomed and James and John were taken to the hospital. He had healers there and I watched as they carefully washed John's wound with wine and vinegar before carefully removing the arrowhead. It was good that he slept for the barbed arrow had to be dug out. The healer used a candle to ensure that nothing remained within and only then did he pack the wound with bread, honey and more vinegar.

He turned and smiled, "I believe we have saved your squire's arm and his life, my lord."

"He is my son."

The monk made the sign of the cross, "Then I am glad I did not know that, my lord, for I would have feared your wrath had we lost the battle."

I shook my head, "I am a warrior and I know that wounds, however innocuous, can be fatal."

Absalon said, "James, lives, my lord. The bleeding has been staunched."

The abbot had watched it all and said, "You will have to stay here for some days yet, my lord. These men still hover between life and death."

We buried the dead the next day. Our two men were buried in the cemetery of the abbey. When the abbot heard that the knight had ambushed us and had been a rebel, he buried him in unsanctified ground. We left a week after the ambush. I gave the purses we had taken from the dead to the abbot and we left to ride, mailed and armed, back to Houghton Regis.

John and I had spoken often during our stay as he recovered from his wounding. He was not dismayed by his wound. He told me that he knew he could have done nothing about it. He was just pleased that he had managed to kill two of his attackers. "Until I slew them I knew not if I could kill. It was the sight of William's body that steeled my heart. I knew that if I did not kill then I would be killed and I want to live. Do you think I will ever become a knight?"

"Our men think you will and they are the best judges of such matters. The question is, do you still wish to be a knight?"

"I do but I fear, Father, that you have set the bar high. I will never be the knight that you are."

"And I will never be Sir William Strongstaff. It does not matter that we do not achieve perfection, only that we try."

Epilogue

We had been away longer than was expected and when we reached my home the empty saddles told the tale. John had decided not to wear a sling and the first his mother knew of his wound was when she hugged him and he winced. I think that the resulting fuss and attention he had from every one of the women in the house was worse than the wound. He did, however, enjoy the praise from the soldiers who had seen the callow youth fighting like a seasoned warrior in the wild woods of Wales.

It was not until we retired that I was able to tell all to Isabelle. She was pleased that I had gone to tell Owen. "It is only right and proper. It is as though Margaret has been reborn for him."

"He may call and visit us."

"And I do not mind but Margaret must never discover the truth of her birth. Better that lies in the grave with the Queen."

I nodded, "And now Father Bertrand. I will have to tell Father John on the morrow. He will be sad."

"And you, husband, is your mind now at rest?"

I smiled. "I should have done this years ago. I think the queen would have wished it."

"She gave that responsibility to us, and I think we have discharged it well."

The next day, after visiting our priest and giving him the sad news, I wrote a letter to the Marquess of Suffolk. The king needed to be told of the danger from the Welsh. I wondered if they would tell the Duke of York too. As I sealed the letter and handed it to Absalon for delivery, I knew that I had done all that I could. I had behaved as a knight should, with honour. That other knights had not done so was nothing to do with me. I hoped that Jack and John would both do as I had. As Sir William Strongstaff had discovered, it did not always bring rewards, but a man slept easier knowing that he had done the right thing. I hoped, as my messenger headed south, that we were in for a period of peace but when I trained with my son, archers and men at arms, we would be preparing for war.

The End

Glossary

Alaunt - a hunting dog similar to a wolfhound
Aketon - a padded garment worn beneath the armour, also called a gambeson
Ballock dagger or knife - a blade with two swellings next to the blade
Barbican - a gatehouse which can be defended like a castle
Besagew - a circular metal plate to protect the armpit
Bodkin dagger - a long thin dagger like a stiletto used to penetrate mail links
Brigandine - padded jacket worn by archers, sometimes studded with metal
Crowd - crwth or rote. A Celtic musical instrument similar to a lyre
Chamfron - metal covering for the head and neck of a warhorse
Chevauchée - a raid by mounted men
Codger - the man who carries the cadge (a rack with hunting birds upon it.)
Cordwainers - shoemakers
Couvent - the French word for monasteries and nunneries
Cuisse - metal greave
Denizenship - rights that are given to a foreigner to live in a country
Esquire - a man of higher social rank, above a gentleman but below a knight
Familia - the bodyguard of a knight (in the case of a king these may well be knights themselves)
Fauld - hooped skirt which hung from a breastplate
Fowler - a nine-foot-long breech-loading cannon
Galoches - clogs
Gardyvyan - an archer's haversack containing his war gear
Glaive - a pole weapon with a curved head and short spike
Gravesham - Gravesend
Gules - a heraldic term for red
Houppelande - a lord's gown with long sleeves
Horsed archers - archers who rode to war on horses but did not fight from horseback
Hovel - a simple bivouac, used when no tents were available
Jupon - short surcoat
Langet - a metal collar protecting the top part of a pole weapon
Livres tournois - French gold coins
Manchet - the most expensive white bread, served for nobles.
Marchpane - marzipan
Mêlée - a medieval fight between knights

Mesne - the men who follow a knight
Pele or peel tower - a simple refuge tower with access to the first floor via an external ladder
Poleyn - a metal plate to protect the knee
Pursuivant - the rank below a herald
Pyx - a small, well decorated and often jewelled box used to take the host to those too sick or infirm to visit a church
Raveled - Yeoman's bread with bran left in
Rondel dagger - a narrow-bladed dagger with a disc at the end of the hilt to protect the hand
Sallet basinet - medieval helmet of the simplest type: round with a neck protector
Sack - generic name for wine from Spain, Portugal, and France
Sennight - seven nights (a week)
The Pale - the lands around Dublin and Calais. The land belonged to the King of England.
Yling - Ealing

Canonical hours

There were, of course, few clocks at this time but the services used by the church were a means of measuring the progress of the day. Indeed, until the coming of the railways, there was no need for clocks. Folk rose and slept with the rising and setting of the sun.

- Matins (nighttime)
- Lauds (early morning)
- Prime (first hour of daylight)
- Terce (third hour)
- Sext (noon)
- Nones (ninth hour)
- Vespers (sunset evening)
- Compline (end of the day)

Classes of hawk
This is the list of the hunting birds and the class of people who could fly them. It is taken from the 15th-century Book of St Albans.
Emperor: eagle, vulture, merlin
King: gyrfalcon
Prince: gentle falcon: a female peregrine falcon
Duke: falcon of the loch
Earl: peregrine falcon
Baron: buzzard
Knight: Saker Falcon

The Knight's Tale

Squire: Lanner Falcon
Lady: merlin
Young man: hobby
Yeoman: goshawk
Knave: kestrel
Poor man: male falcon
Priest: sparrowhawk
Holy water clerk: sparrowhawk

Historical Notes

For the English maps, I have used the original Ordnance Survey maps. Produced by the army in the 19th century they show England before modern developments and, in most cases, are pre-industrial revolution. Produced by Cassini they are a useful tool for a historian. I also discovered a good website http: orbis.stanford.edu. This allows a reader to plot any two places in the Roman world and if you input the mode of transport you wish to use and the time of year it will calculate how long it would take you to travel the route. I have used it for all of my books up to the eighteenth century as the transportation system was roughly the same. The Romans would have travelled more quickly!

Queen Catherine had four children by Owen Tudor although there was a rumour that when she wed Owen, she was pregnant with Edmund Beaufort's child. The children were Edmund, Jasper, Owen, and Margaret. Margaret was born and then disappeared from history. There is no record of her death although one uncorroborated Tudor source claims she became a nun. On that flimsy evidence hangs a plotline for my story. Owen was entrusted to the monks of Westminster and he died in 1502, being the longest-lived of Catherine's sons although there is much conjecture about his existence. The dates I give for the illness and the queen's death are accurate. She died on the 3rd of January but was not buried for a month. The boys were taken to Barking Abbey but they did not enjoy the adventure I gave to them. Owen Tudor did seek sanctuary at Westminster Abbey although not immediately after the funeral. I have changed the timeline for a day to make a better story and to try to give an insight into the character of Owen Tudor. The Welshman did himself no favours by seeking sanctuary at Westminster. Although King Henry did give him an audience when he finally presented himself to the king and allowed the Welshman to return to Wales, it was the Duke of Gloucester who sent men after him to arrest him for breaking the rules of his parole and to incarcerate him in Newgate Prison. Perhaps Owen Tudor had reason to be paranoid.

Sir John Talbot was the great hero of the 100 Years War but he was doomed to failure. He held off the French for many years but after his death, in battle, England effectively lost France apart from Calais.

William de la Pole did negotiate the marriage of Margaret of Anjou and King Henry. The attack is fiction although if there had been an attack it would have been kept a secret for obvious reasons. The Duke of Gloucester's downfall came when his wife was accused of witchcraft and trying to kill the king. She was imprisoned for the rest of her life and the Duke of Gloucester became marginalised.

Books used in the research:
- The Tower of London - Lapper and Parnell (Osprey)
- English Medieval Knight 1300-1400 - Gravett
- Norman Stone Castles - Gravett
- The Armies of Crécy and Poitiers - Rothero
- The Armies of Agincourt - Rothero
- The Scottish and Welsh Wars 1250-1400
- Henry V and the Conquest of France - Knight and Turner
- Chronicles in the Age of Chivalry - Ed. Eliz Hallam
- English Longbowman 1330-1515 - Bartlett
- Northumberland at War - Derek Dodds
- The Longbow - Mike Loades
- Teutonic Knight 1190-1561- Nicolle and Turner
- Warkworth Castle and Hermitage - John Goodall
- British Kings and Queens - Mike Ashley
- The Wars of the Roses - Dan Jones
- Tudor- the family story - Leanda de Lisle
- Ordnance Survey Original series map #81 1864-1869

For more information on all of the books please visit the author's website at http://www.griffhosker.com where there is a link to contact him.

Griff Hosker
January 2024

Other books by Griff Hosker

If you enjoyed reading this book, then why not read another one by the author?

Ancient History

The Sword of Cartimandua Series
(Germania and Britannia 50 A.D. – 128 A.D.)
Ulpius Felix- Roman Warrior (prequel)
The Sword of Cartimandua
The Horse Warriors
Invasion Caledonia
Roman Retreat
Revolt of the Red Witch
Druid's Gold
Trajan's Hunters
The Last Frontier
Hero of Rome
Roman Hawk
Roman Treachery
Roman Wall
Roman Courage

The Wolf Warrior series
(Britain in the late 6th Century)
Saxon Dawn
Saxon Revenge
Saxon England
Saxon Blood
Saxon Slayer
Saxon Slaughter
Saxon Bane
Saxon Fall: Rise of the Warlord
Saxon Throne
Saxon Sword

Medieval History

The Dragon Heart Series
Viking Slave *
Viking Warrior *
Viking Jarl *
Viking Kingdom *
Viking Wolf *
Viking War*
Viking Sword
Viking Wrath
Viking Raid
Viking Legend
Viking Vengeance
Viking Dragon
Viking Treasure
Viking Enemy
Viking Witch
Viking Blood
Viking Weregeld
Viking Storm
Viking Warband
Viking Shadow
Viking Legacy
Viking Clan
Viking Bravery
The Vengeance Trail

The Norman Genesis Series
Hrolf the Viking *
Horseman *
The Battle for a Home *
Revenge of the Franks *
The Land of the Northmen
Ragnvald Hrolfsson
Brothers in Blood
Lord of Rouen
Drekar in the Seine

The Knight's Tale

Duke of Normandy
The Duke and the King

Danelaw
(England and Denmark in the 11th Century)
Dragon Sword *
Oathsword *
Bloodsword *
Danish Sword*
The Sword of Cnut

New World Series
Blood on the Blade *
Across the Seas *
The Savage Wilderness *
The Bear and the Wolf *
Erik The Navigator *
Erik's Clan *
The Last Viking*

The Vengeance Trail *

The Conquest Series
(Normandy and England 1050-1100)
Hastings
Conquest

The Aelfraed Series
(Britain and Byzantium 1050 A.D. - 1085 A.D.)
Housecarl *
Outlaw *
Varangian *

The Reconquista Chronicles
Castilian Knight *
El Campeador *
The Lord of Valencia *

The Anarchy Series England

The Knight's Tale

1120-1180
English Knight *
Knight of the Empress *
Northern Knight *
Baron of the North *
Earl *
King Henry's Champion *
The King is Dead *
Warlord of the North*
Enemy at the Gate*
The Fallen Crown
Warlord's War
Kingmaker
Henry II
Crusader
The Welsh Marches
Irish War
Poisonous Plots
The Princes' Revolt
Earl Marshal
The Perfect Knight

Border Knight
1182-1300
Sword for Hire *
Return of the Knight *
Baron's War *
Magna Carta *
Welsh Wars *
Henry III *
The Bloody Border *
Baron's Crusade*
Sentinel of the North*
War in the West*
Debt of Honour
The Blood of the Warlord
The Fettered King
de Montfort's Crown
Ripples of Rebellion

Sir John Hawkwood Series
France and Italy 1339- 1387
Crécy: The Age of the Archer *
Man At Arms *
The White Company *
Leader of Men *
Tuscan Warlord *
Condottiere*
Legacy

Lord Edward's Archer
Lord Edward's Archer *
King in Waiting *
An Archer's Crusade *
Targets of Treachery *
The Great Cause *
Wallace's War *
The Hunt

Struggle for a Crown
1360- 1485
Blood on the Crown *
To Murder a King *
The Throne *
King Henry IV *
The Road to Agincourt *
St Crispin's Day *
The Battle for France *
The Last Knight *
Queen's Knight *
The Knight's Tale

Tales from the Sword I
(Short stories from the Medieval period)

Tudor Warrior series
England and Scotland in the late 15th and early 16th century
Tudor Warrior *

The Knight's Tale

Tudor Spy *
Flodden*

Conquistador
England and America in the 16th Century
Conquistador *
The English Adventurer *

English Mercenary
The 30 Years War and the English Civil War
Horse and Pistol

Modern History

The Napoleonic Horseman Series
Chasseur à Cheval
Napoleon's Guard
British Light Dragoon
Soldier Spy
1808: The Road to Coruña
Talavera
The Lines of Torres Vedras
Bloody Badajoz
The Road to France
Waterloo

The Lucky Jack American Civil War series
Rebel Raiders
Confederate Rangers
The Road to Gettysburg

Soldier of the Queen series
Soldier of the Queen*
Redcoat's Rifle*
Omdurman*
Desert War

The British Ace Series

1914
1915 Fokker Scourge
1916 Angels over the Somme
1917 Eagles Fall
1918 We will remember them
From Arctic Snow to Desert Sand
Wings over Persia

Combined Operations series
1940-1945
Commando *
Raider *
Behind Enemy Lines
Dieppe
Toehold in Europe
Sword Beach
Breakout
The Battle for Antwerp
King Tiger
Beyond the Rhine
Korea
Korean Winter

Tales from the Sword II
(Short stories from the Modern period)

Books marked thus *, are also available in the audio format. For more information on all of the books then please visit the author's website at www.griffhosker.com where there is a link to contact him or visit his Facebook page: GriffHosker at Sword Books or follow him on Twitter: @HoskerGriff or Sword (@swordbooksltd)
If you wish to be on the mailing list then contact the author through his website.

Printed in Great Britain
by Amazon